SHACKLETON SHELF

SHACKLETON SHELF

Nicollette Petrou

Dedicated to those who inspired this book. I hope you read and enjoy it, someday.

I

2001

The Scottish storm purged through Dob's Inn, which hindered the ancient secrets of the quarry. The rain seeped through a tear of a campsite tent and licked the honeycomb pendant around the neck of Halley Makillen, to steal what was lost years ago. The fossilised butterfly, technically, it was a Clifden Nonpareil, a moth, but given Oren's enthusiasm to have thought it were a butterfly, Halley never said anything.

She emerged from the sleeping bag, grabbed duct-tape from the backpack and leant toward the slit in the tent. Another purge of fresh rain slammed into her face. Her mouth filled with smoke-laden water and the brunette hair plastered to her cheek like cobwebs.

Halley emerged from the tent and sat atop a boulder beneath the portable shelter and bit into a monotonous breakfast bar. After so many days they became tasteless. She watched the storm embellish the mountain terrain of Dob's Inn. It was a major set-back, another days' work lost due to the weather. Her stomach dropped into her spine, the only hope now was that the rain subsided and soon.

Halley knew the quarry like no other, she knew the river valley was lined with limestone, the perfect habitat to find fossilised brachiopods, crinoids and anthropoids—ancient findings of the sea. The mountains behind were constructed of moss and melanin shale where they uncovered a trilobite yesterday and from the valley to the tent it was short of three-hundred steps. Footsteps trudged over the shrubbery and broke her concentration. It was Isaac, with his mattered blonde hair. He puffed his breakfast cigarette. "Well would you look at that."

"My hopes have gone to shit. If we work in this weather, we won't get further than a sprained ankle," she sighed.

Isaac drew another puff. "Should we call up the University of Bristol or take another day?"

"We can't let Bristol know, your job is hanging in the balance … Best see what the others say." Halley hid behind the mask of patience but the fate of his jobs lay in Dob's Inn.

"My job? What about you?"

"This will be my last trip with you, I'm going to work full time at the lab but I'll return one day."

"You better keep in touch." Isaac watched the rain through squinted eyes. "Something tells me we don't have much time left and I don't think Bristol will be patient like last time." He exhaled a cloud of tobacco smoke.

"They can't cut us off that easily, we've worked there for over two-years. That deserves some level of respect."

From the last tent emerged the remaining two palaeontologists, both of whom Halley had already forgotten her name and she placed hands on her hips. "Not such a good morning after all. If the weather forecast isn't promising, perhaps we should relocate."

Before Halley could speak, her phone buzzed. She pulled it out of her pocket and read the latest text message; *Don't forget what you came for. We need it by Thursday, Gabriel.*

Halley gulped, that was the last thing she needed, as if the pressure from Bristol wasn't enough. She placed a tooth pick in the corner of her mouth. Gabriel already had it in for her and Halley knew if she didn't find what she needed, there would be no use to return home.

"Hal?" The palaeontologist asked. "If we produce nothing short of a fossil, Bristol is going to cut our pay-checks."

"Right down the middle," Halley agreed.

"It's too dangerous, we can't climb those mountains like this," added Isaac's friend.

"Do we have a choice?" Halley asked.

The palaeontologists crossed the valley and walked along a narrow base of two conjoined mountains. They walked a straight line which soon grew difficult and half the group walked to the right and the other half to the left of the strict path. The distant mountains were obscured by dark fog and potentially rain. The air stung Halley's nose with cold wilderness, a reminder she was a guest to the alpine. She treaded across then shrubs when a rustle sounded from a nearby boulder. Halley's eyes widened and she outstretched her arm. Halley raised a finger to her lips. Something moved through the greenery and headed in her direction. Halley tightened her grip around her handheld shovel and raised it to her cheek. She closed in on the boulder and the icy air dared her to cough but she fought the urge. The grass parted and Halley lunged forward. To her dismay a red squirrel emerged from the foliage. It darted between her legs and up the mountain.

"Caught yourself a friend?" Isaac taunted.

Halley couldn't help but laugh. "I'm just trying to lighten the mood."

"Mission accomplished."

As the team emerged into the Northern hemisphere of the valley, the mountains parted and revealed a river stream. Halley dropped to the back of the group and followed Isaac's squelching boots. He scraped over loose rocks which skidded down the mountainside and plummeted into the river below and the splash echoed through the valley. Her knees burned with inflammation and she lost focus, she slipped over the shale rock. She forced her feet sideways to stop the slide, when one of the palaeontologists pulled up alongside her. "Another squirrel?"

"A snake actually, mind your step," Halley giggled.

The girl shrieked and darted sideways.

"Here!" Isaac yelled.

He held a chipped white fragment on the axis of his hand. Halley swung her bag around and pulled out some nails and rope. The team mapped the ground around the bone shard and they chiseled away. The tools drilled into the virgin ground but Halley moved slow, careful not to damage the hidden wonders. She worked with precision and soon found a fossilised trilobite around two-hundred-fifty-two million years old. One of the palaeontologists produced a tube of Vinac to stabilise the fossil. "We did it."

A heavy load lifted from Halley's shoulders, they were in the clear now a fossil was produced for the Bristol research department. Although the relief didn't last long once she remembered Gabriel's message. Her chest tightened as reality set back in. The palaeontologists found the fossil too quickly, which meant the trip would soon be over and that didn't leave her much time to find Gabriel's fossil. The team followed an invisible path through the quarry. As the terrain steepened, Halley hunched forward. She paused.

"Come on." Isaac gripped her shoulder. "We're almost there."

Halley grabbed a melanin ledge and pulled herself up but her fingers quivered against her weight. The pointed ledge sliced her hand Halley wailed. She let go. Shit. She dropped down the mountainside, her belly slipped over the moss. She kicked the foliage and tore a hole through her pants. Fuck. She splayed her legs out and lodged her right foot into a crevice.

"Hal!" Isaac called.

With her body curled inwards, there was nothing to hold onto. Halley's only hope was the small foot ledge. Sweat dribbled down her forehead and sticky hair clung to her glasses. She peered upwards, between the strands of hair and saw she at least ten feet from the top.

"I'm coming!" Isaac barked. He secured a rope around his waist and leaned over the mountain. His mouth dropped open, this wouldn't be easy. Halley's toes became numb and she shut her eyes. Her body skidded down the mountain and she desperately searched for something, anything. Her belly slid over the foot ledge and the shale fragment sliced open the jacket. The cold moss chilled Halley's skin and dared slice her open. She pleaded for mercy as the rock travelled beneath her neck and she tilted her head backwards. She groaned against the pain and the fragment pressed against her forehead. Halley scraped over rocks and the friction trimmed foliage toward the river and splashes of water stung the wound in her leg. Her tired arm was knocked back by a blunt force. Then she realised it was a ledge. She reflexed quickly and grabbed hold of it whilst her body dangled mid-air. She swung herself inward and held the ledge with both hands.

"Halley!" Isaac yelled.

She glanced upward and was confronted with space, too much space between herself and the others. "Hurry!"

Isaac slid down the mountain, supported by a rope. "I'm coming."

Halley bit her desperation into her lower lip when something caught her eye. Between the shale and moss was a glimmer of amber. She reached for it, while her other arm quivered and held her entire weight. Her fingers slipped. "Shit."

"Stay there!" Isaac called. He was four feet away. Halley reached forward again and this time her fingers locked around the yellow fragment. She pulled and her legs swung in all directions.

Isaac reached forward. "Take my hand!"

Halley's fingers burned.

"God dammit, take my hand!"

Halley pulled one last time and the fossil slid out of place. She caught a glimpse of what was enclosed, a stick-figured bug. A mosquito. The business trip ended in the evening hours and adrenaline was replaced by fatigue. Halley slumped against into the cream couch in her cottage home. She barely ate dinner and the French Bakery candle made her stomach gurgle. Her right hand leg were wrapped with blood-stained bandages that protruded from the knitted blanket. The wounds soaked in the warm embrace from the fireplace that crackled metres away. Max was sprawled across Halley's chest with the blanket pulled up to his pudgy cheeks and his face nuzzled into the crevice of her neck. She grinned at the brush of Max's flossy red hair, a proud reminder of his Scottish foundations. To be honest, Scotland was only part of his heritage and Halley was guilty for hindering the rest of who he was. She never knew her birth parents and was lost in the cold hands of foster care, where answers remained a mystery. Max rose and fell with each of her own breaths, at only fifteen-months-old, He appeared double his age. Halley reached for her mobile phone halfway across the couch but her hand throbbed as the wound split open. Dobb's Inn left its' mark but it was a small price to pay. The front door slammed shut and footsteps crept down the hallway. Oren emerged into the room and ran pale hands through his hair, ginger as autumn leaves. He caught sight of Halley and his chestnut eyes smiled but not for long. He uncomfortably paced back and forth, and he mumbled under his breath.

"Oren," Halley whispered.

"Gabriel's been on my back all day," he paused. "For that damned fossil. As if I don't already know what's at stake."

"There's something I need to tell you." Halley stroked Max's head and lulled him into a deep sleep. He was too young and innocent to be exposed to the complications of the outside world. Oren spun around and placed his hands over his mouth. "Please don't tell me Bristol called. You can't lose your job."

"I found it."

"You found …," his voice trailed off. "A fossil … For work? That's great." He dabbed at the dribble of sweat down his forehead.

"No, I mean I found 'it'."

"You found the fossil?"

Halley nodded. "An amber-coated mosquito, that means we're onto phase two of the experiment."

Oren's jaw dropped, he could hardly breathe. Halley swore she saw tears in Oren's eyes but he turned around too quickly for her to be certain. "Are you sure?"

"I know what a mosquito when I see one. I'm going to call Gabriel." Halley gestured at the phone across the couch and Oren passed it to her. "Wait," he began. "We're have a meeting with a potential tissue donor. I think it's a good idea to go ahead considering we don't know if that fossil has the DNA intact. It could have disintegrated by now."

Halley nodded, Oren was right. There was no way of knowing if the DNA within the mosquito's belly was still there. DNA was fragile and there was a good chance it didn't make it through the years. "I understand where you're coming rom but if the DNA is inside this fossil, that means we can get to work quicker instead of wasting our time."

Oren leaned before her face. She embraced the sweet kiss, her lips danced and she tasted the brandy on his tongue.

"What happened to your hand?" Oren felt along the crusted bandages and turned her hand. "I need you to be careful, I can't have anything happen to you." Oren's eyes pleaded for sincerity and his freckled cheeks flushed red.

"I know, and I will be but I couldn't walk away with nothing, not again."

"I don't care about that. I need you to promise that you will be alright."

"I promise." Halley peered down at Max and a tear trickled down her cheek.

Oren placed a kiss on her forehead. "It's okay. I know what you're thinking when you look at Max. I can see it in your eyes. It doesn't matter if he never knows the other half of who he is."

"He might walk around with a chip on his shoulder."

"No." Oren raised Halley's chin by the tip of his finger. "You know what I see when I look at him? I see a little bit you and a little bit of me. Nothing else matters." He wiped away a tear from the corner of her eye.

"I'll tell Gabriel to come over tomorrow night for a celebration," Halley changed the topic.

"Only after we sign that contract with the donor," Oren winked.

II

2001

From the office window of L2S, Level 2 South, Halley watched the sunrise reflect off the River Clyde. The Clyde Arc reached from Finnieston to the Auditorium and a thin line of cars crossed the bridge. Rain propelled off the windows and the haloed bridge shadowed the cars like a dome. The sight settled Halley's nerves. The process was generally smooth but there was always the fear of losing a client. That thought hummed through the room. Footsteps emerged down the hallway and Halley swallowed her anxiety. She tucked hair behind her ears and trailed her fingers along the pleated white skirt that swayed beneath the lab coat. Her pointed glossy shoes matched her angelic appearance, a good impression was needed. Oren and Gabriel emerged into the office followed by a lady in her late twenties. Her auburn hair was pulled back into a bun and Butterfly earrings dangled by her cheeks. She wore a slim pink drink that encompassed her body with a black tunic to match her handbag. Halley greeted her with a warm smile. "Good morning, it's lovely to meet you. I'm Halley Makillen, scientist and palaeontologist."

The lady reciprocated the handshake. "Diane Thomson."

"Please take a seat."

Diane Fiddled with the handle of her handbag and glanced around the room, from the Bog Myrtle plant in the corner to the bookshelf besides the desk. She read the titles of the science

textbooks and her eyes locked onto *The Human Cloning Debate.*
Halley grinned. "The debate that has been around for many years, I don't think it will ever end to be quite honest."

"I guess the answers will come."

"I hope so. Now, may I grab some details from you?" Halley ran through a series of questions; age, gender, contact details, demographics. She paused at the next question and twisted the pen in hand. "Ah - background?"

"Half Swedish, half Irish but I have my Scottish husband's last name."

Halley jotted down the information. How wholesome, to know where you were from and what a lovely combination it was. She blinked away the tears, now was not the time.

Halley pushed a fresh contract and pen across the table. *Phase 0: The Benefits of Genetic Mutation and Embryonic Cloning for the Human Race.* "Before I start running through the contract did you have any questions?"

"Genetic mutation ... That doesn't sound very beneficial. Why would you make an experiment where you alter someone's genes?"

Halley smiled. "Do you have children, Mrs Thomson?"

"Yes, I do."

"Good to know. Well, our research focuses on cloning and the potential benefits for the future of science. Not only that but genetic mutation could help the health of children and babies. In this experiment we are focusing on an accelerated growth hormone. If we can increase the pace at which an embryo develops into a foetus, then we can make someone grow faster."

Diane remained silent and her monotone expression remained unchanged.

"We can help premature babies grow faster. If a neonate is born too young their lungs are likely to be under-developed. Currently we are using steroids but that can have side effects. So we are working on a preventative method rather than a treatment one."

"That's great!" Diane looked over at Gabriel.

He smiled. "Our goal is always to help the future generations the best we can."

Oren nodded. "That's right and this experiment could save lives."

Diane thought for a moment. She scoured the contract again. Her eyes fixated on the title that was written in bold writing. "Phase zero," she read aloud. "I don't understand, what does that mean?"

Oren interlocked his fingers and leaned forward until the white tunic tightened around his freckled neck. "Phase minus one, zero, pre-human, if you will. Our experiment hasn't been tested in humans yet. It will be conducted within our laboratory and the embryo will not be implanted back into you or another female host. It's the law, according to the government, a cloned human embryo can be experimented on but must be destroyed by the fourteenth day."

Diane twisted the handle of her handbag and her cheeks flushed red. Halley leaned across the table. "The embryo won't resemble anything of a child, Diane. It is only a cell and won't have a heartbeat or any features comparable to that of a baby. Which is why the experiment is terminated by the fourteenth day, to avoid that situation."

Diane smirked and her Butterly earrings danced as she cocked her head to the side. "I only want to help people, well, other mothers that went through what I did, the death of a child. My son was a stillborn."

"You can help prevent that and so much more."

Diane dabbed at the corner of her eye with a handkerchief. "Oh, well, that's terrific news." She watched Halley and a telepathic empathy encircled the two mothers. "Will it hurt?"

"You might be in a little pain when we extract the embryo, yes. But I promise Diane, you are in good hands and the pain won't last long."

"Will the embryo hurt when you kill it?"

"No. It's not alive and will feel no pain. By definition, the embryo would not yet have a brain or heartbeat."

Diane nodded whilst stretching the leather handle between her fingers. Her eyes darted back and forth and she appeared to choke on her own words. She thought for some time before looking at Halley again. "How is the embryo cloned?"

"Great question. I'll let Gabriel take this one."

Gabriel appreciated the spotlight and clapped his hands together. "I think the first question is why? Why are we cloning this genetic information? Genetic mutation is only half of our experiment but the other half is cloning. So, this will help with elements of IVF and choosing favourable characteristics or eliminating diseases from an embryo. Cloning can help bring back those who have passed on. A clone would have their genetic makeup but not appearance, traits or memory. It would be a twin and this can be extremely helpful to lessen a parent's loss." Gabriel paused and let the information sink in. Diane stared at him wide-eyed. "We extract the DNA from the nucleus from a cell, cell A. We then remove the nucleus of cell B and replace it with that of cell A."

Diane looked at Halley and her eyes beamed with admiration. "You are all doing wonderful things for the future children and I would love to be apart of that. Where do I sign?"

"Right next to the three of our signatures." Halley pointed along the dotted line, below it read *signature of: Human Tissue Donor.*

It was almost midnight but the lights in the Makillen household illuminated the neighbourhood. The aroma of liquor filled the room and tobacco drowned the oxygen from the air but nothing dampened the obnoxious banter. Halley wandered back into the living room with a fruit platter and wedged it onto the coffee table that was crammed with cheese, biscuits, grapes, chocolates, several bottles of wine and vodka. Oren extended his arm and Halley slipped in beside him. After only a couple of drinks her head was heavy and she leant against Oren's shoulder. He was entranced in conversation with Gabriel and the pair practically shouted unintelligible words of the science language, one Halley never fully understood. Oren laughed until he began to wheeze.

"Honey, you need to eat something, you're getting ahead of yourself," Halley ushered.

"Sorry," Oren said disengaged. He grabbed a handful of grapes which lay in his lap. Not quite what Halley meant but it would have to do.

"Can you imagine, brother? Let's say the DNA is in good condition and the experiment is successful, our names would make headlines!" Oren tapped his fingers in turn, "newspapers, magazines, journal articles, interviews. We will be the first to have successfully engineered human embryonic clones outside the womb." His eyes glazed over and could barely focus but still, he leaned in for a drunken kiss.

Gabriel cleared his throat. "I'll let you in on a secret Halley, you're useful to have around, sometimes," he said in a cold Russian accent. His face crumpled was by the bitter taste of romance. Gabriel filled his mouth with vodka and slammed the glass against the table. He watched the pair from the corner of his eyes and beneath the freshly polished bald head reflected the living room light.

"I do know more than I let on. Science only takes up a fraction of my knowledge," Halley said.

"Hal, c'mon, you're a fossil digger not a scientist."

"Palaeontologist." She focused intensely on every syllable, trying not to slur her speech.

"Whatever you call yourself. Besides, you don't have any qualifications in science. Your expertise is based upon what Oren and I teach you."

"Oh please, I've worked on these experiments with you the past five years, that grants me the title of scientist. Besides, I know as much as you do," Halley winked.

Gabriel opened his mouth to retaliate but caught on to the joke and grinned. "Touché." He poured another shot of vodka and flopped back against the couch. His pupils almost doubled in size and he raised the drink to his lips but missed. The rim of the glass pressed against his chin as Gabriel beamed up at the ceiling. Tonight was one of those rare occasions where his inner child emerged beneath the rough exterior. Perhaps it was the liquor but Halley's mind drifted. For the fifth year in a row, they were about to repeat the same cloning experiment. Year after year, they failed. They would extract the blood from the deceased mosquito and attempt to replicate its' genetics. Although Halley attested it would be far easier cloning a live human embryo, Gabriel and Oren had other plans. Their focus lied in cloning the dead for nobody has succeeded before. The experiment could only be possible if the DNA within the fossilised mosquito's belly could weather the years of ageing, trauma and sunlight. It was a long shot and the experiment hadn't begun. Halley pinched the space between her eyes as she went over the process in her head. First the blood would be extracted from the mosquito's belly and then identified if the DNA was present. Then, it would be removed and replaced into the nucleus of another live human embryo. The experiment would be grown and closely monitored, for the embryo would contain the DNA of a deceased human being that would come back to life. Until finally, the microscopic life would be destroyed before the fourteenth day. That thought churned Halley's stomach. To her, the embryo was a life the same as her own, to Oren and Gabriel, it was business and to the government it was ethics. There was nothing morally right about cloning the dead so the researchers were legally permitted two weeks to study the experiment. Even so, that wasn't comforting. The thought of being re-spawning a life and then to kill it wasn't fair and the unlucky soul would be picked at random. "We could always clone a live modern day human embryo."

Gabriel caste a harsh glare. "You know that won't be the case."

"As a backup option."

"No. It's like telling you to dig holes for potting mix instead of fossils. That's not your speciality. We will clone a deceased human from DNA. This is my life's work."

"If the experiment works out," Oren began. "Maybe we can work on the genetic mutation, accelerated growth, the ability to see in the dark," he said whilst snacking on the handful of grapes. "Hearing accelerations. We'd be creating a sub-species of human."

Gabriel drew an invisible line through the air. "Genetically mutated clones of the dead. Imagine all the children, loved ones, pets that could be brought alive again through our research. Not to mention disease free with a highly improved immune system. First thing's first, we need to start this experiment ASAP. I'll be at the lab by dawn."

Halley pondered that idea. "We only have one fossil, I thought we agreed to have at least five before starting over?"

"I'm already onto it, we have more mosquitos coming in the next few days," Gabriel said.

"It's a shame we can't produce results sooner, people would pay great money for something so sweet. I mean, we live, we die, we are reborn. Perhaps one day we shall relish in the beauty of such a life."

"Let's just hope the mosquito will do us justice this time," Halley sighed.

"I've already looked at the mosquito. I saw it," Gabriel cackled. "The DNA is there. We start the extraction process tomorrow."

Halley turned to Oren, whose jaw dropped open. Things moved faster than they anticipated. Before she could speak, Gabriel continued. "I have another mosquito lined up too, donated from the British Museum." Gabriel extracted an envelope and placed it against the table. Halley drew the envelope close to her face and traced her fingers along the edge that was already ripped open. She glanced at Gabriel, who appeared particularly proud of himself. "How long have you known about this?"

"It came through yesterday," he admitted.

Halley stared at him whilst her fingers slipped inside and extracted the folded letter. Oren leant over her shoulder and they skimmed across the formal text. The mosquito was harvested from Britain at coordinates 52.6309° N, 1.2974° E. The letter quivered in her grasp and a gush of emotions clouded Halley's mind. "Are we ready for this? I mean …," she paused, trying to recollect her thoughts. "Do we have enough funding to go ahead with the experiment? If it fails this time, we could be pushed into liquidation." Halley scoured the room and the air stood still. Oren nodded and turned towards her, his tender eyes glowed with sympathy, Halley was right. They couldn't afford to loose another experiment, as it stood, the researchers could hardly repay the business loan. She swallowed a lump in her throat when Oren extended his open hand. "We are together in this and we know more than ever before. Everything will be alright. Do you trust me?"

"Always."

Oren extended his hand, to Halley and they interlocked their fingers. Then Gabriel sealed the deal.

The faintest glimpse of joy broke through their bond. The night ended late and Halley collected the empty liquor bottles when a high-pitched cry rang over the baby monitor.

"I got it," Oren attempted to stand but barely picked off the couch.

"Leave it to me." Halley clambered up the stairs and reached the third door to the left. The room was illuminated by a blue nightlight next to the wooden crib where Max's arms flailed frantically. She scooped Max into her arms, his face was crumpled with distress. She strode toward the rocking chair beside the curtained window. Then Halley realised. "Ah - honey, I forgot the milk." She headed toward the door when static emitted over the baby monitor. Halley listened to the conversation but it was faint. She increased the volume and waited until the drunken silence broken again. Gabriel mumbled something that sounded important and was followed by a prolonged sigh. She replayed the noise in her mind but the words didn't form.

"What can I say?" Oren sighed.

"Forget I mentioned it."

"No, its' fine. You know I sometimes wonder that myself... I can't talk about it with Halley, it's a real tender topic."

Max wriggled against Halley's chest and wailed as she rocked him. He was now quiet but on borrowed time.

"Would you like another drink?" Oren slurred.

"What?"

"Did you say something?"

"Gabriel, I think the vodka has hit you hard." Then the sound of laughter and clink of glasses emitted over the speaker. Halley frowned, she went over the conversation in her head, again and again. The whispers appeared an encryption and left a disturbing sensation swirled within her belly. She emerged back into the living room but this time the banter was replaced with silence. Oren and Gabriel had passed out before midnight. Halley cleared the table but a strange thought crept into her mind. One that she could not push aside. What was Oren and Gabriel talking about?

III

1821

Atop the vault of the flint Cathedral, a mosquito descended into the smog and tobacco of Great Britain. It buzzed past the silhouette of top hats and petticoats before it landed on the cheek of Henry Gilchrist. Although it was missing a leg, it still plunged the needlelike mouth through his skin. He slapped the mosquito away but the bastard stole what it came for, his blood. An unfair trade-off it was and enough to dampen the day. Henry returned to the letter in hand, now a crumpled mess. He relaxed his fist and pressed the steel point of the fountain pen against the paper atop his knee but beneath the movement of his leg, the ink smeared and ripped through the parchment. He sighed and dated the letter: *January 20th 1821*. Before he could continue, a bony hand clasped his knee and Henry stuffed the paper into his coat. He peered down to see John stand beside the wagon, he bore a wrinkled smile that was short of a front tooth. He appeared much older than a man of forty years.

"Another letter?"

"Yes." Henry jumped down from the wagon and wiped the invisible dust from his shins.

"How is your brother anyway?"

"I don't know. He hasn't written back."

John raised an eyebrow. Henry wasn't quite sure why his twin brother hadn't replied. Maybe he forgot, perhaps the mail was late or was it something else? He waived the thought aside.

"You'll help me with the geldings, won't you? They could use a drink."

The men made their way to the front-end of the wagon and attended to the two black gelding horses. Henry's fingers danced around the reins of the younger of the two, it was still a foal. He unbuckled the bridle and the foal jerked its scrawny head in every way. Henry tightened his grip and wrapped the leather strap around his hand. "I must take to the road. At least the weather is promising."

"I disagree with you there." John gestured to the sky, staring at the hazy clouds. "That may hold you back. Anyway, where shall the road lead you, sire?"

"The East Midlands and after that, Winchester."

The men rounded the mortar Cathedral and it's hundred-and-something windows. The rooftop was over three-hundred-feet high and touched the Heavens it preached of. Henry bowed to the trinity before he went about his way. They slowed down at a pothole, where he unscrewed his vessel and filled the hole with water. The black horse lowered its' head and began to drink but the foal faltered. It thought for a moment before it gulped the water at an incredible speed. Henry broke the silence, "I best be off. I prefer taking to the road before dawn, for it does get rather busy."

"That it does but first, can I ask a favour of you? My crops haven't produced as they should this spring and my profit reflects that."

"What shall you do?"

"That is why I need your help. I need you to sell my crops in

Winchester."

Henry cackled at the poor joke and after some time recollected himself. He cleared his throat and tucked a strand of dark hair behind his ear. "I appreciate your desperation, John, but I can't do that. Selling crops of such poor quality would tarnish my name and that is something I cannot afford."

"I will offer you commission."

Henry tilted his hat. "No, thank you sire. Now if you'll excuse me."

He reached for the bridle of the foal, when the musty stench of John's rotten teeth thickened the air. He whispered. "Take my produce with you. Unless you want your wife to find out about the mistress."

Henry's jaw froze shut and the world around him deafened. He gulped, convinced he misheard John's words. "What are you talking about?"

"If you don't sell my crops in Winchester, I will make known the love affair between you and the mistress."

Henry breathed heavier, his face crippled with disgust. "Liar! I haven't done anything like that." He clenched his fists and plunged closer to John and pulled the foal with him but its' tender cry went unnoticed.

"I wouldn't do anything stupid if I were you!" John snapped. He peered around before lowering his voice. "If you cause a scene right now, you are going to draw unwanted attention to yourself. I wouldn't do that." John grabbed Henry's shirt. "My crops are withering and that is no lie. So I suggest that you help me."

"It isn't true though. I am not unfaithful."

"True, not true, what does it matter? Whatever I choose to speak of will be true. I'll cast you the infamous man to an unfaithful marriage and I don't fancy that title, do you?"

Henry pulled away, unable to look John in the eye. His head pounded from the inside out as he tried to comprehend the proposed deal. "Sell your own crops," he spat and faced the dirt ground.

"That would be far too out of character. I made my offer clear. If you cannot fulfil it by the end of this week, then you know the outcome."

John began to walk away and turned back around. "Henry, I can only hope you understand my desperation. Help me, friend."

Henry hate to admit but pity clouded his mind. For the first time, he saw angst in John and it was almost forgivable. He lifted his gaze and saw the moscato sunrise glisten over the Cathedral that reminded Henry of his duty to the ministry. He sighed, embellished in sin as he shied away from his friend's cry for help. He swallowed his pride and looked John in the eyes, it was a small favour after all.

Henry sat atop the wagon which shifted, as eleven-year-old, Little John loaded the final carton of potatoes. It was a fair trade-off, Henry sold his father, John's, produce, and in exchange Little John offered a hand where possible. Well, that was the original agreement. Now John took matters into his own hands but Henry swore himself to secrecy. It kept the fib of his mistress at bay and after all, Little John shouldn't carry on the same legacy of infidelity as his father. Little John was a friend but also a snitch, he knew hard work and stood for nothing less.

Henry tilted his hat. "Good work."

"When shall you be back?" Little John toyed with his suspenders and peered at such an angle he would get a stiff neck.

"I'll be back by dusk."

"Can I not come with you this time? I promise to be quiet and I can look after the horses for you." Little John squinted against the sunlight.

"Enough with the questions!" Henry stretched out a fist and dropped five pence into Little John's hand. "Don't tell anyone." He winked.

"Now I must be off."

"Bye, Mister Henry!"

"It's Henry." He whipped the asses of the gelding horses and the wagon jolted forward. He was headed a little over ten miles toward the East Midlands. He worked as a coach for twenty years. Well, that was not quite right. Henry worked from an early like Little John but it wasn't until many years later that he earned his status as an official coach for his own farmland. Nowadays Henry earned four pound a week, enough to support his young family. That was another fib. His eldest son was sent to work in the factory and the younger would start in a few months, they would earn their living and help pay for food. Henry's weight shifted as the wagon bounced by the lead of the geldings. He knew the horses like the back of his hand, only this time the gelding to the right was a replacement for his previous one that broke its leg on a trip. The new horse seemed to move slower but would soon learn its purpose in life. Henry felt the parchment through his pocket and grinned as it crinkled. Working seven days a week meant Henry had little time to visit his twin brother, Urian, nor the newborn his wife bestowed upon them. Besides, Urian relocated for Norwich, which would take many days to reach. The cloudy sky forecasted the long slog ahead which would be an exhaustive journey for the horse, at least they didn't know it. Morning spun into evening and Henry focused on the dirt road whilst the gelding ploughed through the busy terrain that swarmed with people.

IV

1821

Henry pried open the edge of the wooden window frame and picked at the letter inside. He re-read his own letter from the basement window of his house on the prairie. He tapped the envelope against the glass in thought, he would hand deliver the note to his twin, Urian. He raised the glass of gin to his mouth, the liquor should have dissolved the day away but the memory lingered like a foul smell. Winchester was not a light journey and now Henry would be accompanied by John's offer. Desperate bastard. He was a poor sod that was for sure, always pitied himself, never saw the light of an opportunity. His head spun. The alcohol had set in. He thought about John and his crops, they were withered as were his profits but that not enough reason to lie. Henry was a faithful man and prided himself for it, until now, his reputation hung by a thread. He sighed. John had a family and hungry mouths to feed. There would be no income without a sale and the crops were in such poor state, they offered no nutrition. Henry shook his head, there was no way around it. He wobbly headed up the basement stairs and slammed the door shut.

Little John worked about a half-a-mile from the front porch. He pressed a handful of potato spores into the ground and buried them by the heel of his boot. He took a break, his shoulders heaved with exhaustion. He only noticed Henry's presence by the footsteps that vibrated the ground and Little John bowed his head. "Master, I heard from father that you are headed to Winchester tomorrow. Is that true?"

"Yes." Henry swung back the gin. "Don't call me that."

"Yes, sire." From the pen over, pigs ploughed through mouthfuls of corn. "Shall we be taking the pigs to Winchester?"

"No. The beastly animals will make a fine dime when the time was right. That will be all."

Between the redundant questions and the stale odour of the pig's slop, Henry's fury brewed. He would fulfil the favour for John but it would be his last. Upon Henry's return from Winchester, he would pay out John for his rotten produce and the ordeal would end. He glanced down at Little John, who shouldn't be caught in the cross fire, although he was and Henry pondered what would happen to him. He toyed with the glass in hand traced his fingernail along the pattern indentations. Little John's blood coursed with the infidelity of his father and he too would follow the same path someday. Perhaps not anytime soon but it was inevitable. Henry returned his gaze to the moon-crescent sky, it was getting late and Little John had a lengthy travel home. He squinted at the darkened clouds and rummaged a hand in the pocket of his pants.

"Open your hand. The extra shillings are yours if you meet me at dawn. And be sure to bring your fathers' produce."

Little John tugged at the tight straps over his shoulders and grinned. He stuffed the shillings into his pocket and turned around. By the time Henry polished off the gin, Little John had disappeared.

The dining room was cluttered with cabinets filled with porcelain plates. Henry who sat at the head of the table whilst Clara plated his meal; cubed potatoes, onions and one sausage. Beside him was his eldest son, David, who at thirteen years old worked at the local mine. He noticed his father's gaze and ploughed through the plate of dinner, all the while, he avoided eye contact. To the other side was Arthur, who begun at the cotton mill. He toyed with the potatoes.

"Son, you're going to eat that aren't you?"

Arthur nodded. "Yes, sire." He diced the sausage into bite sized pieces and a squelch oozed. The sleeves of his over-sized coat trailed into the oiled onions and brought with it the stench of grease.

"Did you enjoy your day at the mill?" Henry asked.

"I don't like it there."

"That's the way it is." Henry cut another portion of potato. "You have it better than the orphans on the other side of town. You could be working away from your family but now you work on a full belly and when you're older you work where you choose."

"You mean when I'm your age?"

"Yes." Henry cleared his throat. "Anyway, tomorrow I will leave for Winchester." He nibbled at the potato with his fork. He choked on his own words and would give nothing away from the deal with John. He foot jittered and the vibrations rang through the table but his family seemed too engrossed in their own meal to realise. He wiped a hand over his face when he caught Arthur watch him. Henry ploughed through a mouthful of dinner. "I should be back within the week."

Clara tilted her head to the side. "You will pass on my greetings, won't you?"

He winked and she blushed.

Henry awoke before dawn for sunlight had not yet reached the hill. He slipped the link of the suspenders into place whilst he climbed down the stairs of the basement to collect the leather satchel. He double checked the letter was inside and was about to leave when a silhouette outside the window caught his eye. Henry squinted through the darkness and realised the petite silhouette was Little John, poised beside the buckboard wagon. He wore a sack coat three-sizes too big. He always knew to arrive ten-minutes ahead of schedule.

Little John paced as he awaited the boss, his boots kicked up a plume of dust that encased two sterilised tin containers filled to the brim with potatoes. "Good day to you sire!"

"Good morning!" Henry pointed to the crate. "Let's start with that one."

Little John loaded the crate, which must've weighted as much as himself, into the wagon, which was now cluttered by rice, turnips and potatoes, covered by a canvas cloth. The pair headed for the geldings who munched on an early breakfast.

"Sire, do the horses have names?"

"No." Henry reached for the bridle slumped over the fence.

"Why do they not have names, they work like I do?"

"If you're not careful you should not have a name either and I'll call you horse."

Little John gulped but Henry laughed, perhaps the joke was a by-product of his nerves, for he had not forgotten the deal, sell the produce and salvage his marriage.

"Very well then," Henry shielded his eyes. "We better leave before the sun rises. Little John I have a proposition for you. Today shall be the day I teach you to control the wagon. You may steer the geldings, all the way to Winchester. You must to learn to control them if you are to be a farmer one day, like your father and I."

"Of course, sire." Little John placed the lamp between his feet and gathered the reins. Henry leant across, when the sudden stench of over-ripened vegetables soured the morning air and he coughed into his elbow. Henry demonstrated how to hold the leather straps and Little John rearranged his hands multiple times. His tongue slipped out the side of his mouth in concentration and his hands became entangled in the reins. The musty smell of rotten vegetables stung Henry's eyes and he ended the demonstration early. He glanced back at the house and Clara emerged from the door. She unfolded her arms, pressed two fingers against her lips and raised them into the air. Henry reciprocated the act and swallowed against the lump in the back of his throat as a wave of heaviness coursed through his chest. The dreaded adventure into Winchester would soon end and John would bite his tongue, never to speak again about lie of Henry's love affair. Henry nodded and Little John whipped the geldings. The wagon pulled away from the farm and the journey to Winchester begun. Only a hundred-thirty-five miles remained. For Henry the journey was as he expected, pleasant and nothing but farmland to distract him. But Little John's stern frown spoke of the gruelling task of navigating the wagon. His knuckles whitened and his tailbone bones ached from resting in the same position for endless hours. He shifted atop the wooden seat but it offered little relief. "Will we get a break soon?" He moaned.

Dusk was upon them and Henry decided it was time for an inevitable rest. "You make a good point."

Little John shivered as the winds howled but Henry was a friend to the cold. "There's a blanket or two in the back if you wish." He demonstrated how to pull the wagon aside of the imaginable road, there was no way to know where it started and ended for it was a muddy mess. The wise knew not to travel the roads at night. Henry was desperate. The geldings collapsed and Little John placed a blanket over their face, he only left their snouts exposed. Henry grimaced, Little John had a heart of gold but not that of a man. He had compassion and too much of it, he needed to toughen. Henry pushed the containers aside, curled into the corner of the wagon and used the canvas cloth as coverage. Little John blew out the lamp and lay beside him. Henry felt the warmth from Little John against his back which disrupted his attempt to sleep. Instead he rolled over and gazed at the night sky, which was almost black as the ocean depths but between the stars, fragments of snow trickled down, it was what Henry dreaded most.

"Sire, how much further is the trip?" Little John Whispered.

"Two more days if we continue at this rate."

"That's good because my father will be needing me back on our own farm by the end of the week. He says the horses will need moving into the next paddock and my brothers' broken his leg, he cannot work." Little John rambled on but Henry's mind drifted with the sky. He would be home soon and all would be normal once this trip had ended.

"Sire, I'm cold."

"Then use the cloth."

"I'm already wrapped up in the cloth. Can I sleep beside you?"

Henry hesitated. "Alright, but only for tonight." Little John who hunched into a foetal position along Henry's backside. There they lay, not quite warm and not quite comfortable either as the unforgivable snow came down. They made do with each other's warmth and slept somewhat through the night.

V

2001

Halley shovelled her hands into the pockets of her jumper, an attempt to stop from wiping away the heavy bags beneath her eyes. Oren left before she awoke and for good reason, she wouldn't want to be seen in such a state. The three-storied laboratory loomed ahead with large pillars on either side of the entrance and a rusted metal fence that encompassed the small car-park. Halley opened the door and the familiar scent of detergent and hand sanitiser flooded her nose. It would sicken her on a good day. She slipped into a white lab coat and headed towards the winding staircase and down to L2N, Level 2, North wing. The narrow corridor lead to a pair of frosted glass doors and she punched a code into the black keypad. The doors parted and revealed a lab that was crammed by the array of medical equipment and glass cabinets. The windowless lab was airtight but embodied a strict ventilation system. Halley raised an eyebrow at Gabriel, who was dressed in an identical white coat.

"Two casualties and five successive DNA extractions from the mosquitos," Gabriel muttered as he transcribed the results in numerical value onto a blank page. "That brings our losses up to twenty-one. Twenty-one fossils wasted over the last four years."

Halley sighed as a heaviness filled the room. The mosquito subjects were either donated by museums, tissue donors or purchased by universities at a steep price. "Do you think the experiment will work this time?"

"I know what you're asking and that won't happen. We've practiced this experiment for five years," Gabriel spoke in a pressured voice. "We have the DNA, it won't be like the last time, not if we move quickly. You know as well as I do that we have two weeks left of this experiment, so let's make the most of it."

"So tell me, did you and Oren clone the DNA this morning?" Halley wasn't a scientist and the fate of the experiment was out of her grasp. The DNA presence was only half of the problem, it must be extracted with accurate delicacy. She scoured Gabriel's face for answers but behind the rough Russian exterior, he gave nothing away. Through the concrete walls a muffled whistle sounded, the tune trailed down the corridor and Halley's stomach fluttered with passion. Oren entered the room, he whistled the tune of The Beetles' Blackbird. His hands were tucked into his pockets and cheeks sucked inwards, he showed off his etched jawline. He slipped an arm around her waist, his face said it all. He was smitten with glee.

"It worked didn't it?" Halley asked.

"It sure did."

She perked herself up by her tiptoes and pressed a kiss against Oren's lips. Her face tingled with sweet excitement. It was great news.

"Show me."

Gabriel led the way over to the bench along the back wall hunched over. Halley tried to understand what Gabriel looked at. Then she realised. There was a row of five petri dishes, all of them with a code written on the masking tape around the base.

Each petri dish had a small blob inside. It was an embryo. Halley glanced over the subjects, to the far left was B-400, X-313, M-000, Z-201, X-313 and E-250. The alphabetical codes differentiated the specimen's and the numbers described their age, well according to her calculations. The specimen to the far left, B-400 was the oldest, approximately four-hundred-years old, the petri dish to the far right, E-250, was two-hundred-fifty-years-old and somewhere in-between the embryo M-000, a specimen that was never born. The DNA from the blood within the mosquitos was already transferred into a human embryo. Halley ran her fingers through her hair, she almost couldn't believe her own eyes. Gabriel pulled up an office chair before the petri dishes. He daren't look away.

"What are you doing?" Oren asked.

"Waiting." Dark bags encased Gabriel's eyes and tears dropped to the floor from the lack of sleep. Time was short but Gabriel's need for sleep was shorter. "I'm going to monitor this experiment on a twenty-four hour basis and make sure these embryos grow. This is going to work."

"You're not doing that job alone, we will help you," Oren insisted. "How did the embryos take to the accelerated growth hormone?"

"So far, so good. Only time will tell if they will make it though." Halley's hands shook and she clasped them together. The cloned embryos would not age at a normal pace, instead the growth hormone would double it. By the end of the fourteen days, they would be size of an eighteen-day-old foetus. The thought chilled Halley to the spine, the experiment had never gotten this far. She turned to Oren and tears prickled her eyes, a combination of fear, glee and everything in-between.

"It's okay." Oren stroked her hands.

"I know, I just can't believe we've made it this far. May I?" Halley gestured towards the microscope.

"Please."

She placed the microscope above the petri dish labelled subject X-313 and twisted the knob until the view blurred into perspective and there it was. A cluster of identical cells encapsulated by a thick circumference. Its sole purpose was to flourish and at the pace of the researcher's discretion. Although, it appeared a cluster of microscopic cells, multiplying into a greater mass, to Halley it was much more and she whispered a prayer of thanks. Her heart pumped with adrenaline and a million thoughts, more so, questions, crossed her mind. Everything was going to be alright, this time. There was a future beyond the experiment and all the years of failure would finally contribute to something. A strange but wholesome sensation pulsed through Halley's body and she felt content. There was hope for all their crazy science. "I'll be in the library if you need a hand."

"Dim the lights on your way out, won't you Hal?" Gabriel asked.

In the darkness the embryos were almost invisible and to society the embryos never were but to the researchers the experiment worked. Halley emerged into L1W, level one west wing, the only wing on that level in fact. She entered the library and pressed her back against the door. As Halley's eyes shut, she surrendered to the tranquil blackness. The memory crept into her mind:

It was April and overgrown grass was dehydrated along the roadside and the mountains were a distant blue-grey. Halley shut off the radio, it made her head pound as they travelled to Dr Innley's office. Nobody spoke, even Max remained silent. His grey-blue eyes squinted against the morning light from the car window. At only a few weeks old and in the tenth percentile, he hardly gained any weight. The three of them entered the blue-and-white clinic and were guided into a consult room where, Dr Innley greeted them with bulging blue eyes and thick rimmed glasses. He looked far too young to call himself a paediatric oncologist. Dr Innley remained silent and Halley searched his face for answers, uncertain if she wanted them or not. Her heart sank into her stomach, this wasn't going to be easy. Dr Innley grabbed the bundle of pages and fiddled with the edges.

"As you know we have Max's results back and I thought it would be better to tell you in person. His pathology results indicate an abnormally high level of white blood cells and consequently his red blood cells are very low." Dr Innley clasped his hands together, maintaining a professional face but Halley swore his eyes darkened. He seemed to choke on his own words. "Max has CML."

She leaned forward and searched the blood results on the table but nothing made sense. The numbers blurred and her head spun. Dr Innley's words radiated through her head, CML. A heavy guilt flooded Halley, was she suppose to know what CML was? She repeated the abbreviation over and over, hoping the answers would come and although they didn't Dr Innley's tone was enough to suggest something dire.

"What is CML?" Oren interjected.

"I am very sorry but Max has Chronic Myeloid Leukaemia."

The words sucked the air from the room and Dr Innley spoke again but Halley wasn't listening. She turned towards Max and stroked his cotton-soft cheeks. His petite face burrowed a frown and then flopped into her hand. Max was forced to carry a heavy load by a fragile child-sized body. How unfair to expect him to bear the weight of Leukaemia. "Ninety-percent survival rate," Dr Innley's voice echoed inside Halley's skull. For some reason that statistic didn't make her feel any better. She reached for the trash can and poured her stomach into it.

Upon returning home, Halley watched Oren lay a feeble kiss on Max's head and lowered him into the cot. Max slept in a peaceful realm with his stubby hands tightened around a bunny and the scent of Johnson and Johnson's baby conditioner lifted through the air. Halley clenched her jaw, somehow this was her fault, for bringing Max into this world, for the Leukaemia, for him not thriving. She twisted the hem of her jumper in her teeth and bit down until her jaw thumped with ache and heavy tears drenched the fabric. She slid down the cot, pressed her forehead against the wooden bars and gripped Max's hand, toying with his little fingers. She pressed her lips closer to the cot. "I'm right here Max, I'm not going anywhere. You're going to be okay," Halley's eyes filled with painful tears. "I promise you that."

A piercing clash emitted and Halley's heart skipped a beat. She leapt down the hallway was confronted with a pile of shattered glass that emitted from the bathroom. She burst inside, where Oren hunched over an abstract splatter of fresh blood dotted the sink. The mirror was shattered and the crimson blood dripped down his balled fist. Neither of them spoke for what could be said?

Halley leant against the doorway. It all made sense now, Max's lack of appetite, weight loss, fatigue, all of it. She thought it was a phase or the flu. There was hope before that day and it honestly seemed stupid but not having a diagnosis was better than having one. Only this time was different, it was worse than she predicted. There was a glass fragment lodged within his thumb but it was far less painful than the pain inside. That day a part of Oren's spirit died and it took Halley with him.

Halley wiped a tear rom the corner of her eye, everything seemed to be shaping up. First Dr Innley said Max is doing well and now the experiment worked. Her fingers trailed along the circular oak table and she focused on the bookshelf along the back-wall. Rows of novels reached to the ceiling and the warm scent of paper wafted through her nose. Her fingers fumbled along the shelf, following the indentations of each book but not the one she sought. She glanced over her shoulder at the door but it remained shut. Halley was alone. She encircled the bookshelf and slowed at the same spot, two-hundred-sixty-fifth books to the right and pulled out a crimson novel, with gold engraving on the front, *The New Gulliver*. Someone wise once said placing a negative within the realms of beauty, would bring great things. Perhaps that was happening now. It was nonsense but when you are desperate, fibs are the way to brighten a mind. Sometimes the right amount of lies can make you believe it's true and there's no harm in that. At least, Halley didn't think so.

She placed the book on the table and followed the red ribbon bookmark to where a bundle of letters lay, each of them sealed and dated. Some were in pristine condition, others aged with yellow-edges but they none were ever read. Most were drenched in Halley's tears but she knew the tenderness of the letters and handled them feeble as moth wings. Amidst the blurred black ink, each letter was addressed to Max. She extracted a fresh blank page from her pocket and laid it out. She pressed the pen against the page and tried to write but the pen simply quivered on the spot. Halley grit her teeth and exhaled a deep breath. She wanted to write, it was something that had been done for months but the exciting news was almost too good to be true. It seemed almost sinister for life to be so sweet. Halley pressed the pen harder against the page and a speckle of black ink drained but remained within the circumference of the pen-head. Being grateful is enough sometimes and didn't mean the blocked ears of these blank letters needed to know. They only knew as much as she told them. Halley breathed a sigh of relief and the pen began lucidly moving, back and forth. The cursive words transcribed onto the page.

Max is in remission.

Dated 03/03/2003

That was all that mattered. It was most possibly the shortest letter of them all but those words were magical. Halley quickly shovelled the letters back inside *The New Gulliver* and placed it on the shelf. Since Max's diagnosis, she hardly discussed it with Oren. It seemed easier to suffer alone and so she transcribed her thoughts and emotions into letters. She wiped her cheeks and rearranged her hair when the door knob jiggled and Oren entered the room. He clenched his chiselled jaw and his over-grown hair licked the cuff of his neck. "Hal, what's the matter?"

"Nothing."

"You're crying?" Oren stroked her cheek.

"I cry at the best of times, you know that," Halley laughed.

"That I do know but you have let me in on this secret though, if it's that happy I want to cry too."

"It's Max. I'm going to call Doctor Innley's office again."

"Didn't he call already?"

Halley nodded through the blurred vision. "Yeah but I want to hear it again. And again and again and every single day."

Oren laughed and wrapped his bear-sized arms around Halley's small physique. There they stood, within the realms of each other's embrace until their arms grew weak and tears soaked each other's clothing. Neither of them were quite sure where the pain ended and relief began but in that moment, it all felt the same.

Later that night, Halley was awoken by a distant voice. Through the blur of sleep, her alarm clock read 3.05am. She rolled over and planted her face into the pillow. Then she heard it again. A familiar voice. She forced her eyes open. "Oren ," Halley mumbled.

No response. She headed downstairs and made her way over to the front porch, where a full crescent moon watched Oren pace back and forth with a cellphone pressed against his ear.

"Yeah I know, just let me know when to come - ," he cut himself off as Halley stepped through a bundle of leaves.

Oren spun around and held one hand in the air. "One second - Sorry, honey, it's Gabriel."

"Gabriel?" Halley frowned. She wrapped her hands around Oren's waist as he ended the call and tucked the blackberry cell back into his pocket. "How many times have I told you that you need a new phone?" Halley taunted.

"I don't see anything wrong with it ... Besides it being old."

"It's outdated. Anyway, why is Gabriel calling you at this hour?"

"He's making a schedule for around the clock monitoring of the embryos." Oren grinned and the sweet dimples re-appeared. "It's a little beyond me to be honest. I'll have to go into the lab soon, he hasn't slept in almost twenty-four hours."

"Yeah, you don't say he looked like shit. Do you think he's a little dramatic?"

"Of course." Oren wrapped his arms around Halley and pressed his head against her's.

"Should I be worried?"

"About what? Everything is going fine, Gabriel's always dramatic. He's running off of adrenaline and probably hasn't eaten since yesterday."

"Take some left overs when you go in. How are the embryos?"

"They're great. We're now in the blastocyst stage now and they've almost doubled in size since Gabriel tampered with their growth hormones." Oren sighed. "The experiment will be over before we know it, all the lead-up and anticipation will be gone.

Don't get me wrong, I'm thankful it worked but having to kill off the embryos in twelve days days is just too soon."

"I think we always want more time on this Earth … If you had more time with the embryos, what would you do?"

Oren thought with his chin pressed against Halley's forehead. "I don't know. There's so many reasons I want to keep the embryos alive, so much I want answered but now you ask, I can't think of anything." He cocked his head to the side. "If I had more time in this life I do know what I would do though." Oren cradled Halley's body and nibbled along her jawline. The wet kisses forced her eyes shut and her body relaxed in his arms. "C'mon, let's get to bed. What time are you going to the lab?"

"Six."

"I'll meet you there once I drop Max off." Halley walked towards the porch but noticed Oren wasn't behind her. She turned around and folded her arms. His face was shadowed by the dark but his eyes glistened beneath the moonlight. "I love you," he whispered.

"I love you too." She waited for him.

From atop the microscope, Halley watched the petri-dishes of the cloned embryos or, what she considered, children and to a premature world that was not ready for their existence. They would never be granted the gift of humanity for their unforgivable emergence would eternally be condemned. Nobody would welcome the embryos with open arms like it would a child born within the four white walls of a hospital. The embryos would be despised not for who they were but what they had become and in that alone, their death had long foretold long before their creation. She focused on subject X-313 and wandered who he was in his old life. The cloned DNA would tell the truth of their past. Halley looked over subject ER-250, the being she gave life to, beneath the microscope. It reached the morula stage and was comparable to a mulberry. The cluster of sixteen cells morphed within the zone pellucida. The cells were undefined and fuzzy as they melted together and the biological fluid compressed the cells and they matured into the experiment. It worked as expected. The lab doors parted and Halley swivelled around in the chair as she heard fast-paced footsteps. Gabriel punched through the air in his pristine lab coat that was buttoned neck-high.

"Morning Gabriel."

He hunched over the petri-dishes. The glint of white teeth protruded over his bottom lip. He muttered something in harsh Russian but the euphoric expression on his face spoke of the upmost contempt. "Morning my little ones." He sighed, still focused on the embryos.

"I'm still here and not going anywhere, unfortunately," Halley said.

Gabriel cackled. "I wasn't talking to you."

"The subjects were doing well. I just checked over E-250 and X-313."

He turned back to the embryos and the light reflected off his polished bold head. "Not all of them are thriving. Subject M-000 isn't coming along as fast. It's a little behind." He strode towards the cabinet filled with formulas and medications. "Nothing a little growth hormone can't fix."

"Is that necessary?"

Gabriel cast a dominant glare and Halley soon realised her remark was a bad idea, she gulped down the coffee, filling her mouth with something other than words. "Here. I got you one."

Gabriel sipped the coffee. "It's warm? How many times do I have to tell you, hot coffee isn't good for anybody. Throw a few ice cubes into it and let science do the work." He grimaced at the sight of the coffee. "Hal, you shouldn't have food in here, you know that."

"I was just heading off."

VI

1821

The snow melted and mud puddles formed through the trails of Great Britain. The geldings grew weak as the sticky roads clung to their hooves. No matter the pain inflicted by the whip, they refused to pick up the pace. Henry bit his lip, there had to be a faster way to Winchester but it seemed another break was needed. No, the snow would melt faster and the mud would thicken. He was sure another heave of frost would fall again, it always did. That would only make matters worse. Little John held the canvas cloth over his shoulders to stop shivering against the May winds. He annoyedly gnawed on a carrot, chiseled away at the skin and tossed it over the side of the wagon. He was a fussy eater and chewed loud. Henry grimaced, the sloppy chewing disturbed his train of thought. Little John pinched off another piece of carrot skin by his teeth and toyed with it absent-mindedly. He examined the specimen, then leaned forward and offered it to the foal, who smacked its' lips and demolished the carrot. The foal cocked its' head sideways, it awaited another piece and the wagon began to shift in the direction his head turned. Henry straightened the foal and snapped a carrot in half, he offered a piece to each gelding. He was the strong link even though he ate rations and offered whatever warmth he could for Little John.

"Don't worry, we are almost there," Henry said through chapped lips.

"I'm not worried, not even cold."

"Not the slightest?"

"No, sire."

Henry cackled.

"Sire, what do you think happens when we die? Mama says we go to Heaven and never come back."

"Do you want to know what I think?"

"Yes, sire."

"I think we live beyond this life." Henry pointed to a by-passer. A man rode a caramel Clydesdale horse whose long-hair was covered in mud and ploughed across the mountain. The man tipped his hat to which Henry reciprocated the act. "That man could be you in the after life."

"I don't understand, sire."

"I think that when we die, we are reborn. I don't think we live once and that is the end. We keep coming back in another form."

"How does that happen?"

"Faith. God. Research. Science. Who knows. Perhaps you, Little John, will be a horse in the next life. You know the job well so hopefully you don't need much training."

Little John gasped and almost toppled over the wagon. Henry laughed and returned his focus to the map sprawled across his lap. They were on the brink of Winchester but the next few miles would be difficult. Up ahead was an unbridged river and the stream was high. Henry cussed, he looked across the sidewalk which was a muddy mess as the snow began to disintegrate. It would act as quick s and swallow the geldings. Henry's heart pounded in his mouth, it wasn't an easy task. "We take to the river."

"But sire!"

"The roads are uneven and muddy, the horses will tire much quicker. Besides the river is a short cut, on the other side is the nape of Winchester. We will be right at the foot of the town."

The wagon stopped along the edge of the river which flowed viciously, the waves toppled over themselves. Henry gulped, he knew what had to be done. He whipped the asses of the geldings and they reluctantly took to the river. The foal squealed, it had never seen so much water before. It's mane flicked in every way and Henry struggled to hold him in line. There was no choice, the foal plunged forward beside the other horse. Their front hooves soon submerged in a water current that threatened to knock them sidewards. The geldings attested but he urged them onwards and the wagon tilted as it climbed down into the river and then straightened. Henry held his breath, the horses had not made a stream this high before. The foal entered the river and its' head barely protruded above the surface. He already regretted the decision but the latter option wasn't any easier. The geldings became entrenched by the heavy current and pushed their muscled legs through the stream. The foal hardly pulled his weight. Water splashed into the air and the foal's front legs struggled with all of its' not-so-mighty force. Little John held onto the side of the wagon for support but his body bounced. He clawed the wood and splinters flew through the air. Crack.

Henry heard something snap. "Where did that come from?"

"I don't know!"

He twisted the reins around his hands and peered back. The

wood snapped and echoed again. Then he felt it. From somewhere below, the wagon gave out and the icy water seeped inside. Henry's boots were coated in a fine layer of water as the river raged and splashed against the wagon. The foal suddenly plunged forward. His head flung in every way as he wailed. Henry whipped the foal but it did not budge, his snout kept above water but Henry wondered for how long. Then he realised, it was stuck. His stomach dropped. "Here, hold on tight."

Henry passed the reins to Little John. He leapt atop the wagon, which threatened to throw him off, and held onto the wooden beam. He delicately placed one foot before the other and jumped onto the back of the black horse. Who wailed and flung its' head all around. Henry pat its' back and the gelding calmed. He scoured the horse but couldn't find the problem and then jumped into the water. The current was stronger than Henry anticipated and he held onto the wagon for support. The river prickled his legs with numbness and Henry couldn't feel himself move anymore. He stroked the mane of the foal and whispered words of comfort. He reached his hands into the stream and felt along the foal's leg which pulled back. Then again. Harder.

"I'm going to have a look! Hold on tight!" Henry yelled above the river.

He held his breath and plummeted down. His face stung as if shards of ice were beneath his skin. Henry forced his eyes open but saw nothing other than green blur. He guided himself down by his hands alone. Then he felt it. There was a mud-hole by which the foal's front hoof was stuck. Henry's lungs gasped for air and he was forced to re-surface. He sucked in a mouthful of oxygen. He glanced over at Little John, who appeared on the brink of tears. "I'm alright."

Henry plunged into the river again, this time he dug at the muddy ground around the foal's leg. He dug away the mud and soon the hoof was free. He moved aside in time for the foal to slam down against the ground. He pushed through the river as he urged the geldings forward but though their fear stricken faces , they were hard to manoeuvre. "That's it, now come on the both of you." He flicked away the beads of water from his eyes. "That's it," Henry ushered.

Little John whipped the geldings and this time they pounded forward.

"Gently, don't push them too much," Henry urged. He balanced himself and walked backwards and the horse followed. Turbulent waves burst out from beneath the wagon, it now reached ankle-length on Little John. Although it was still shallow, his face grew pale. He couldn't swim.

The river knocked the back of Henry's knees and he fought to let the river force him down. He leaned against the thick necks of the horses, who groaned obnoxiously. He grit his teeth and forcibly steadied himself. "Keep coming!"

Henry was drenched in the cold river and heavy water loaded the pockets of his coat. He stumbled backwards onto dry l and the geldings followed. The foal panted and Henry pat his back. "Good job."

VII

2001

The lights were dim and a vanilla-and-cinnamon candle brightly burned in the centre of the table that encompassed two untouched plates of roast chicken dinner. Halley's head slumped over a balled fist and she picked at the chicken with her fork. It was cold and hard. She blew out the candle and the smoke trailed through the air, it contorted into abstract figures. The kitchen was silent and bumped up the volume on the baby monitor beside her elbow. The static puff of a faint breath emitted. Her fingers trailed along the edges of the baby monitor. Two hours already passed. Halley threw the napkin over her food. Then the front door creak open. She sighed, Oren shouldn't have come home. He staggered into the room, a complete mess. His mattered hair was plastered against his face that dripped in sweat and the foul smell of body odour wafted. He glared at Halley wide-eyed and attempted to recollect his breath that seemed to never catch up.

"Happy anniversary." Halley pointed at him. "Please don't start with the excuses and no … I'm not mad." She swung back a long gulp of champagne.

"I'm so sorry, love." Oren puffed. "You don't understand, at the lab - "

Halley pointed the champagne glass towards Oren. "Don't start on me about the lab. We're not talking about this. Especially not tonight!"

"Halley, firstly, I didn't forget our anniversary. I have your present in my back pocket but I also need to tell you something. I wouldn't be late unless this was extremely important." Oren shadowed her through the kitchen. "Please."

Halley reached for the tea towel that hung from the oven handle and wrapped it around each finger. She vigorously rubbed away the moisture from the webs of her fingers. "Can it wait?"

Oren bit his lower lip.

"Hal, you need to hear this!"

Halley poured another glass of Armand De Brignac Gold champagne. She swallowed the expensive taste, something she was saved all year. Her heart cracked, she didn't seem important to Oren anymore. The lab had become the very purpose of his life and where did that put her?

"Six years Oren. It's our six year anniversary. We're not doing this tonight."

Oren's solemn face flooded Halley with guilt but that night, she didn't share the same passion for the experiment. Every year He welcomed her with a bouquet of withered flowers and Halley was just as surprised. But not this year, she was presented with more conversations about the lab and nothing romantic seemed to be up for discussion.

"Alright." He reached into his jeans pocket and extracted an envelope. It was addressed to Halley and in the corner it read AncestryDNA. She stared at the letter confused. Halley threw the tea towel into the sink, where the soap bubbles engulfed it. "What is this?" She asked in a pressured tone.

"A gift."

Halley accepted the letter and tore open the seal. Her fingers were damp and clung to the paper. Impatience crept into her hands and she roughly pulled out the letter. She flicked it open and scoured the contents. There was a diagram in the centre, unrecognisable names and paragraphs around it.

"I traced your DNA, I know being an orphan has taken a chip from your shoulder. I thought if you knew where you came from, it may offer some comfort. Happy anniversary."

Halley traced her fingers along the edge of the letter and handled it with tender care. The family tree encapsulated a long list of names and although they appeared meaningless, these people were her family.

"I collected the saliva sample when you were asleep. I have planned this for a while."

Halley paid attention to each name and then she locked her eyes on her parents. Her vision blurred, as if the final reveal was too good to be true. Oren rested his hand against the kitchen bench.

"Now can I need to tell you – "

"You're unbelievable." The thought of Halley's parents suddenly disintegrated into nothingness and her heart burned with fury. The moment she waited for so long exploded into darkness and the family tree soured. Oren ruined it for her. Halley folded the letter and stuffed it back inside the envelope. She grabbed the champagne glass and gulped back a large mouthful.

"Would just listen to me?"

"No." Halley slammed the champagne glass against the counter and her hands shook. This was a joke. "Did you try to win me over with my gift? Out of all the damned nights, it had to be tonight! You couldn't wait till tomorrow? You'd rather put that stupid experiment before me?"

Oren nodded. "You're right you know, you're absolutely right."

He reached forward and stroked Halley's hand. His eyes pleaded for mercy. "I'm sorry. I'm sorry I missed our anniversary, I'm sorry I've been so caught up with work but please read the letter."

Halley dropped the champagne glass into the sink and a fine crack emitted as the glass broke. She flapped the letter open and scoured her eyes over the family diagram again.

A lump grew at the back of her throat and her fingers shook. She had to find out who she was and where she came from, something she longed to tell Max. "My father was British. I'm actually British and American?" She gasped. "My heritage dates back to York, Great Britain." The tears blurred her vision before she could read the names of her parents. She crouched to the ground and Oren slipped his hands beneath her armpits in time. He drew Halley close to his chest and she sunk her face into his shirt. It was too much to fathom and somehow, she was not ready to have all the answers at once. She would look over the letter another day, for now, Halley understood a fraction of her foundations and that was enough.

Oren rambled an apology but she placed her index finger against his mouth and shushed him. She leaned forward and gently kissed his cold lips. "Come upstairs."

Halley heard the rapid heartbeat beneath his freckled chest. Their inter-woven fingers lay on his belly and Halley glared at the scar along the knuckle of his thumb. She traced the pink defect surrounded by hardened skin. It was a memoir from only months earlier. Halley recalled the memory as if it were yesterday:

Oren became mute. He Lost his appetite and deteriorated faster than Max. He left Halley in limbo. For six months neither of them exchanged a glance much less a conversation. She was always the 'strong one' as if that was something to be proud of. She watched from the doorway as Oren poured himself another whiskey shot. Her heart sunk into her back, he never drank. He mumbled to himself and paced the circumference of the living room. Halley crept down the stairs, silent as a child. Oren plunged the shot glass down on the coffee table and reached for the journal article. He drew it close to his face and guzzled back the contents from the whiskey bottle.

"Yes, now that makes sense," he mumbled and walked in a circle. Halley traced her fingers through her greasy hair, it reeked of dandruff. She took a deep breath and walked towards Oren. He turned away and buried his face in the papers.

"You can't even look at me." Halley whispered above the lump in her throat. "Look at me."

Oren's eyes were clouded by a drunken haze. His lips drew apart and he breathed heavily but he remained speechless and his soul rot within the barricades of his own mind. How long could Oren survive without proper human contact?

Halley felt along his cheek where the over-grown stubble prickled her fingers. Oren pulled away. "How much longer are you going to push me away for? You won't come near me!"

"Not until I find a cure for our son." He raised the papers in the air. "I'm going to help him!"

"We will help him together but I need to be sober!"

"Fucking man up and help me! You always leave me all alone to deal with Max while you get drunk!"

Oren spun around and the edge of the whiskey bottle smashed against the corner of the table. Glass rained over his hand the caramel liquor stained the cream carpet. Halley wished she could erase Oren's memory of that day and take it all back. She felt along the scar of his thumb. Maybe if the scar was removed, he would forget. She was forced back into reality as Oren shifted.

"What did you want to tell me earlier?" Halley asked.

"I think it's better I show you in the morning."

Before 8am, Halley and Oren entered L2N, where the freshly mopped floor smelt of bleach. She moved fast, this better be important to have missed the anniversary. The frosted lab doors opened and the lights flick on. There was a messy splay of paperwork along the wooden desk, a pillow and takeaway coffee cup. Gabriel obviously slept there and the foul odour of morning breath wafted . Halley gagged, it was off-putting.

Oren looked at her with a fond smile.

"Well, what are we doing here?"

"Okay, so you know how the experiment is now up do day seven?"

"Yeah."

"Wrong. Today is day fourteen."

Halley extracted a toothpick and her tongue danced with the

symphony of frustration. It was a bad habit, especially now her teeth decayed but it kept her nerves at bay. Between Oren's redundant questions and the odour of the room, she became impatient. Oren smirked with pride and waited for Halley to catch on. "Fine, don't tell me."

"Honey. Think about it. These cloned embryos have been given accelerated growth hormone."

Halley spun around. "If you aren't going to be clear with me, then I'll go see for myself."

She marched over to the petri dishes and placed subject E-250 under the microscope. Halley increased the fine adjustment notch and the test subject blurred into vision. Her eyes widened and stung when she refused to blink. Her heart almost pounded out of her chest. The embryo matured and far too quickly. Along the caudal end of the cell, Halley saw it. A black groove had emerged. It was the primitive streak. A new sign of life, the embryo had developed into the next stage, where the definitive endoderm would form. At some point Gabriel entered the room and stood beside Oren.

"What the fuck is wrong with you two?" She spat, tears poured down her cheeks.

"It wasn't meant to happen this fast, I had no idea. How could we know this would happen?"

Halley pointed a shaky finger at the petri dishes and walked forward. "The primitive streak. Do they all have it?"

Gabriel nodded. "We can fix this."

"How can you fix it?" Halley spat through gritted teeth. "These embryos are seven days old, this shouldn't have happened and you know it … The primitive streak forms on day fifteen, one day before we should have ended the experiment. How did this happen so soon?"

"The accelerated growth hormone. We've never tested it before and I didn't know it would be that fast."

"You've broken the law. Those cloned embryos are not allowed to have a primitive streak, the first sign of actual life. This never should have happened. By the end of this stupid experiment … In another seven days, those embryos will be closer to a fucking foetus! So tell me, how on Earth can you fix this."

"I have it all under control," Gabriel barked.

"Oh, really? What comes next in your big plan?"

"We end the experiment today. It can't go on anymore!"

Oren burrowed a frown. "That's too soon."

"We don't have a choice," Halley whimpered. "This is all your fault! What did you think was going to happen? You gave those subjects accelerated growth hormone, of course they were going to grow faster. How could you miss that?"

"I didn't know it was going to work!" Oren bellowed, he was shattered. He knew the laws of science but couldn't comprehend what had to be done. "I know, okay, I know what we've done is wrong. But this is my life's work, my ultimate passion and I can't believe it has to end so soon." Tears streamed down his flushed cheeks. "It's not fair."

Halley closed in on him. "I can't believe you. This is why you missed our anniversary? Your life's passion should be me. I should come before those damned embryos. It should be Max and me."

Oren cupped Halley's face and kissed the top of her head. "Let's end this madness."

She pulled away. "End it now."

Oren turned to Gabriel bowed his head. "It's time. Hal can you please pass me the petri dish, we will start with subject X-313."

"No. Do it yourself, I need to be alone." Halley stormed out of the lab.

IIX

2001

With the embryos gone, an eerie silence hung in the lab, there was nothing left to discuss or work on besides the final research report. Goosebumps covered Halley's body and she appeared a plucked chicken. She made her way out of the library and down the hallway of L2N. Oren pulled up beside her and reached for Halley's hand but she jerked away. She didn't blame Oren for what happened, it was nobody's fault but she was angry at the situation. Oren forced an arm outward and stopped Halley in her tracks. She glared at him confused and then she heard it. Voices. There was two of them and they were speaking a foreign language, it sounded Russian.

"What's going on around here?" Halley pondered.

Footsteps clambered up the staircase and soon enough Gabriel and another man appeared, he was about six-foot tall with a buzz-cut and blue stained tattoos covered his neck. The pair were immersed in a fit of laughter.

"Hello," the man said in a thick Russian accent. His left eye was opaque, he was partially blind. Over the left-breast of his overall's. An embroidered circle read *Piper's Plumbing*.

"This is our plumber. Sebastian," Gabriel introduced.

Sebastian grabbed the thick straps over his shoulders and heaved forward. A black backpack bounced from behind.

Oren extended his hand. "Oren, nice to meet you!"

Halley folded her arms. The goosebumps now creeped along her neck to where the hairs stood on end. "May I ask what plumbing problem we have? I didn't know there was one."

"Down in the basement, you had some leaking pipes. Anyway it's all cleared up now."

"Is that so?" Halley raised an eyebrow toward Gabriel.

"I'll show Sebastian the way out."

They muttered in Russian and both their faces turned serious for a moment before he broke out in laughter. Halley never understood Gabriel's attempts at humour. Perhaps Gabriel was joking half the time and she had no idea. She reached inside her pocket and placed a toothpick in the corner of her mouth. The basement has never been used. It was run down without any electrical supply and the floor was sunken in, at least the last time Halley had ventured there three years ago. She turned to Oren, who shrugged.

Back at home, Halley straightened herself and glanced over the sunflowers. Max sat upright on the carpet floor in a U-shaped yellow cushion. He laughed and clapped the stubby hands whilst him build a block tower and tore it down. Oren cackled and extended his hand to stop Max toppling over. Max waited for Oren to build another tower.

"What have you found so far?" Oren called.

"I can't find anything," Halley said.

"Don't worry about it honey, we should be grateful the basement was taken care of."

"I can't wait for it to be done but I don't know why I can't find anything about it online."

"What was the name of the company again? The one Sebastian

worked for?"

"That's what I'm trying to look up. Ah – P … P … Plumbing something."

Halley scoured the internet. When she found the name she would know but nothing seemed to stand out. She could remember every other detail, Sebastian's buzz-cut head, deep voice, blue overalls with the silver buckle, freshly polished black shoes, the emblem over his left breast but the name was absent from her mind.

"Maybe you're not looking hard enough."

"It's on the tip of my tongue. Pip … Pipes … Ah … plumbing." She tapped the keyboard. "Piper's Plumbing," she exclaimed.

The search results were endless for the words 'Piper' and 'plumbing' yet none of them were conjoined. Halley slammed the computer screen shut. "It doesn't matter, I'll message Gabriel."

A strange thought gnawed at Halley. Maybe she looked too far into the situation and it was nothing more than a piping problem. Gabriel was notorious for the lack of communication but this was different. Not even Oren knew about the plumbing problem. Halley rubbed her temples, she was already on edge from the morning and this nonsense made the day worse. Her skull seemed too small as her brain throbbed from the inside out.

Max smashed the stacked wooden blocks and Oren knocked one of them against his forehead. Max broke into a laughing seizure. Oren scooped him up and headed toward the couch. "I'm sorry about earlier."

"No, not in front of Max," Halley said.

"Okay. Don't think too much about the basement. Anyone in their right mind would say Gabriel is on the spectrum and we know intelligence gets the best of him. He can be a real odd ball at times. I mean, he probably hired this plumbing man from a family friend. It can't be a coincidence he spoke Russian?"

"It's not a Russian name though."

"We are in Scotland, they would need a simplified name that everyone can understand."

Halley thought for a moment before she changed the topic.

"Oren, the anniversary present was amazing, thank you. I'm going to look further into this. Now that I have answers, I want to really understand what they mean. Where did I come from in America and Britain? I want to someday tell Max. How was his temperature anyway?"

"A bit high, that's why I unwrapped him."

Max had his entire fist in his mouth and drool dripped down his chin while he chewed all five fingers. Behind his hand, Max smiled at Halley but she solemnly returned the gesture by a tear that trickled down her cheek.

IX

1821

Winchester was a small town but the infrastructure was great in size. Little John guessed the library must have been twenty-stories high but Henry reassured him it was no more than seven. For the first time in days, Henry saw civilisation and it made him smile even through his wet attire. It was not that he forgot the sight of towns and people but it was the scent of warm bread, perfume and tobacco he missed. This time Winchester seemed smaller, perhaps it was the absence of wagons and the crowd literally halved. He exchanged one pence for a small loaf of bread which he shared with Little John, he offered crumbs to the horses. They ploughed through the town, made a sharp right turn and then a left into a residential street. It was not long before they caught sight of the familiar white house ahead with a steel fence and ferns along the porch. It was the home of Urian. Henry knocked at the front door and Little John tied the geldings to a steel post. Henry sighed, he left the produce exposed to the sun another day defeated the purpose of selling John's veggies fresh. But a break was needed, at the very least a change of clothes and a decent meal. The door slipped open and a sweet face appeared. "Oh, hello. I didn't know you were coming."
"Not to worry, Wendy. My friend and I were stopping past, I had a letter for my brother but as you can see I'm a bit wet and could do with the cheapest pair of Urian's suspenders."
"Come in," Wendy whispered.

The walls displayed vertical wooden planks and greenery filled every cornice of the room. There was a small coffee table in the centre and a crocheted blanket laid over the rocking chair. The house was quiet, almost too quiet for a new family. Henry spun around to see Wendy shut the door and peer outside the laced curtain.

"Please take a seat."

Henry sunk into the floral couch and his knees almost reached his shoulders. A string of fabric dangled from a hole in the fingertip of Wendy's glove. Her nail poked through and fumbled with her violet petticoat which began to fray. She bit her lower lip. "How was your journey?"

"Fine, besides the mishap with the horses. I think the foal needs more training. Where is my brother and the child? I have a niece to meet, so I believe."

Wendy's face grew pale. "I am surprised you travelled all this way considering, well, you know."

Henry stared at her, dumbfounded.

"There is a plague," Wendy's eyes glimmered with tears. "Have you not heard?"

"No, we have been on the road."

"It's struck a couple days ago but so many have been cast down in this town and it's not that I want you to leave but I think it would be best."

"I did not see anybody ill on the way here."

"Many have left the town and those that remain stay inside their homes."

"How is my brother?" Henry's voice quivered.

Wendy bowed her head and allowed the visitors to enter the room, here was a double bed and a cradle beside. Henry held his hat against his chest and walked over. A scrawny figure lay sprawled beneath the white sheets that clung to every crevice. It was Urian. The bruised eye-bags and sunken in cheeks cast him unrecognisable. The halo of mattered hair shadowed his face. Henry knelt beside the bed. "Brother, what happened to you?"

Urian turned his head, puss-filled blisters and blood-crusted sores were sewn into his skin. His eyes half-opened and rolled back into his head. "Brother." Urian's voice was a whisper. "You came."

"Shhh, don't speak. Savour your energy."

Wendy sat along the edge of the bed with a bucket in hand. She wrangled the excess water and dabbed at Urian's forehead. "He has been ill with a fever and can hardly keep anything down. People all around are dying. You must go, get out of here!"

"How far has the plague travelled?"

"They say it reached York."

"No." Henry shook his head. Tears filled his eyes. "My wife and boys, what is to happen to them?"

Henry leapt up and pounded toward the door. Little John spun around and knocked against the pale of water, which doused him head to toe. Amidst the commotion, the wail of new life sounded from the cradle. Henry was hypnotised by the child's plea. He turned around, reached inside the crib and lifted the newborn girl, all wrapped in white satin with a bed of dark hair. She wriggled beneath his grasp and her hungry mouth searched in all directions. He passed the baby to Wendy. "I'm sorry, I have to go."

In a midst of panic, Henry ripped the horses from their grass breakfast and buckled the wagon. Wendy watched from the front porch, a stream of tears dripped down her cheeks and Henry whipped the geldings. Little John shivered beneath the heaviness of his soggy clothes but that was the least of their worries. The horses ran through the town and civilians jumped out of the way.

"Little John, I need you to listen to me and not touch anything, not so much as look at anyone."

"Yes, sire."

They rode in silence and this time surpassed the river, he took to the muddy road instead. The wagon fled across the rocky landscape faster than before and the pair bounced in their wagon seats. Fear was the only perpetrator that urged them forward.

X

2001

August twilight dwindled and the summer breeze danced along the River Clyde. Even the lab was warmed by the summer night. Inside the library of L1N, the walls radiated with heat. Halley shovelled *The New Gulliver* into the empty place. She jumped back, Oren now stood behind her and as if he forgot her strangeness, paced forward. "How are you today?"

She walked past him and remained silent.

"Are you still mad at me? Even after all this time?"

"You kept those embryos growing when they shouldn't have. To say I'm angry is an understatement."

"It's been months! I'm sorry, it was out of my hands."

Halley watched Oren over her shoulders. "No more lies."

"You're right, no more lies. That was wrong of me. Now please, let's go home, it's getting late." Oren placed his hands atop his hips. "Can I ask you something? Did you end up looking into AncestryDNA?"

"I haven't had time, it's been so busy here."

"Then let me help you."

"It doesn't matter for now."

Halley pressed through the front door and was welcomed with a summer shower. The green hills wafted with the scent of fresh grass and mud. The rain plastered the hood against her cheeks until Oren opened the umbrella. They walked towards the red Nissan 4WD, where, through the distance the Clyde Arc bridge towered over. It represented a dome over the car and the city lights glistened around it. A blunt force knocked against Halley's arm. She looked at Gabriel who smiled beneath a grey beanie and a black trench coat with the collar pulled up around his neck. He held a cardboard tray which began to cave inwards beneath the weight of the rain and the three coffees titled lopsided.

"I brought us all coffee," Gabriel passed one to Oren and Halley in turn. He titled his head back, as the cold shards of rain smacked into his face and exploded into a million pieces. Although, he did not shudder and instead embraced the shower.

"Gabriel, the coffee!" Halley yelled but it was too late. The soggy tray collapsed in half and hot coffee splashed over her legs but was soon cooled by the rain. She reached toward the ground to collect the cup and paused.

"That coffee was hot."

"I know, there's nothing like a hot coffee in the rain," Gabriel exclaimed.

"You hate hot coffee."

Halley awaited a scientific reason behind why hot coffee was a fantastic source of antioxidants and good health but it never came. Gabriel laughed as beads of rain dribbled from his lip. Something was definitely not right. The only time Halley had seen him ever laugh was, never. "I love you guys. You know what, swing past my apartment tomorrow night."

"Gabriel are you alright?"

"Alright? Am I alright?" Gabriel laughed but the noise rattled Halley's brain. She threw the virtually full coffee into the bin, for she would rather not find out what made Gabriel so joyous. She climbed into the car, plucked the glasses from her face and wiped the lenses by the hem of her jumper. "Oren, what's going on with him?" Halley asked confused.

"Let's chat about it tomorrow night."

"If you're keeping something from me again, I swear - "

"We'll talk tonight."

Dark bags encased Halley's eyes and could be mistaken for bruises and her mind was boggled with questions. Maybe it wasn't as bad as she anticipated but yet again, something was up. Something odd and Halley was going to get to the bottom of it. She sunk into the cream couch and clutched at the glass of water, as if she were a child about to be lectured by her parents. She held her breath against the foul aroma of mould and dust, the apartment was small but made even smaller by the cluttered pot-plants and busy floral carpet. Halley reached forward and pressed the glass of water against the table, stuffing it in-between a bundle of magazines, wilted plants and silver bowls filled with cat biscuits.

Gabriel emerged from the kitchen with two glasses and a fresh bottle of ouzo. He slumped into the couch which almost engulfed him, then passed one glass to Oren and held the other close to his chest. The room was silent for some time as if the built-up excitement was too valuable to share. As if Halley knew about this secret, it would be no more. She sighed, not quite sure if it was from relief, fear or something else. Nobody made eye contact but the telepathic secrecy was uncanny. They were entranced in a speechless world of their own. Halley's heart skipped a beat. "Alright. Does someone want to tell me what the heck is going on?" Halley snapped.

It took Gabriel by surprise and he blinked into focus. He swung back the ouzo and smacked his lips together. "Pitsiladi, only the best around. You know there is evidence of such consumption dating back to five-hundred BC and since then ouzo evolved in the nineteenth century and – "

"Gabriel!" Halley shouted. A fire brewed within Halley's stomach and she swallowed the rage at the back of her throat.

He glanced over at Oren, he searched for answers that never came. A silence congested the room and for some unknown reason, Halley could taste bitter malice on the tip of her tongue.

Gabriel bowed his head, not able to look her in the eye. "Halley. It's the cloning experiment. I know you're going to be mad but just listen to me. The embryos are not dead but alive. They have entered the foetal stage."

Halley's jaw dropped open and that could be heard was the heaviness of her breathing. A million questions raced through her mind, the information was far too much to bear.

"No, that's not true. Tell me the truth."

Oren held her hands. "Gabriel's right, the cloned embryos are alive and I know it sounds crazy but we are doing great things!"

Oren hid this secret from her for months. She ran her fingers through her hair. Then it hit her. The late night phone calls, the primitive streak, they planned this all along. Oren's eyes glimmered with something she had never seen before. A kind of passion or vengeance, that was not him.

"I don't believe this. How can they be alive? We killed them months ago – ," Halley cut herself off. She saw Gabriel destroy the experiment. She thought for a long time. No, she did not, she left before the deed was done. Of course, how stupid to leave the experiment at the hands of Gabriel. Halley faltered. Gabriel was a scientist, he had every right to execute the embryos. It would have made no sense or difference if she were there. Halley felt her heart stretch in two. At first, she pitied the death of the embryos but that was only her human consciousness speaking. Her mind knew the truth and if they kept the embryos alive, it would bring dire consequences. But there was no going back now.

"Halley," Oren began but she was hardly listening. "The embryos are thriving, it's the most beautiful thing I have ever seen."

"Are you insane? Both of you?" Halley spat. "You know better than anyone else those embryos cannot be alive. I don't know how to be any clearer!"

"You don't need to be. I'm the one who taught you most of what you know of the science industry. I'll fill you in on the blanks but only the important bits," Gabriel winked.

"What the hell is that supposed to mean?" Halley turned to Oren who raised his hands in the air.

"Do you think I would do something like this if it was not important? C'mon Hal, you know me. Calm down and I'll explain everything to you," Oren encouraged.

"No, apparently, I don't know you anymore so start explaining right now," she puffed. "Better yet, why didn't you start talking sooner?"

"We have tried to unlock the secrets of cloning for so many years and it's finally happened. With these embryos alive, we can keep experimenting, keep doing what we are doing. This kind of research is priceless."

Beads of sweat dripped across her neck. The oxygen evaporated from the air and she breathed in nothingness. "Are you kidding me?"

"You never wanted to kill the embryos off anyway, you felt sorry for them!"

"Of course I pitied the damned things but it didn't mean I wanted them to live! They are clones of the dead and that thought alone is petrifying but not as much the fact that we just broke the law. I don't know what's worse."

"I know it's a lot to take in but if we are careful, this can all work out. It's going to be okay."

"Nothing will ever be okay again, we are going to jail."

Halley grabbed the car keys from the coffee table and made her way toward the door. Each step was more difficult, as if she forgot how to walk. Her mind was clouded with nothing but peril. They were criminals, all of them. Adrenaline coursed through her muscles. Halley grabbed the door knob, when Oren laid a hand on her shoulder. She paused, clutching the cold metal.

"Why would you do something like this?"

"Let me explain. Gabriel started all this before I had any idea and it was already too late to back down. Do you trust me?"

Halley thought for a moment. Gabriel never cared about the embryos, it was all just money and science to him. Since when did he pity them enough to keep them alive. Nothing added up. As if he read her mind, Oren broke through her thoughts.

"Gabriel doesn't care about the embryos Hal, he doesn't pity anything but we need to study them more. It's too soon to end the experiment when it was developed so well. We don't have all the information we need and now we can keep testing out the accelerated growth hormone. Our work on saving premature babies from early death can keep going. Our experiment isn't over yet because it has just begun."

"Try and explain that when the government finds out." Halley's eyes were unforgiving. Oren reached forward but she slapped him away and the palm of her hand burned against the blunt force. "Don't come home tonight," Halley mumbled through broken words.

The king-sized bed felt empty and the branches racked the window, which made it hard to sleep. Halley grabbed the letter from AncestryDNA and walked into Max's room instead and pulled him onto her chest. They sat in the rocking chair and the wood creaked, it lulled Max to sleep. She listened to the pant of his breaths whilst she watched the tranquil stare of moonlight over the pitched rooftops. In the early hours of the morning, the city of Scotland slept, oblivious to the experiment and to Halley's pain. Her heart pumped adrenaline and fear throughout her body. Never before had Halley felt so vulnerable. The cloning experiment worked and the offspring were alive. A tear trickled down her chin. Nothing was alright and it seemed as though it was never be. There was no going back. No way out. This time there was a narrow path with no room to turn around.

Her intestines knotted with the sensation of betrayal, that she expected from neither of Oren nor Gabriel. Sure, Gabriel had a rough exterior, no doubt about that but he followed protocol in the strictest manner. He dare not veer in the slightest and now he was a perpetrator of illegality in the upmost form. Worse yet, Oren, her sweet Oren kept a secret too large to fathom. Of all people, why him? A part of Halley wanted to believe him. To believe that the embryos were kept first by Gabriel and he found out a few weeks later. Maybe it was not such a far-fetched idea after all. Still yet, this was his 'life's passion.' The words made Halley's stomach churn.

She watched a white fragment from the sky descended. She squinted, it was an owl. It perched atop their sandstone fence and the owl's wings folded neatly in place. The yellow eyes amidst the grey glorious feathers stared at her. She looked down and noticed Max reached a hand forward and grabbed the empty air, in the direction of the owl. Halley rested her chin against his head, he smelt of home.

Halley clenched her jaw and regathered her thoughts. "Everything's going to be okay. It's all going to work out just fine. Dad will be home tomorrow and this nightmare will end before we know it. I promise you, Max. I promise."

But Halley knew better than to make promises she couldn't keep.

XI

1821

The trip back to York was long and made even longer as Henry and Little John barely engaged in conversation. Their lips were frozen shut and too weak to speak. The geldings slowed and Henry whipped them again. Then, an unfamiliar sniffle sounded and Henry looked over. "Little John?"

No response.

"Boy."

Little John turned his attention back to the road ahead. His stern face gave nothing away but the bitter tear that trickled down his cheek said otherwise.

"I need you to answer when I call you. Why are you crying? Boys don't cry."

"I'm worried, sire. Is York safe?"

"Of course it will be, now no more of this nonsense."

"Yes, sire."

Henry clenched his jaw. Truth be told, he too was overwhelmed with unspoken panic but a man never showed emotion. He focused on the road and tried to push aside any pessimistic thoughts that crept into his head. Questions filled his mind without answers. Dirt crackled and the shuffle of footsteps followed, Henry peered around but saw nothing. Then there was a sneeze. He glanced over his shoulder and to his surprise, was confronted with a girl about sixteen years old tailed behind the wagon. She held a letter in hand focused on the ground. Her once pink gown was replaced with thick layers of dirt that matched the mud stains along her cheeks. Henry pulled the wagon to a halt.

"What are you doing?"

The girl trailed her fingers along the wagon and stumbled forward. She now stood beside Henry. He gulped at the sight of her. The girl's left eye was glazed with an opaque film and her face was smeared with dirt.

"Where are you from?"

"From afar."

"What are you doing here? Why are you following us?"

"I am blind in one eye and can't see too well." The girl toyed with the envelope in hand, she folded over one edge. "I was using your wagon as a guide and hoping you were going in the same direction."

"I am headed for York, where are you going?"

"York."

"Where did you come from?"

"Nordstrom."

"What's in York?"

"I have family there. I don't have anywhere else to go."

Henry thought for a moment and glanced over at John who shrugged his shoulders, seemingly unconvinced by the additional traveller. He looked back at the girl. "Where are your parents?"

"My mother passed away."

She offered the letter to Henry but in the wrong direction. Then Henry realised, she was loosing sight in the other eye too.

"I'm sorry but I can't give you a lift, since there is a plague."

The girl thought for some time but remained silent. She kept her arm extended and the letter blew in the wind. Henry dismissed the conversation and the wagon jolted to life. He peered over the wagon to see the girl stood in the same position. Her hands by either side and a solemn expression across her face. She was pale and pondered why she was covered in dirt but didn't say a word. He let the thought go.

XII

2001

Halley's sweaty fingers fiddled with the plastic buttons of the lab coat. She exhaled and stood at the staircase with the coat sprawled over her shoulders, unbuttoned. She broke strict policy but there was no such thing anymore. She released a deep breath she did not know she had been holding. Her hands trailed through her mattered hair. "Let's go."

"Not yet." Gabriel reached forward and removed the hem of her lab coat that was snagged on the staircase. "You're breaking policy and if you think -," Gabriel silenced as footsteps emitted.

Oren strode towards them, hands tucked into his side pockets and a groomed smile etched across his face. He clasped a hand on Gabriel's shoulder and whispered, "watch your tone with my wife or watch your back." He turned back to Halley. "It's good you're back honey."

"Just show me the embryos. I need to see them."

"Of course, they're in the basement."

Halley was about to speak but before she could, Oren raced down the hallway. Then she realised. Piper's plumbing worked on the basement only a few weeks ago. She no longer wanted to see what exactly was had grown in there. But she knew that she couldn't turn back back.

Oren twisted the door knob and Halley shut her eyes. She dug her hand inside the coat pocket but could not find what she was searched for. The door creaked open and chills coursed through her blood, it numbed her bones. Consciousness urged Halley to open her eyes, to peek at the embryos and all their glory. But the fear of what the experiment had become was too much to handle. Her fingers scuffled around the coat pocket. Then she pulled out a silicone box. Halley's finger nibbled at the hole and extracted out a toothpick or perhaps two.

"Open your eyes," Gabriel whispered.

Halley felt the warmth of the basement light and her eyes unwillingly flashed open. She gasped and the box of toothpicks dropped to the floor, wooden splinters splattered across the basement as the secrets were truly revealed. It had to be the most beautiful but sight that petrified her then most. Almost too surreal to comprehend. Three meters away were five egg-shaped tanks surrounded by an abundance of wires and a monitoring box above each. A neon blue light radiated from the base of the tank where a black pump was connected. It filtered the fluid that bubbled into the tank. Halley stepped over noodles of electrical wires. The entire ecosystem functioned around the life inside the tank, a baby. Five were lined up side by side but within the confinements of their own space. Halley's jaw dropped open as she pressed her hand against the tank. The glass was heated and she could feel the buzz of electricity from inside. A baby was coiled in a foetal position, its' stumpy body bundled and small fingers trailed across its' face. The baby moved in tune with the current of the fluid. Its' fingers opened and closed around its' petite nose. Hidden beneath the seaweed of brunette hair was a squished face. The masking tape along the bottom read *Subject E-250*. Halley bent her knees and lowered her head to clearly see the baby's face when she noticed something strange. Its' bogey eyelids were translucent and were masked by a film and Halley saw the iris behind. It was blue. Her breath fogged the class exterior and the baby's opaque fingers splayed open before they recoiled into a fist.

Oren's hand trailed from one tank to the next as he circled them. "Artificial amniotic fluid, it practically mimics the mother's womb. That's where the name came from, artificial womb, it sounds more respectful that way."

Halley no longer listened, it was too much to take in. Her mind and heart didn't share the same consciousness. She felt disjointed. Through one lens, Halley was petrified of the clones. They were replicas of the dead and she had no control over who they would become. Not only that, this was no longer an experiment and the cloned babies were illegal. They shouldn't be alive. But at the same time, she was intrigued by their being. All those years of research, trial and error, paid off. The experiment worked in every sense of the word and she was apart of that. Guilt coursed through her body, she should be ashamed.

"The best part?" Oren continue. "The accelerated growth hormone has really kicked in. These babies are full term at only five months. They have doubled their growth and not even born yet." Oren clapped his hands together.

"What have you done?"

Oren rubbed Halley's hands. They stood there for some time, entranced by both their the mess and success. Halley hardly recognised her own husband in that moment. His eyes shone in a way she had never seen before and chilled Halley to the core.

The name Diane Thomson crept into Halley's mind. She remembered the tissue donor with all her glee and triumph for the experiment. The vision of Diane's Butterfly earrings sway as she cried for her stillborn son and blushed with hope for the future. Diane never agreed to any of this and Halley owed it to her to set things right.

"They're all orphans, just like me. Do you realise what you've done? You resurrected the dead and now these kids will never know who they are. Do you understand the pain they will go through? On top of everything else, the clones have to deal with not knowing who they were in their past life. Just like I had too."

"You're different," Oren stepped forward.

"How am I different? I am just like them. An orphan who wanted answers. They have every right to know where they came from."

"They don't have a voice. Is that what they might want or is that what you want?"

"Both."

"You want to perform the AncestryDNA test on the clones?"

"You say it as if it's so absurd. Find some humanity for them." Halley pulled back and headed toward the door.

"Where are you going?"

"I can't look at you anymore."

A bitter tear trickled down her cheek and into her mouth. Somehow she felt responsible. Halley's ignorance convinced Oren and Gabriel to breed clones was a sane idea. The tears poured down full force and Halley bolted through the door. She felt sick.

Oren stood on the back porch with a fresh glass of whiskey. Beyond the white floor-boards, he watched the sunset. It washed away the truth that day but the pain remained. He heard Halley's bare-feet over the floor. "Everything is under control."

"How can you say that?" Halley exclaimed as she bit into a toothpick from the corner of her mouth.

"Lower your voice, the baby is asleep."

"I'm obviously not involved in this experiment anymore. It's between you and Gabriel now."

"Now you're being ridiculous."

"Am I? Or is it you who has cloned dead people?"

"After seeing the embryos I couldn't walk away. Not like that." Oren paced back and forth.

"When did you find out?" Halley folded her arms. Her frontal lobe and jaw throbbed.

"A while ago." Oren tossed a hand over his head.

"You're lying! That cloning experiment took place five months ago."

"Christ! I only found out a few weeks ago!"

"You didn't think to tell me then?"

"You wouldn't have bloody listened! We would be where we are right now."

Halley's eyes were hollow as the crusted residue of volcanic ash. She had enough and no longer wanted to tip-toe around the topic. "Tell me when you plan on killing those clones."

"It's too late. Clone or not, they are living, breathing human beings. They have rights."

"What are you saying?"

"I'm saying that by the time I found out there was nothing I could do," Oren's whisper disappeared into the backyard.

Halley's heart almost burst out of her chest. Cloned children. The world had never heard of something so atrocious and it was all for science. Never before had a cloned embryo reached this stage of life and that was because no scientist was stupid enough to follow it through.

"What's the plan Oren?" Halley's voice broke off. She remembered subject E-250's eyes and pudgy body. He was alive and had a mind just like every other righteous child. He deserved more than this. Oren swung back another sip of the whiskey. He allowed an ice cube to slide along his tongue and he chewed his anger into the frozen water. "Like any baby, conceived naturally, through IVF or lab, it has rights. The clones, the same for any child, they have legal human rights. If we kill them, we are murderers."

Halley felt the remainder of blood drain from her face. The hairs on the back of her neck pricked upright. She knew what she heard but it was too hard to be sure. "I … I don't understand."

Oren clenched his jaw. "I'm not worried about the government finding out that we kept the cloned embryos alive past the fourteenth day. Nobody would ever find out, its' an easy secret to keep. What I am worried about is killing those clones when the experiment is over and getting caught for murder."

"Oren." Tears filled Halley's eyes. "They are clones of the dead. Who have we brought back?"

"That won't be any of your concern. Given the right environment, anybody can flourish. I promise, nothing bad is going to happen."

Halley raised her hand in the air and slapped Oren across the face. His head smacked in the opposite direction and ice flew out of his mouth but the red imprint remained on his cheek. The whiskey glass shattered against the floor.

"We don't even know what we're dealing with in that damned basement. We've not only bought the dead back to life but tampered with their genetics. You've engineered those clones to become whatever you want."

"You should be thanking me I didn't kill the babies. We would all be in jail by now if it was up to you."

"So long as I wouldn't be in the same cell as you."

Halley ventured into the bedroom and curled up into a ball, still dressed in the attire of that day. Time was the enemy and it seemed to move slowly. She shut her eyes and tried to summon sleep but it was not a friend that night. Every time her eyes slipped shut, she saw subject E-250. She saw those blue eyes that watched her from behind the translucent eyelids.

XIII

1821

The wagon pulled aside as Henry and Little John polished off the crumbs of the bread loaf.

Henry forced the meagre meal down his dry throat.

"Sire, my head is really sore." Little John clutched his temple.

"I know, me too. You need a warm shower and a descent meal. We will be home soon."

Little John blinked through the pain and leant over the wagon, he emptied his stomach onto the ground. Henry pulled the canvas cloth to his chin and curled into a foetal position, he used his hand as a pillow. "Get some rest."

Henry felt Little John's warm body press against his backside but put up with it. Perhaps it was the fatigue that riddled his body or the fear that he denied, either way, Henry and Little John were strangers to the hard journey but together they were. His eyes slipped shut and sleep came easier than expected.

The following morning, the foliage was covered in a fine layer of frost but a speckle of sun parted through the sky and began to melt the ice. Henry awoke, although it seemed he hardly slept. He turned to Little John who was curled up and faced the rear end of the wagon. Given the circumstances, Henry decided he would benefit from the extra rest. He draped his half of cloth over Little John and moved toward the front seat. Henry whipped the geldings and they ploughed through the road. He dreamt of a warm shower to wash away the journey but couldn't seem to get Urian out of his mind. The once strong man but succumbed to a vegetative state. He hardly went a day without work and to see him bedridden was compelling. Henry gulped, he could only hope for the best. A few hours passed and Little John was still asleep. Henry decided it was time he lent a hand either with the lamp or take control of the reins.

"Boy!"

Silence.

"Little John, get up." Henry peered over his shoulder to see him coiled into a ball. He cursed, Little John's slumber would set them back. The journey was already more exhaustive than planned, this couldn't go on. He pulled the geldings to a halt and their feeble cries filled the air. The wagon screeched over the dirt. He climbed into the back beside Little John. Henry tried to shake him awake but he didn't move. Henry pulled Little John onto his backside and a trail of crusted vomit dribbled down the his chin and his face was covered in boils. Pus exploded over Little John's cheek and his chapped lips were blue. Tears filled Henry's eyes. "BOY! GET UP!"

He cradled Little John's head which moulded to Henry's grasp. He was limp.

"Please don't leave me! Don't leave me alone!" Henry wailed and shook the stiff, cold body. He couldn't fight back the tears and they dribbled down his face. There was not much time left. Henry had to be quick. He needed to think fast. The wagon was heavy and would take longer to reach York especially now that the horses were weak and fathomed. Henry leapt from the wagon and yanked Little John down by his coat. He dragged the child over the edge and slumped him over his shoulder. He grit his teeth against Little John's weight and held him by the back of his knees.

"Hold in there, boy!"

The foal wailed as Henry unbuckled its bridle single-handedly. It stood still and stared at him expectantly. Henry slapped its' back.

"Leave you dumb animal!"

The foal squealed and ran into the distance. Then Henry turned to the other gelding, unbuckled the bridal and flung Little John's body over the front saddle. The gelding stepped backwards from the newly mounted weight atop its' back.

"Hold on, Little John! We're almost home!"

Henry climbed atop the sire and it began to gallop. Then Henry smacked it again and the gelding ran. It moved faster without the weight of the wagon. All the while, Henry guarded Little John with his life.

XIV

2001

Halley's vision blurred and she pressed her hands against the lab bench for support. She faced the floor, trying to focus on her boots, to get a grip. She could feel the heartless steel knife against her thigh and the unforgivable sharpness through her jeans pocket. She had no sympathy and would follow through with her plan for Halley was colder than the knife. No, she wasn't. She couldn't even fool herself. Halley bit into the sleeve of her parker and twisted the loose thread of fabric between her teeth. Emotions choked Halley and she clenched her jaw to stop from screaming. She dropped her hands by her side, which left a fine handprint amidst the dust from the bench. The lab had been abandoned since all the focus turned towards, she choked on the thought, the clones. It almost seemed as if she spoke of the clones, it would make them disappear, something Halley only hoped for. She extracted her cellphone from her back pocket and the line rang. "Hey, it's me, where are you?"

"I'm in the basement," Gabriel replied.

"Of course you are."

Halley placed a toothpick in the corner of her mouth and toyed with it for some time, unable to look inside the basement. "Gabriel."

"I'm here, Hal. What are you doing?"

"I – I'm coming."

She exhaled and strode into the basement, where the artificial wombs greeted her. The monitors danced with numbers that calculated the vital signs of the clones in real time. She stared at the one closest, Subject M-000. He seemed bigger this time. The clone wriggled around and its' foot was entangled in one of the black cords. Halley's breath fogged up the glass. The clone was fully formed with a human face and the translucent eyelids were no now replaced by fatty tissue and chubby cheeks. She reached inside her jeans pocket and clutched the meat knife, the cold numbed the blood that pulsed through her fingers. Her breath quivered as she fought against the lump in her throat. If she was to go through with the plan, Halley had to change her mindset to that of mindless cold metal. She had to be as ruthless as the knife itself. Human consciousness was the only thing that held Halley back in that moment. She wished for nothing other than normality but it cost a steep price. She had no idea how she would deal with the aftermath of what she was about to do but it seemed a better exchange than the resurrection of these clones. They could never live past the foetal stage. It was not right and she knew it. Subject M-000 turned the other way and Halley saw his face crumple. The hairless eyebrows burrowed a frown and his thick lips drew apart. Beneath the blue illumination, his skin was porcelain pale. A rush of pity flooded Halley, she couldn't do it.

Gabriel walked around one of the artificial tanks and leant his elbow along the rim. "They're bigger. In a few more days they will be born." He pointed to Subject M-000. "This one is one of the largest of the boys."

His innocent face was that of pure life yet his genetic make-up fuelled who he once was and would be. Maybe this baby was a reborn sinner, or perhaps a gentle soul. Maybe he deserved to live. That thought tore Halley apart. There was nothing morally correct about what she would do but there was nothing right about the clones' existence either.

"We need to look at a set up for them." Gabriel winked.

"Don't look at me, I'm not helping with this."

"Maybe so but we are changing history."

"I bet the government would like to catch wind of this turn of the century."

Gabriel leant forward. "I bet the government would place you and Oren in a separate prisons. You would never see Max again so I would be careful next time you decide to threaten me."

"I'm not the one going down, you are."

Gabriel's lips almost brushed against Halley's ear. "If I go down, we all go down."

Halley's blood curdled. She peered at the clones once more, the tranquil babies floated within the artificial womb, oblivious to the conversation of their life. They were shadowed by the truth and would one day find out. She made her way towards the door and with every step, the knife pinched through her back pocket. It was a constant reminder of her unfinished business and one that may never be fulfilled but the sweet face of the clone was etched into her mind. Maybe Oren was right, death was out of the question.

XV

2001

The clones' due date was upon them. Halley stood with her back pressed against the wall. She was anything but ready and nothing could prepare her for something so life changing. The monitor above subject Z-101 alarmed and the baby's heart rate sky-rocketed. He bounced to life and droplets of amniotic fluid splashed onto the monitor. Oren nudged Halley by the corner of his elbow. "Honey, do you want to sit down? You look like you've seen a ghost."

"Maybe that's because I have seen a ghost. Five clones of the deceased."

Halley outstretched the white towel in her hands and waited. Her mouth grew dry and she swallowed nothing but air.

Gabriel looked over. "Ready?"

Oren nodded and walked forward as he dropped the lab coat to the floor. He rolled up the sleeves of his flannel top and took one last look at Halley but she couldn't face him. He reached inside the tank of Subject Z-101. The blue-illuminated amniotic fluid creeped up his arms as he clamped off the black cord, connected to the clone's belly, with a Gilles forceps. The baby wriggled uncomfortably as the oxygen and nutrient supply was shut off.

"How are we looking?" Oren called.

"The heart rate is two-hundred," Halley said with her eyes fixated on the monitor beside the tank. "Two-ten." She watched as the trace danced. Oren disconnected the cords attached to the clone and the monitor showed nothing.

"Do it," Gabriel said.

Oren slipped his fingers around the clones' waist and pulled it out of the tank. Waves of thick fluid splashed over the floor. He raised the clone in the air but it was limp. Halley breathed a sigh of relief, the experiment was unsuccessful, the clone could not live outside the tank. It was a stillborn. There was some sadness to that thought but it was out of her control and under the guise of mother nature. Oren pat the clone's back and the he began coughing. Subject Z-101 gasped for air, followed by a shriek cry. Oren plunged the baby into the towel of Halley's arms. She wrapped the clone in the towel and for the first time his eyes opened.

They were blue.

XVI

1821

Henry was weak and his head thumped with unbearable pain. He cried until he could not anymore and clutched the reins with the remainder of his strength. The morning fog was thick and beneath Henry's' puffy emerald eyes, he could barely see a two feet ahead but he no longer cared. He whipped the gelding again but barely inflicted a pinch. The minster of York loomed in the distance. The church welcomed Henry. It beckoned him into the comfort behind the large wooden doors, they were home.

"See? I told you, we made it," Henry whispered. He spoke to the minster of York, to the chiseled concrete and castle pitched roof. He was only meters away from home and would protect his family, protect them all. His vision began to haze and his shoulders dropped. He tried to sit upright but felt as though he carried twice his weight. He reached a hand forward and almost touched the minster until something caught his eyes. Henry drew his hand toward his face to see a round blister on his finger tip. No. There was more. His entire hand was coated with puss-filled boils. Henry focused on the minster and with each wheeze, it became harder to breathe. Almost as if a straw was plunged into his lungs and sucked out twice as much air as what he inhaled. Henry's vision blackened. His body began to slip sideways.

Thump.

Henry hit the dry ground. His eyes slipped open in time to see the gelding gallop through the congregated fence, with Little

John slumped over its' back. The boys' face was a deep purple and his eyes shut. Henry breathed out. It seemed as though he breathed on-top of another breath. To breathe became a chore too painful and difficult to coordinate. His chest rose and fell. His fingers trailed across the gravel, he searched for help that never came. His lips parted and a cold breathe escaped his mouth. His emerald eyes slipped shut for the last time.

XVII

2001

The artificial amniotic fluid was warm and the lucid current circulated Subject X-313. As he breathed out, a plume of bubbles rose toward the surface, they burst into circular ripples and expanded into nothingness. A large hand wrapped around his little body and Subject X-313 was pulled from the warm embrace. The time was 07:20 pm when his eyes flashed open for the first time. They were an emerald green. A supernatural remnant of a life more than two centuries, yet he did not look a day past four-minutes old. Life outside the womb was different, it was cold and an abundance of intrusive noises filled the air. He missed the blurred sound in the womb. The clone's crumpled face dripped with the essence of amniotic fluid as Gabriel wrapped a towel around him. Subject X-313 had been re-birthed in the name of therapeutic research and his life blurred the lines between humanity and science. He just doesn't know it yet.

Halley's eyes widened as seven-pounds of squirming life was placed in her arms. She clutched Subject X-313 and proceeded to wipe away the fluid from his face. He shrieked and thrust his face away from Halley. The clone needed to replace the fluid in his lungs with air but his meek wail broke her heart. She rocked the baby and he cried at the top of his lungs. Halley gave in. "It's okay, I've got you."

She swaddled the blanket around Subject X-313 and placed him upon her chest. The fresh scent of new life wafted and his tender breaths blew against her skin. A lumped formed at the back of her throat, to think she tried to murder him the other was a memory she wished to erase. Only it couldn't be replaced and she was forced to live with the burden.

"I'm sorry little one. I'm so sorry." Halley whispered into the clones ear, whilst she stroked his delicate face. Gabriel's stern eyes focused on the clone. He studied the symmetry of his face and the proportionate details of his body that were comparable to a porcelain doll. "It worked."

"And now we have five children to raise, nice going."

"Don't be so sour."

"How are we suppose to raise these kids? You do realise they will grow up and then what will we do?"

"I have a plan." Gabriel leaned towards Halley. "Funny how you spoke of eradicating their life the other day. To erase their very existence and now you're rocking that baby like nothing ever happened."

"I spoke of what I thought was best but he's here now."

The clone gazed up at Halley, through the green-rimmed eyes. His heavy head dropped back onto her chest and the peach fuzz atop his head brushed Halley's chin. She would never forgive herself to have wished death upon him. Halley only wanted what was best for everyone but murder was never the answer. "Who were you in your past life, subject X-313? Those eyes, who were they?"

"Alright, Halley pass him to me," Gabriel said. He reached for the clone, all the while holding an injection between his teeth.

"No!" Clone or not, these babies will be safe. Halley shook her head and backed away, all the while clutching subject X-313. "You are not going to do more experiments on it. Now get that damn needle away from him."

"She's right you know," Oren interjected. He pressed his hands atop his hips and as if through telecommunication, Gabriel backed off, he whispered something in Russian. He slammed the needle against the bench and exhaled heavily.

"The only test we will perform is AncestryDNA. Treat them with some respect, as the unfortunate future of humanity." Halley placed a kiss atop subject X-313's head.

Over a matter of days, the basement was transformed into a nursery, if you could call it that. There were five bassinets lined up, the windows were covered with thick velvet curtains and held in place by masking tape. Halfway across the room was a small television sat atop a milk crate and the scent of baby powder never seemed to leave. Halley leaned forward and placed the clone in the bassinet, she was wrapped in a thick pink blanket and beside the four other clones that were dressed in soft blue. She couldn't help but think of her as a daughter. Did that make her a parent for these clones or maybe it was a non-consensual adoption? Even though the clones were the offspring of science, they were still children and would be raised as such. The clone squirmed and grunted. Halley pat her belly and then her large head dropped to the side with sleep. Halley extracted five tests from her handbag and slit open the packaging. She leaned over Subject E-250 and opened his lips, where she swivelled the white swab around the gummy mouth. The clone crumpled his face but Halley pat his back and he silenced. She gathered the swab from all the clones and smiled. It was time to find out who they were. One day, when they are old enough, she would hand them the results. Halley slipped into the office chair and placed her elbows atop the desk. She shuffled through the papers and searched for the observation sheet. Her index finger trailed down the column of page 346 and she marked a small x into the diagonal boxes that lined the page, to update the clone's sleep and feed schedules. Halley leaned back and switched on the soundless television, she flicked through the channels and settled on the latest series of Burnistown. She kept track by the subtitles along the bottom. In less than twenty-four hours life with the clones had become a somewhat normal.

Footsteps entered the basement, a sign Halley would be relieved of her duty. Gabriel reached for the observation chart and pulled it out of her hand. Gabriel covered his face with the chart and thoroughly scanned the observations. He tapped the page. "Subject E-250 had more formula at six-thirteen tonight. I wonder why that was."

"They grow you know. Not every one of them are the same, even if they are clones. Welcome to fatherhood."

Halley stood up and grabbed her coat.

"How did subject Z-101 do?" Gabriel asked, he still avoided eye contact.

"We can't keep calling them subjects anymore, Gabriel. They need actual names."

"No, no they don't." He watched at Halley from the side of his eye. "They are science, if we name them it means we have attachment. That, is something we cannot afford."

"It's a bit late for that don't you think?" Halley taunted. She re-arranged the collar of her jacket. "The girl, her name is Kiara and Subject X-313 is Rex. I'll think of the others within a few days. See you later ... Dad."

As Halley headed toward the door she heard a few gently cries. The chair skidded across the floor and Gabriel muttered something beneath his breath. He knew Halley would settle them within seconds but not given his attitude. Her duties were over until tomorrow, the day after and the day after that. This was her new life.

XVIII

2001

The sickening aroma of sweet sugar filled the air. Within the confines of the dining room was a crowd of family and friends separated by green and blue balloons with the occasional over-sized Ben-10 ones. Streamers lined the walls and a stack of presents were shovelled into a nearby corner. None of them were opened yet but the small scratches at the wrapping said otherwise. Halley tugged at the elastic band of the party hat beneath her chin. She ushered her way through the crowd of joyful faces and reached the dining table. She placed a kitchen knife to one side and lighter to the other.

"Say cheese!"

Halley looked upward in time for the camera to take their picture. Then she leant forward and kissed the scrawny freckled cheeks. "Happy birthday, honey."

"Thanks mum!"

On the table was a sponge birthday cake decorated with an edible image of Ben-10 and his fellow aliens. The buttercream frosting read *Happy 10th Birthday Max!*

Max interlocked his fingers, he cracked each knuckle. A new habit, and one Halley would normally scold him for, but today none of that mattered. Max smiled beneath the amber hair and his buck-teeth protruded, whilst he glanced down at the cake. He searched among the crowd. "Aaron! Check this out, it has heat-blast on it!"

Aaron now stood along the side of the table. "Oh and Ghost freak!"

The boys high-fived but Halley cringed whilst their sleeves dangled above the candle blaze. The boys got lost in conversation and a small crowd of children formed around either side of the cake. One of them dipped their fingers in the icing along the side and plunged it into his mouth. He closed his eyes and savoured the moment. Max did the same and then again. The cake was soon a massacre of green mush, all apart from the Ben-10 image, of course. Halley leant forward to pull the boys in line. Then, Oren slipped his hand around the waist of her floral boutique dress.

"Not now my love."

"There won't be cake left and if there is nobody will want to eat it. I mean, look at them."

"Does it matter? Who cares about the cake. Max is happy."

Halley sighed, he was right. The cake was for Max and however he wanted to celebrate was his choice. "It took me weeks to find that cake you know."

"Did it? And how did you do such a good job?"

"Oh don't worry, Max helped me! He wrote down a list of all his favourite aliens."

"Do you think Gabriel is going alright with the clo-," Halley was cut off.

"Shh. Not today, let's not talk about them for now. It's Max's day."

Clumps of wax drooled down the candle body and from

somewhere within the crowd the tune to *Happy birthday* begun and it soon spread throughout the room. Even the boys straightened their backs and chimed in. The room of three generations sung out of sync but that's what made it perfect. Max was plastered between his parents and the small family peered upward as an array of lights flashed through the room. They turned in all directions, as if captured by the media along the Hollywood carpet. Then the crowd began to clap and cheer. Oren whispered into Max's ear. "Make a wish sonny boy but don't forget to close your eyes or it won't come true."

Max shut his eyes so tight that his face crinkled. He silently mouthed his wish and shifted atop the chair, hardly able to contain his excitement. Then Max leaned forward and with a deep breath. He blew out the candles. Trails of circled smoke lifted through the air and seconds later Max had disappeared with his friends. Halley scooped another bite of sponge cake into her mouth and returned back to the now two-way conversation of the latest cloning technologies between Oren and his old colleague. Something Halley could hardly focus on, not on an occasion like this. The talk of science came across as unintelligible for Halley had no ear for it. Instead, she glanced around the room and her eyes settle upon Max and his friends who were perched along the rim of a pot-plant. Max was in the centre and focused on the latest present, a Nintendo. His fingers slammed against the black buttons and his friends were hunched over his shoulder.

"What are you doing, Max?" One of them called and clasped both hands over his temples.

"Go left, go left!" Aaron shouted back.

"I know, I got it." Max said.

Silence. Then a burst of cheer as the boys screamed over the Nintendo which Max raised victoriously into the air. Halley clapped her hands and Max caught sight of his mother. He waved his hands above his head. It almost seemed as though Halley celebrated two parties at once and both equally as important. Max had been in remission for nine years. For him to forget the Leukaemia would be Halley's only birthday wish.

The next morning, Halley nursed a cup of coffee by the kitchen sink and peered around the room. It was an absolute mess. Shredded streamers and fallen balloons created a colourful maze and if you dare step on one it would pop with shock. She picked up the kitchen knife and sliced another piece of cheese into the opened piece of bread.

"Max. You need to get up for school!"

No response.

"Max! C'mon, we're both going to be late. I have to go to the lab soon!"

Silence. Halley dropped the knife and darted upstairs. She grabbed the hem of her gown and climbed the stairs, two at a time. She swerved along the corridor and thrust the bedroom door open. A lumpy mass was hidden beneath the bed sheets. Halley crept forward and sat on the edge of the bed, she placed one hand over the sheet and it shifted.

"Max …. Honey are you sick?"

The upper half of the sheets moved, it almost appeared a nod.

"Talk to me, what's going on?"

No answer. She drew back the blankets to see Max curled up and he bit his lower lip. He laughed and covered his hand over his mouth, to mimic a cough instead. Max avoided eye contact and his grey eyes stared at the floor, an attempt to find some seriousness. Halley's blood boiled and her fingers trembled.

"MAX!" Halley gripped his shirt. He no longer laughed and sat upright.

"Don't you ever, ever do that to me again! Do you understand? That's not funny!"

"I …. I'm sorry mum, it was," Max gulped. "It was just a joke."

Halley wiped her face. "You … You're right. I shouldn't have gotten angry."

"All my friends did the same joke to their parents, that's all. Mum, why did you get so angry with me?" The innocent puppy eyes stared at her.

"It's time to get dressed, okay?" Halley said over the lump in her throat. "I'll make you some breakfast, how about sunny-side up?"

Max smiled and appeared to have forgotten the entire ordeal. It was a joke, a childish joke. She knew she had to relax, but how?

XIX

2001

The once white roof was now stained with mould. Water dripped into a metal bucket on the floor and the stench of rotten vegetables never seemed to leave. The growth hormone injections had stopped some time ago but the effects were ongoing. The researchers maintained a red book for the past nine-years old the binder gave out. Each week the researchers documented the date and today it read;

1.02.2010: Clones are 9/18

The abbreviation meant the clones were nine-years-old in numerical value but behaved and developed as eighteen-year old children. To the researchers' surprise, their intellectuality and behaviour also reflected that of a teenager.

Subject X-313 was renamed Rex. His crusted lips inhaled the toxic fumes of tobacco and he puffed another ring of smoke. He practiced the art for weeks and now he mastered the skill, the excitement had died. He reached into his jeans pocket and felt for the packet of cigarettes, which was empty. Rex shrugged his shoulders, he would borrow more from Gabriel's stash in the afternoon. The obnoxious symphony of Metallica blared that morning. He cocked his head to the side. The Rage music channel was cranked to the max by the television that sat atop the milk crate. "Would someone lower that shit down? It's going to snap the crate it's so loud."

The musty cologne drifted from his clothes and his damp hair hung shoulder length. He pressed out of the chair that was all-too-small and smudged the cigarette embers into the concrete with his bare foot. Rex's shadow towered over the chest of drawers beneath the window and he picked out a flannel shirt, where the sleeves were cuffed around his biceps. He tugged at the collar so as to not choke himself then he jumped atop of the drawers with one leap. He scratched away at the tape that pinned down the velvet curtain.

"It's beautiful isn't it."

Kiara now stood beside him and remained silent, her eyes narrowed on the new house that was being built across the road. Construction workers moved through the wooden infrastructure like ants that fixed a nest. The windows were up today.

"Yeah, it is." Kiara tucked the side-fringe behind her pointed ear and leaned closer, she pressed a hand on Rex's shoulder for support. Her freckled nose touched the window and her breath fogged the glass. That familiar aroma of Victoria's Secret lifted through the air.

Rex turned away but still the smell lingered and he bit the inner of his cheeks, she smelt like Heaven in the morning. Kiara noticed him blush and leant closer, she flirted with her exotic scent. Rex gave into the silent game, he always did. He placed a feeble kiss against her neck, to which Kiara held back a smile. It reminded him of when they were younger. "You haven't grown up," Rex whispered.

"Should I have?"

"No. I want to remember you this way."

"You haven't changed either, you know that." Kiara tossed her glossy hair over her shoulder.

"What's that supposed to mean?" Rex asked.

"You know what I'm talking about. You've always been a dreamer. You showed me the outside, I would have thought it would have been me who discovered it first."

Rex cleared his throat and allowed the memory into his mind:

He reached for the velvet curtain but his fingers fell short, so he poised himself up by his tip-toes and this time grabbed the hem of the curtain. He tugged hard but the tape kept it shut. He lifted one foot off the chair but he quivered and he wobbled. Rex crouched forward and placed his hands on either side of his feet, which secured his balance again.

"Good morning," Kiara yawned and wiped sleep from her eyes.

"Come up. I think you are a bit taller."

She climbed onto the handle of the chair and up the backrest. Rex made room and held onto the window frame as he inched his feet across the thin chair which pressed into the soles of his feet. The pain was obsolete, he needed to see this. Kiara followed suit, her feet now where Rex's were seconds earlier. She had one pink sock painted with butterflies pulled up to the knee but her other foot was bare.

"You can have one of my socks if you want," Rex gestured.

The offer went unnoticed as Kiara focused on the task at hand. She slipped her tongue out along her top lip and groaned. "I think I can almost reach it."

"Remove the tape."

Kiara frowned, she wasn't stupid. She scratched away but her short finger nails barely touched the surface. She worked on it for some time. "I got it!"

Kiara pulled the curtain aside and morning light entered the room. The clones peered the window. They watched the treetops reach the Heavens and the flock of ducks that honked across the sky. Rex gasped at the rosé sunrise. It was something he had never seen before.

"What is that?" Kiara was astounded.

"Do you think this is what they call outside?"

The basement door flung open and in its place stood a tall figure who was drowned out by the black room. Rex knew it was Gabriel by the bald head. He trudged across the room, reached for the clones and dropped them onto the floor.

The outside was magnificent and nothing in the basement compared. Rex would never forget it. He whispered into Kiara's ear. "One day we will go outside."

"How will you do that?"

"I don't know but I will find a way."

He snapped back into reality when the door knob jiggled. He thrust his arms around Kiara's waist and lowered her to the ground, then pressed the tape against the curtain. He slammed it flat by the palm of his hand.

"Good morning everyone, breakfast time!" Oren called.

Halley pushed a two-tiered tray into the room when the smell of eggs and toast evaporated through the air. Rex gestured an open hand to which Kiara led the way. One of his brothers pushed past him. The clones fought to choose the best rashes of bacon and freshest fruit as if they hadn't eaten in days. Rex noticed someone was missed and pulled back. He rounded the bed and to no surprise there was Chino, curled into a foetal position. He crouched on his haunches, and wiped away the iced white fringe that covered his eyes. It was a pleasant barrier to his shy interior and thus the name was a perfect fit. Chino, short for chionophile, someone passionate for the cold. After all, Chino despised the heat and for good reason, his albinism restricted him from sunlight. Chino's grey beady eyes caught sight of Rex.

"Brother, lets' get something to eat." Rex lifted Chino's chin by the tip of his finger. There was a red scratch and a purple bruise across his cheek. Rex clenched his jaw, those fucking bastards, they couldn't leave the poor kid alone. They were family, show some respect. Rex combed his fingers through his long hair. He knew Chino was tender hearted, which made him an easy target. He would try harder to keep an eye out. After some encouragement, Rex turned his attention back to breakfast and plated his own breakfast once Chino began to eat. He shovelled a string of bacon into his mouth as a thick film of oil trailed down his chin. Apollo sat beside him and beneath the bed of spiked brunette hair, he winked. Rex knew what that meant. Kiara strode past and as she did, Apollo puckered his lips. He was a slow learner. "Looking gorgeous today, Kiara."

"Better than you, right Apollo?"

Apollo's cheeks blushed and his smitten eyes widened. Although his lust was short lived once he noticed half his breakfast was sprawled across his lap. His jeans dripped in oil and scrambled egg found their way into his pockets. Rex winked and ploughed through his breakfast.

XX

Rex is 9/18

The bathroom was a makeshift timber cell in the corner of the basement and with the lights dimmed Rex could hardly see. Despite the clones' disagreements, Chino's albanism was something they all respected. The four brothers leaned over the double bathroom sink and watched as Oren covered the lower half of his face with shaving cream. He worked the foam along his chiselled jawline and down his neck. "Alright boys. Work your shavers gently down your face, moving in one direction," he instructed.

Rex skimmed the razor over his face and the stubbled hairs snapped off. He tapped the excess shaving cream against the rim of the sink. Besides him, Chino frowned. "I don't feel anything." "You've got it back to front little brother." Rex flipped the razor to the sharp end.

Cyrus rolled his eyes and continued to shave with an abundance of confidence. He winced and examined his face in the bathroom mirror to see a puddle of blood drip down his cheek. It stained the foam and Rex cackled, served him right. Cyrus pulled his shoulder-length hair into a low pony tail and got back to work. He wouldn't acknowledge his embarrassment. 'Oren, I have a question for you," he said.

"What's that buddy?"

"Why do I look so much like Rex?"

Cyrus and Rex were twins. Not identical, their eyes were dissimilar, hair was a different tone and texture but their facial features and mannerisms were almost the same.

"You were both cloned from the same DNA." Oren paused his demonstration. From the mirror reflection, he watched Cyrus, whose face split in half by a crack in the glass. "When we extracted the DNA from a mosquito, many years ago, we used the same sample for both you and Rex. That's why you look similar but like any strand of DNA, you have your differences. No clone will ever be the same."

Rex wasn't particularly phased, he always suspected there was some link to Cyrus. His train of thought broke as Chino flinched and scraped the bruise across his cheek.

"Oren." Rex watched him from the mirror reflection. "Where did the mosquito come from?"

"The outside."

"Where is the outside? What does its look like?

"Beyond the basement." Oren sighed. "I think you know the answer to that. You've seen it on the tv many times."

"But when will we go there?"

The clones awaited a response. Rex, Cyrus, Chino and Apollo fixated their gaze on Oren. They had never stepped foot outside but Rex suspected it was bigger than the basement itself.

"You can't leave here."

Rex slammed the razor against the basin. After all the times he stared outside the window, his curiosity only grew. The lack of answers bubbled a rage within him. Why couldn't he go outside? Did everyone go outside? The researchers must. The clones were, yet again, suppressed by the glorified authority of the researchers. Rex even enjoyed Oren's classes for it broke the intensity of the basement but at times like this, he was reminded of their differences. He dropped the razor in the sink, grabbed a hand towel and stormed out of the bathroom, which was an entire five steps to the left. He wiped the shaving foam from his face and threw the towel against the floor, dismissing Oren's lesson early.

"You're next life lesson class with be with Halley at two-pm!" Oren called.

"Oh goody." Rex whispered. "I wonder what it's about this time."

"Ecology."

"Oh," Rex replied, he didn't realise Oren had eaves dropped in on his own self-talk. Once again, the confines of the basement meant for a lack of privacy. Rex gnawed on his own questions. If the outside existed that meant there was an entire world to be discovered. Well, according to the television anyway. At least that couldn't hide any secrets. Rex sat on the edge of the bed and reached for the remote when Oren emerged from the bathroom.

"I need you back in my lesson."

"I need answers," Rex breathed.

"You will get them in time. C'mon, Rex. This isn't like you. Where is all this coming from?" He placed his hands on his hips. "You're normally so placid, what's gotten into you?"

"I grew up."

Oren scratched his head. "I know, okay, I know. You're older now and you want more than I can tell you." He thought for a moment. "I gotta idea."

Oren disappeared from the basement and returned within the hour. He brought a casket of Belhaven Ale and handed one to each of the clones. Rex examined the blue and white label. Beer. He turned to Cyrus who took a sip and cringed at the bitter sensation. Rex looked over his siblings, who seemed appalled by the beer, even Kiara winced. Rex tossed the thought over his shoulder, it couldn't be that bad. He guzzled the beer and air-pockets of bubbles exploded inside his mouth and the drink was bittersweet alcohol. The odd sensation dribbled down his throat. He smacked his lips together, it was like nothing he had drunken before. Rex sipped it and again until the sensation normalised. Oren sat into a foldaway chair and hung leaned his elbows atop his knees. He swallowed the beer incredibly fast. His face daren't waver, he was clearly accustomed to the odd taste and there was a second beer beside his boot. "You all want answers. So, if you think you are big enough to get them, then you need to act like it. Beer is for adults only and so are answers." Oren drew another swing. "You all were born into this world but not like the rest of us. You already know how you came to be and now you want to know what the outside is like, so I'll tell you."

"Another lie?" Cyrus intimidated Oren's posture.

"No, no more lies. You deserve to know the truth."

Oren took some time to recollect his thoughts. He swallowed before continuing. "You are all clones of the dead. People who are no longer around, those that have passed onto another life. That means, you have somebody else's genes. If you go outside, there is a chance you could be recognised. We had no control over the similarities between you and the previous host. My guess is that you would resemble them in some way and we're worried Scotland would notice."

"I don't understand," Apollo twirled a strand of spiked hair. His buggy brown eyes fixated on Oren.

"The chance of you looking or acting like the person you were cloned from were is very high. According to our calculations, Kiara, you died ten years ago. Chino was hardly alive, Apollo, you died a hundred years ago but I think that estimate could be a lot sooner than we think. Rex and Cyrus you were deceased for approximately three centuries, it was so long ago that our fear isn't so much about you being recognised but genes do play a part for generations to come. That is our worry." Oren placed the empty beer bottle on the floor and reached for the other one. He plucked the lid off by the hem of his shirt and took a sip. "If someone recognises you, any of you, us researchers would go to jail. As for the rest of you ... Well, I have no idea. You would probably be experiment on, imprisoned or something worse. If the world found out, there's no telling what would come next."

"What do you mean something worse?" Rex asked.

"I don't know. No clone has ever lived as long as you all have. It's not allowed and I can't guarantee you would be safe. You could be prosecuted for being a clone and yes, I know it's not your fault but it is a possibility."

Rex's head began to spin. He opened his mouth to speak but he felt sleepy. He switched his gaze to the beer, there was some kind of peaceful arousal to it. Damn. Strong stuff.

Halley entered the room. It was time for ecology class.

XXI

Rex is 9/18

Rex slipped into a pair of boxer shorts and a white singlet top. He examined the hole in the middle but it was his last fresh shirt. It would have to do. He searched the basement but Cyrus wasn't around. Rex shrugged and combed through his wavy black hair. He slicked it backwards by a finger of styling gel, to reveal his almost perfect hairline across his sculpted face. He glanced around and realised a light illuminated the floor. He crept behind the bathroom and awaited his cue. Rex poised his elbow against the timber frame. When Cyrus emerged with his hair shorter, almost chin length. The edges were jagged from the fresh cut. He always butchered it. Rex lunged forward and thrust his arms around his twin's shoulders. He cackled as Cyrus spun around, dazed. Rex coiled his limbs around Cyrus' waist. "What are you going to do now?"

Cyrus sighed. "Nothing. You win."

"You bet 'cha!"

Cyrus thrust himself backwards and they slammed against the floor. Rex took the brunt of the fall. He groaned in agony and clutched his elbow. That was unexpected but he should have seen that coming, it was an old move. Rex thought quickly, he needed a rebound. He extended his leg. Cyrus tumbled and fell face first. It was the perfect opportunity and Rex mounted his back, pulling Cyrus' wrist into the air.

"Hey," Cyrus wailed. "I need a break. Time out!"

Rex relaxed and Cyrus somersaulted sideways. In a twist of events, Cyrus pinned him down. He held Rex's neck in place by the heel of his foot. Nice move. It locked Rex's jaw into place. He took mental notes.

Cyrus folded his arms. "I know you're moves too well."

"Oh yeah?" Rex reached behind Cyrus' knee and flung him sideways. "So do I!"

Cyrus' cheek plastered against the floor. "That's new." He groaned. "Alright, help me up."

Rex reached his hand forward when Cyrus grabbed for his shirt. He yanked Rex and crowned his knees to his chest. Cyrus kicked off. Rex flew across the room. He craned his head to his chest but his limbs flailed in all directions, when he slammed against someone.

"Knock it off!" Apollo wailed as he dropped to the ground. "You're mucking up my hair." He twirled the spiked hair clumps.

"You think your mug needs any more gel? Looks like you've used the entire bottle!" Cyrus taunted and Rex covered his mouth.

"C'mon Rex, you know how long this took me." Apollo headed for the bathroom, comb in one hand gel in the other.

Cyrus winked. "Nice work with Oren. I didn't know you had it in you."

"What's that?"

"A brain."

Rex panted and flapped his top from the heat of the fight. "You mucked up my last singlet." It was virtually torn in half.

"Really? I think it's an improvement."

Rex thrust the singlet on the floor and drips of sweat trailed between his pecs. He admired his body's defined glory. He knew Cyrus watched without even looking. He always did and his glare was invigorating. Poor sod, couldn't gain much more than fat. He got the poor end of the genes. Rex walked towards the chest of drawers. He pulled the handle but it fell off and instead Rex pried the edge open and rummaged around the sweaters and hoodies.

"How about one of those cigs?" Cyrus called.

Rex frowned. He pulled out a black jumper and broke into a sweat at the sight of it. "I got none left."

"C'mon."

"Seriously. I need to hit up Gabriel."

Cyrus thought for a moment and folded his arms. "Tell you what. When you get some more, hand me one."

"What's in it for me?" Rex returned his attention to the drawer and searched for something lighter.

"A new singlet."

"Hmm." Rex extracted a red flannel, pulled it over his shoulders and rolled up the sleeves. "There's just one more thing I want." He strode towards Cyrus and ruffled his collar. "Lay off Chino. Enough with the taunting, scratches, the bruises. Knock it off. I don't give a damn if he's weak. All the more reason to leave him alone."

"Two cigarettes."

He offered a hand Cyrus shook it. Deal.

Rex picked the basement lock with one of Kiara's hair pins. He slipped out and crept up the staircase. He pressed his head against the wall and peered upright. The coast was clear but Rex knew to play it safe. He soon reached the top step. On L2 the office door was shut and through the glass window, he couldn't see anybody inside. Rex crossed the corridor and stood at the frosted lab doors. He knew exactly where Gabriel kept the cigarettes, to suggest they were well hidden would be a lie. A door shut from somewhere near. Shit. It sounded like the front door. Rex peered over the brass railing of the staircase and saw a shadow but couldn't make it out. This hadn't happened before. If it was Gabriel, he would be busted and there would be no more cigarettes. He decided to make a run for it. He dodged for the lab door and when he reached the black pad his mind went blank. In a fit of anxiety, he forgot the code. He punched a random code into the pad and it alarmed. Whoever entered the lab heard the buzz and ran for the stairs. Dammit. Rex turned around and sped towards the office instead. He jiggled the handle but the office was locked. Damn it. That just made more noise. The footsteps were close now. This was it, his cover was blown, that didn't take long. Halley emerged from the staircase. "You scared me. What are you doing?" She dropped her hands by her side.

Rex avoided eye contact. He had to think of something and fast. He wouldn't want to disappoint her.

She strode forward. "Hey? What's happening?"

"It's not like we have any other excitement in the basement. I only wanted a cigarette from Gabriel's stash," he mumbled. "I swear, I've never done it before."

Halley raised an eyebrow. "Come with me." She walked towards the lab.

Rex paused, temporarily dazed by the change of events.

She peered over her shoulder. "Are you coming?"

He didn't think twice and fastened his pace but was sure to stay behind Halley. "You're not mad?"

"I knew about the smoking for a while. I smelt it on your clothes. Good thing I wash them before anyone else notices."

"You don't care?"

"To be honest, I'm not too fond of Gabriel myself. I don't see any harm in a fag." She entered the code into the pad and the lab doors opened. Rex darted inside and sat atop the wooden desk. He opened the second drawer. He opened the packet of cigarettes and extracted two. Then he remembered his deal with Cyrus. Four it was. He thought in silence, Gabriel might notice that many missing. He switched his gaze to Halley and her eyes shone with guilt but Rex wasn't sure what for. Halley folded her arms. She allowed the memoir into her mind. "I'm surprised you never figured it out. You're smart and … This is where you were created."

Rex frowned. The lab was his place of conception. For some reason that shocked him, it never crossed his mind before. He glanced around at the lab in a new light. The steel bench top, windowless walls and pristine cabinet was where was spawned. It was a heartless environment and there was nothing that welcomed him. He never suspected a place so cold would be where he came from. He pondered where other babies were born. Perhaps the movies were right and it was within a hospital with a crowd of expectant people. Parents. It seemed sweeter than here. Tears stung his eyes. "How?"

Halley bowed her head. "Come with me."

She walked to the back wall. Rex watched as Halley grabbed a glass jar filled with an amber substance with a stick-figured mosquito inside. She dragged it along the edge of the bench. He lowered his gaze and moaned as his back ached from the play fight with Cyrus. He looked into the hollow eyes of the mosquito. It's body was translucent and didn't appear to be as much of a thrill as he expected. It floated in the preservative residue. An eternal prisoner to death.

"This is where the DNA came from. We used an embryo and when you were absolutely tiny, you grew inside this." Halley placed a petri-dish before him. "Her name was Diane Thomson, her embryos cloned you and Cyrus. The others were derived from other women."

"Is she my mother?"

"No. Her embryo was just the host. Your genes came from the mosquito who sucked blood out of someone."

"Who was that?"

"We will never know the answer to that."

"Does that mean I don't have parents then? Do you have parents?"

Halley gulped. Her cheeks flushed bright red and she bit her lower lip. Enough said. Rex was an orphan. He redirected his attention back to the mosquito. It was short of a leg and its' long snout was fine as a pin. That's where his true identity came from but it still didn't answer all of his questions.

"Come with me."

Halley entered the office and extracted a textbook from the shelf. Along the corner, each one was printed in green and blue writing AncestryDNA. Handwritten codes and names were written on the front. Halley handed a letter to him, it read Subject X-313, Rex. "It seems like my life is one big hidden letter. Anyway, I know how it feels to not know who you are. I can relate to that. When you were all babies I had this test done to find out where you came from and held onto the results until you were older."

Rex flipped the letter over. It was still sealed. "Why didn't you open it?"

"I wanted this to be your choice. This is my gift to you and the others. To reveal more of who you are, is up to you."

Rex hugged Halley and his biceps crushed her neck. She gasped for air and he loosened his grip. He resorted to a warm hand against her cheek.

Back in the basement Rex stuffed the five letters into the top drawer. Cyrus bolted towards him with hungry eyes. "What took you so long?"

Rex avoided the question. He walked away but Cyrus extended a hand to stop him. Rex ignored his quizzical stare, sure to give nothing away. There was no need to mention the discussion with Halley. It would only evoke questions among his siblings that couldn't be answered. He decided to savour them the pain. Rex extracted a cigarette.

"And?" Cyrus asked.

"Chino. Leave him alone."

Cyrus extended his hand.

Rex slapped two cigarettes into his twins' hand. He let the trade-off for the singlet go. It didn't matter anymore.

XXII

Rex is 9/18

Rex awoke by the slither of morning light that poured through the slit in the curtain. It blinded him and he pressed his eyes open. The memory flooded back in, Rex was 3/5;

His button nose was sprinkled with freckles but his feet were too large for his age. Sponge-bob played terribly loud but it was better than his brother complain about the missing puzzle piece. Rex sat on the floor, cross-legged. Oren always said that if you sit too close you can go blind but it was too good to miss. He wiped away the thick fringe but it flopped into place. Instead Rex brushed the wavy strands of hair out of his eyes as little make-shift windows. He twiddled his thumbs as his eyes were glued to the screen.

The basement door swung open and the researchers entered the room. Finally, it had been so long. Rex had seen the same episode of Sponge-bob a dozen too many times and his knees cramped up. Oren almost tripped over the flash ball. "Rules are meant to be broken," he shrugged.

Halley scooped up Rex's petite body and poised him atop her hip. He was four-feet taller. He could see everything in the basement, even Gabriel's polished head.

"Honey, where's Chino?"

"He's there!" Rex pointed in the corner of the basement.

Chino sat in the over-sized office chair, where his feet dangled over the edge. He waved with his free hand whilst to the other side Gabriel tightened a blood pressure cuff.

"Ata' boy Chino! Come here and give me five?" Oren winked.

Chino could hardly contain his excitement. He leapt down from the chair and as the blood-pressure cord trailed along the floor. He dodged across the alphabet play-mat, jumped over the flash ball and hid behind Oren's leg.

"Let's look at getting that fringe cut sometime soon."

Chino shook his head.

Oren laughed and made his way toward Gabriel. "They're getting big now. I remember being that age, don't you?"

"I know what you're getting at."

"Then say it."

"What for? You know my answer."

"I do but they don't."

Gabriel leaned close to Oren's ear and whispered. "Stick to the plan or the deal is off."

Rex's gaze switched over to the window that was covered by a tarp. It flapped inwards against the wind that tugged on it from the other side. Rex squinted at the glimmer of light that beamed through a slit in the tarp. There was something on the other side, Rex knew that much but what was it? His petite belly swirled with a crowd of butterflies, one day he would know. He opened his mouth to ask but quickly placed his index finger over his lips. Gabriel always reminded him not to interrupt when the adults spoke. He would try harder.

All too soon, Oren and Halley left and an eerie silence filled the room. Rex switched off the television and felt something throb from within his chest. Being alone with Gabriel only meant something bad would happen. His brothers knew what was to come and already hid under the blankets but someone's pink foot poked out.

Rex was left in the open. He dodged toward the table and curled up with his knees to his chest and tucked his nose behind. Only Rex's innocent green eyes were visible and even then, they were hidden behind his thick fringe. He watched as Gabriel's black boots entered the basement. He gulped. It was time for another vaccine.

Rex was thrust back into reality when the basement door flung open.

"Good morning, rise and shine! Alright everyone, listen up!" Gabriel walked into the middle of the room. Rex shielded his eyes by his hand, it was too damn early for this.

"It's five in the morning and there's something we need to tell you." A letter was raised in the air and he cast looked over the clones. "It's that time of year again and the HFEA will conduct another investigation. That means we need to haul everything out of here asap."

"When is it?" Cyrus asked.

"In a couple weeks. So we need to get a move on, starting today."

Oren nodded. "That's right. Half of you will help me move the beds, Kiara you're with Halley." He turned toward Gabriel. "You, do whatever you do."

The HFEA was the Human Fertilisation and Embryology Association, they regulated places like this. Once a year, the

HFEA would inspect the lab and make sure everything operated as it should. Rex laughed on the inside, the lab was anything but compliant. If the HFEA found out that he was a clone, the researchers would go down big time. But what would that mean for Rex?

He ran a hand through his hair and felt a surge of emotions he could not describe but what he knew it was directed at the researchers. Rex had hardly finished breakfast before he was on his feet for an early start. He lifted the chest of drawers with one hand mounted it onto his back. He strode past Gabriel who yelled in Russian beneath a furrowed brow. He spun around, his lab coat flew through the air and an elbow smacked into Rex stumbled and the drawers each pulled out of place. Bundles of folded clothes sprawled over the floor. Amidst the mess Rex saw a fresh white singlet.

"Seriously," Rex snarled. "I guess it will take me a few hours to clean this up. Let's hope the HFEA doesn't come too soon."

Gabriel dropped to the floor and gathered the clothes in his arms. Rex laughed at his prudish exterior. Cyrus caught onto the joke and winked at Rex and the brothers laughed in sync. Rex wouldn't harm a fly but knew how to make Gabriel quiver. Maybe the start to such a morning was not so bad after all.

Later that day, Rex watched the researchers latest cloning experiment, which focused on marine preservation and oceanic regeneration. Rex was poised atop the office chair, crossed legged. He didn't know what happened on but was mesmerised by Oren's rhythmical hand movements and the inter-twined gloved fingers. Through the white film of Oren's gloves, puddles of sweat formed between the webs of his fingers. He hunched over the microscope and continued the delicate task. Beside him, Gabriel's hands moved steady as if in slow motion. Rex leaned across the table and bumped Gabriel's shoulder, that was the second time. He whispered something in Russian, enough said, Rex moved to the other side of the table and watched from afar.

"I got it." Oren said. "I've removed the nucleus of cell A. How are you going over there?"

Gabriel remained silent.The somatic cell nuclear transfer was well under-way. Now that the nucleus had been extracted from cell A, it would soon be transferred to cell B. Well, when Gabriel was ready of course. Rex rolled his eyes. Okay, he got it, experiments like this required a lot of concentration but Gabriel did over-do it. Apparently the experiment was more important than breathing at this point.

"Psst! Halley?" Rex whispered. "What are they cloning this time?"

"Fish."

"No I mean what was the scientific name? I forgot again."

"A Danio Rio ... Zebra fish."

Rex's stomach churned. These cells were produced for the use of research and disease eradication. That was why Rex was cloned. He pitied the Danio Rio for it would never see the light of day again. As he shouldn't have. Rex battled inner demons when he watched these experiments be repeated over and over again. It tugged at his heart strings some days but others he pleasantly accepted this was their fate. He rounded the table and rolled up his sleeves. He stopped walking. On the edge of the table lay a Danio Rio. Its' slimy corpse watched Rex. Its' life was worthless to the researchers.

"You alright?" Halley placed a hand on his shoulder.

"That was meant to be me, wasn't it? All of us never should have never lived."

"Don't say that."

Rex turned to face Halley, his nose almost touched hers. "I was never meant to be alive after the experiment was I?"

Halley face didn't waver and the mutual agreement was telepathic. There was no comfort she could offer. "I'm going to help find out who you are."

Rex turned away.

XXIII

2010

The lounge room resembled a cinema. The salted caramel emitted from a candle on the table and the buttery popcorn sat between Oren's thighs. He scooped another handful into his mouth and reached for the remote. Halley shifted her body to face him. She grabbed a piece of odd shaped popcorn and examined it as if it were the questions that boggled her mind.

"Did you see that?" Oren said, his eyes fixated on the screen. "Hal?"

"Yeah."

"You're a bit quiet .. What are you thinking about?"

"I'm thinking about the beach."

"The beach?"

"The clones have never left that basement. You know, they've never really lived. Never seen a beach, never smelt the bitter salt or felt the sting of water as it cleanses a healing scab. Never felt the sand between their toes."

"Okay. Where's this coming from all of a sudden?"

"It's nothing new, come on."

"Absolutely out of the question."

"Honey, they're just children."

"No. The clones can never leave the basement, do you understand?"

"Don't talk to me like that. Do you understand how hard it must be for them?"

"I don't really give a shit! They're lucky to be alive."

Halley silenced, encased in the realms of her own bitterness. The clones deserved more than that. They were not delinquents but their existence made them such. She felt a gush of guilt. The clones were of age to question their life, they're being and what that meant.

Oren pinched the skin between his eyes. "I'm sorry, I didn't mean to snap but we have been through this before. We can't afford to get caught."

"Then we're at a crossroad. On one hand we can honour their life and give them freedom but on the other hand, we can use their existence and hold them hostage. After all, it's not as if anyone would realise they're clones."

"Clones of the deceased. If someone recognises them - ," Before Oren could finish the patter of feet emerged from down the hallway. Max stood at the base of the staircase, bare foot and rubbed his eye with a balled fist. The hem of his blue-and-red Spiderman pyjamas trailed over the ground. He strode toward the couch and climbed into Halley's lap.

"I had a nightmare."

She kissed his forehead and stroked his bundle of ginger hair that smelt of cotton candy conditioner. Max laid his heavy head atop Halley's chest. He was soon asleep and his head dropped to his chest. She turned to Oren and cast him a serious stare.

"No." Oren whispered. "The clones stay as they are." He pointed two fingers at his eyes and then at Halley. "Watching you." He tried to maintain a serious stare but burst into a giggle.

Halley lifted from the couch with Max cradled in her arms. She returned moments later and sat beside Oren, who then pulled her onto his lap.

"I know where you're coming from," he began. Halley trailed her fingers through his hair that was crusted in a thick layer of gel. The ginger strands moved in clumps. "You need a haircut." She tucked a longer piece behind Oren's ear.

"Well you've gotten pretty good at hairdressing, so why don't you do it for me?"

"I don't know what I'm doing. Besides, the clones are going through a phase where they all want long hair, it's not hard cutting a straight line and I'm not doing yours like that too."

"All besides Apollo."

They laughed. Apollo was the only who spiked his hair, the higher the better, apparently. Oren stroked Halley's cheek by his thumb and she dropped her head into the palm of his hand. He lent forward and kissed her neck. His hands now wrapped around her waist but Halley was tense. "Stop worrying, the clones are lucky to be alive," he whispered.

"They are alive." Halley pressed her forehead against his and scoured the face. Surely he knew where she came from. Oren was caught off guard and looked away.

"What if that was Max?"

"Don't be so stupid, Hal!"

"What if that was Max in that basement?" Halley's voice cracked. "What if our only son never ventured beyond those four walls. We owe it to those clones, they are all somebody's child, sister, son, uncle, brother … Bringing them into this world was a promise we made a long time ago and now it's time to set them free."

"No."

Halley raised her hand but Oren grabbed her wrist mid-air. She felt her pulse quicken beneath his tight grasp. For some reason the crinkles along his forehead in a fight made her heart race. Oren pulled her close to his chest. A trickle of sweat trailed down Halley's neck. She bit her lower lip.

XXIV

Rex is 9/18

At some ungodly hour the lights came on in the basement and flashes of colour danced across the inside of Rex's eyelids. He groaned and realised he was the only one that laid in the king-sized bed with the sheets up to his chin. Rex squinted to see the clones sprawled across the basement. Chino was in the far corner, his hands tucked into his armpits. "Can someone turn off the lights, it's too bright," he winged.

Cyrus exhaled cigar smoke. "I didn't realise you still held onto your blankey."

Rex stumbled across the floor, wearing boxers and a pair of socks. Cyrus folded his arms and pressed his biceps forward. He dropped the cigarette to the floor and smudged the embers with his foot. "Well now that I have your attention... We're leaving." Rex rolled his eyes.

"I think we can all agree that we have had enough of this place," Cyrus continued. "We are tired of the experiments, blood tests and being forced into the boredom of this damn basement! We want to know who we are and we can only accomplish that by freedom." His eyes glowed with the embers of rage.

Chino turned his head in the direction of the others but kept his eyes shut the whole time. "Actually I like these four walls, I don't intend of ever leaving, especially if the outside is like they say." Like always, his commentary went unnoticed. Although there was a hostility in the air that seemed to tear the clones apart.

Kiara placed a cold hand on Rex's shoulder. "He is right you know. We have dreamed of the outside since we were kids. We pondered our identity in the past life." The tender words rolled off her tongue eloquently and the sweet scent of strawberries blew in Rex's face. He bit the inner of his cheeks and faced the floor. Surely Kiara was not fooled by the lies of Cyrus. She was too smart for that.

"We don't know anything about the outside. We need to plan this better."

"Rex, this may be our only chance." Her eyes glistened with unspeakable passion. Kiara leaned close to his ear and whispered. "I need you to come with me, I can't do this without you."

Cyrus paced. "We're all leaving tonight unless you want to stay behind brother."

Rex glanced over the clones. Each of them looked at him for approval. Apollo held his head high and tried not to smile too wide. Behind Chino's sunken face, there was the faintest shadow of excitement. It made Rex's stomach drop lower into his back. Of course he wanted to see the outside and probably more than any of them. But he knew there was no escape without a plan.

"We stay put."

"What?" Kiara gasped.

"It would never work if we just got up and left. How does that make any sense?"

Kiara's face was tense and the tip of her freckled nose tingled. Her face burned and tears filled her eyes. "I don't want to stay here forever."

"Neither do I but we need to play it smart. I've spoken to Halley about where we came from and we need to keep gathering clues."

"The researchers can say whatever they want, we can't believe them. I have a better idea," Cyrus said. The twins stood there for some time. Face to face. "You don't know what's best for everyone so I challenge you to competition. We fight until a leader is born and only then will our future be determined. Only a true leader could guide everyone out of the darkness and towards the answers we desire. Then can we decide whether or not to go outside," Cyrus said.

"I'll fight you," Rex implored.

"No. Leadership is not a privilege, we all must earn it."

The hairs on the back of Rex's stood on end. Beside playful wresting, none of them had ever fought. But he know, that if hr attested Cyrus' proposition, it would be a sign of weakness and if he defended the clones they too would appear weak. Rex glanced across the room, none of them stood a chance but no-one retaliated. Nobody could walk away from a leadership fight, not when Cyrus led the battle. Whispers erupted within the room but the voices were meek and sounded like a contorted mess of blurred language. The once familiar faces now seemed a crowd of distant strangers. The clones were stone cold as they glared at their opponents.

The battle had silently begun and it was all too late to back down. The ground was cold beneath Rex's feet. He wiped away the greasy strands of hair from his face and dare not look away from Cyrus. His fingers trembled with anxiety but his biceps pulsed with thick blood. He was prematurely ready for the leadership fight. Rex nodded his head. "Best of luck to you, brother."

"As to you," Cyrus bowed his head.

Rex peered at Kiara from across the room and his hands trembled. He couldn't fight her, there was no way. He gulped. The first round was about to begin. Rex leant forward and placed his hands over his bent knees. In all honestly, he was ready to back down, to fight his twin brother was the last thing he wanted but there was no choice. He breathed heavily. He needed to change his mentality and fast. He sought after a spark of hatred or some deep emotion within. He needed to find a reason to fight.

Rex clenched and unclenched his fists. He thought of all the times Cyrus tried to intimidate him, of when teased Chino. Then he felt it. A heated bonfire within his belly. He clenched his fists. Apollo clasped both hands around his mouth. "Now!"

Cyrus sprinted forward at incredible speed. Rex threw a punch but Cyrus dodged it, he kept his body close to the ground. Smart move. Cyrus bent his leg and kicked, hard.

Rex skidded halfway across the room. His skull scraped across the floor and a trail of blood followed. His brain raked from the inside and Rex was dazed. Get up, he told himself. Quickly. He clawed the floor but he couldn't stand up. He saw double vision and his elbows shook. There was no time for this.

Slam. Cyrus knocked him back. Rex's head hit the table and his body throbbed. He jumped to his feet and a dizzy spell circled his head. Rex drooled a mix of blood and saliva and wiped his mouth by the back of his hand. He focused in time to see Cyrus jump forward, leg outstretched. Rex spun around and dodged the kick. A weak move but it was enough. He needed a stronger comeback. He panted and thought fast. They circled each other and with each step, Rex felt a trail of warm blood ooze down his forehead. A sign of weakness but he compensated with it by ignorance. The pain was meaningless. He shook the blood out of his eye. He threw a mighty punch but again Cyrus ducked down, his head close to the floor. Rex kicked off the ground, tumbled along Cyrus' back. At the final second, Cyrus whipped around and head-butt Rex's jaw. He wailed in pain and stumbled backwards. His mouth filled with blood and Rex knew in that moment he made a big mistake. He appeared injured and that in itself was an unforgivable price. Rex focused on the matter at hand. Leadership. He needed to lead his siblings through this difficult time and keep them safe. If Cyrus won the fight, it would be chaos. Then it hit him. Rex was wounded but Cyrus fought twice as hard, which meant he would tire faster. It all made sense. So far, Rex would win. He needed to keep Cyrus fighting. Keep him on the move. That was the answer.

With that in mind. He charged forward and simply stood aside. He copied Cyrus' move and dropped close to the ground. Knees bent and head down. Cyrus pulled himself back to stop his fall. His arms flailed. The plan worked. Cyrus tired. Rex raised his fists to his face and bounced on the spot. Cyrus frowned but little did he realise the distraction. His frustration forced him to lunge forward. Rex moved aside and punched Cyrus in the face.

Then he kicked him in the core and Cyrus stumbled back. He kicked behind his knees and dropped to the ground. Rex poised a heavy foot atop him. Rex won and then the clones cheered. The first round of the leadership fight was complete. Cyrus lifted his head off the ground. "Well done brother, well done," he whispered.

"C'mon you gotta get up," Rex encouraged.

Cyrus stood almost straight, placed one hand across his abdomen and bowed before the winner. The upmost respectful act and one of sincere courtesy but Rex felt the despise. It chilled his bones.

"Who's next?" Rex spat blood-riddled saliva at the floor.

The leadership fight lasted what felt like hours but only the second round ended when Apollo was defeated. Across the room the next opponent entered the tournament. Rex gagged on the swallowed blood. He stomach churned, he dreaded this fight more than any.

It was Kiara's turn. The sweet tenderness vanished from her face and she switched over to the poised seriousness of a cold-blooded killer.

Kiara pounded forward and Rex had no choice. They slammed into each other with great force. She whined against the blunt force but her complaints were drowned out by the cheer of the crowd. All of whom probably had no idea which side to favour but the dawn of an official leader was at hand nonetheless. No matter who won, they would all accept their newfound leader with great enthusiasm and respect. Kiara and Rex somersaulted along the floor and then slammed into the far brick wall. Rex's brain splattered against the back of his skull. His head flopped forward. She was stronger than he expected. His vision blackened. It was under a minute when Rex re-opened his eyes and realised Kiara knelt over him. She gripped his throat. Rex choked against her fingernails that pinched his skin and her grasp that constricted his air supply.

He coordinated his body and coiled his knees against his chest. He pushed Kiara off and she was knocked onto her backside. She groaned but not for long, if she dared drop her guard she would lose the fight all too soon. Kiara pressed her feet against the wall, miraculously bounced off and tumbled through the air. She flew over Rex's head and landed neatly. Her fight was skilful and light-footed. The less Kiara tried, the harder it seemed for Rex. Maybe his emotions got the best of him but there seemed no way around it. He couldn't conceal how he truly felt. It was a loosing battle. The clones roared and some of them called Rex's name. The adrenaline made him try again. He pounced forward and was about to catch Kiara in his grip. She threw a punch. Again she stood on-top of him and clasped her hands around his neck. Rex gasped for air and his body convulsed. He gripped Kiara's forearms but he couldn't push her off for she was too strong. Suddenly, his eyes rolled back into his head. This was it. This was how his life would end. Kiara took the fight too seriously but Rex didn't have the audacity to fight her, not with how he felt. Kiara winked at him. She lowered her body and shielded them both from the crowd. "Follow my lead," she whispered. Kiara wailed and flung herself onto the ground and pulled Rex on top.

Rex won. He looked at Kiara confused but she ignored his stare. It didn't make any sense.

The clones yelled and jumped on the spot and specs of blood flew in all directions. Rex bowed back at his entourage and they reciprocated the act.

The fight continued, until all the clones had their turn and walked away with battle scars. Nobody was left unbranded. After some time, the leadership fight came to an end and the leader prevailed.

"I am Rex, your newest leader whom you shall follow. Should anyone trespass me, they would be exiled from this pact. Thank you for your efforts in the leadership fight, I know you all tried your best and now I shall act on everyone's behalf. We are one!"

The clones cheered until their throats were a raspy mess. Rex glanced at Cyrus who was coiled onto the bed with a ragged shirt, drenched in blood, pressed against his head. Cyrus closed his eyes and lowered his head to resemble a bow. He squinted, there was something else in Cyrus' face that night. A hand clasped Rex's shoulder and he was swarmed with words of praise by Apollo. "That was well deserved," he applauded. He clapped his hands together but winced each time they collided.

"Thanks, I hope you're not too hurt," Rex gestured.

"I could be worse." Apollo shrugged. He glanced over the room. "Where's Cyrus?"

"He was right there," Rex pointed dumb-founded to the bed.

The clones searched the room to see Cyrus was gone. He was there a minute ago but obviously had other intentions. Rex salivated with frustration and swallowed the mouthful of blood that pooled at the back of his throat.

"Rex," Kiara whispered.

He looked at her confused and then realised. The basement door was wide open. Rex cussed beneath his breath and was first to bolt out the door. A blood trail led up the staircase. He punched the air and with each step, his body seemed as though it would give out. There was no time for pain. Rex emerged onto L2 and saw the office door was slightly ajar. He burst inside to see Cyrus faced the window. "I have to do this. I can't pretend everything is okay anymore." His shoulders rose and fell.

Rex inched forward. "Come here."

"No."

"What do you want?"

"Rex, don't pretend you're happy." Cyrus turned around and bore a bloody grin. "We need to get the hell out of here. Nine years, nine damned years of that shitty basement!" A tear trickled down his chin. He tapped his temple. "If you had half a brain, you wouldn't stay here."

Cyrus smashed his fist through the window. A cascade of glass shattered over the ground and the storm blew a gust of rain into the office. He jumped out of the window and his body dangled mid-air, held up by his hands alone. Cyrus swung his legs sideways and his foot locked against the gutter but lost hold. He tried again but the rain pried Cyrus' hands open. He swung his legs across harder and his ankle anchored over the metal gutter.

Rex leant his head out the window and hard rain smacked into his face. He was too late, Cyrus was already out of sight. He felt his stomach sink. That back-stabbing dick.

"Apollo, get him."

"Don't worry," he sneered.

Apollo jumped out of the window and next was Kiara. Just like her fight skills, was fast and disappeared within seconds. Rex turned around, his face a mess of blood and rain that trailed down his cheeks and lips. He saw Chino cowered under the window frame. There was no time to spare. Rex poised himself along the window and hauled Chino out.

They were were, with one foot pressed against the gutter and the other along the slanted tiles of the roof.

"C'mon," Kiara urged. She arched forward and climbed outside. Rex was last, he gripped the slimy tiles and was halfway up the roof when the storm raged and thunder shuddered the sky.

"Look out!" Apollo bellowed. A tile skidded along the roof and Rex raised his foot so it slid between his legs. He closed in on Cyrus and almost reached the pitched roof of the lab.

"I can't stay hidden like this anymore," Cyrus yelled. He crouched close to the tiled roof and nursed his arm that oozed with blood. Apollo extended his hand, which Cyrus punched away.

"We will never make it like this, come back inside," Apollo encouraged. Rex watched the scene unfold a few metres away. He crept up roof but was sure not to make any sudden moves. Cyrus searched the sky for answers between the blurred grey clouds and rain slapped his face. He smiled at the storm that washed out his wounds. Then it dawned upon him. For the first time they felt cold, the natural embrace of rain as it smacked into his face. The bodies of his brothers and sister were bruised with the leadership fight and now the rain stung every inch but it was would invigorating. Rex pitied them all. He was guilty, for wanting to lead them back into the lab but knew they would never survive.

"I'm going," Cyrus said.

"No, you are not going anywhere," Rex spat. He reached for the tile above his head and drew his body further up the roof. Gravity pulled him back but Rex used the remainder of his strength to climb. "If you do anything stupid I will have no choice but to have your own siblings attack you until death. I order you to come down from there."

Cyrus' face was overcome with darkness, a hunger for freedom. He grinned at Rex but with broken eyes. Cyrus finally made it but his destiny was short-lived. He stood upright and raised a hand in the air, to gesture a farewell. Suddenly, Apollo lunged forward and tackled him down. The clones battled across the roof but slipped over the edge. They dropped along the slanted tiles. Rex moved aside when Cyrus and Apollo tumbled onto the balcony and their bodies collided into the office. Rex panted. It was all over. Everyone was safe again.

Back inside, the basement was a catastrophic mess. Streaks of blood splattered the walls with sediments of hair plastered inside. There was a cluster of yellowed teeth strewn across the floor that nobody mentioned or own up to. Rex's wounds leaked jagged trails of crimson blood that gravitated toward the floor. He limped across the basement and sat on the edge of the bed. He switched the television on. Being leader was numb sensation, he felt no different. Rex lit a cigarette and drew a long puff as he watched some foreign movie. He hardly followed the subtitles, just traced the images with his eyes.

Kiara stared at the disarray of bodily fluids over the floor. "It was cold outside. It was cold and bitter. There was a strong breeze, rain plummeted down from the sky and the clouds are grey."

"Are you alright?" Rex asked through a cloud of smoke.

"I am better than alright. That was the outside. Rex, we witnessed the outside. "We did it, like we said we would as kids."

Rex cackled and cigarette ashes drop to the floor. She was right, they were outside and it was petrified him but was more beautiful than in the movies. In that moment, Rex forgot the pain from his head that throbbed. Nothing mattered.

Chino carefully placed his feet between the crevices of blood. He shuttered with each step. "Should we not be cleaning this place up?"

"Why would we do that? We want freedom, then let's make a statement. Something that says, we can take freedom if we want but it would be easier with your help." Rex puffed the cigarette. He leaned next to Kiara's ear. "Can I speak with you in private?"

They were glad to leave the basement. The stench of wet dog and blood was gag-worthy. Rex led the way to the library. He crossed his arms.

"Nice fight out there," Kiara praised.

"What was that?"

"I don't know what you're talking about."

"Don't give me that tone."

Kiara sighed. "I let you win the same reason you let Chino win."
"He's the youngest of the pack, I couldn't fight him, not without ripping him to shreds."
"Exactly."
"You saying I couldn't take you on?" Rex leaned close and sniffed her wet hair.
"That too but … I know who I want to be leader." Kiara cast her eyes over his chapped lips and breathed slow.
A fresh scratched reached from the corner of her eye. Rex traced it with his thumb. "Did I do that?"
She pulled away but her eyes spoke of the truth and he would never forgive himself. "Did you know Cyrus was going to try and leave?"
"No, master."
"Please don't call me that … I don't trust him, there's nothing to stop him trying to leave again. That was the whole point of this leadership fight and he's still denying me as leader."
Rex encircled Kiara. He caressed her with his eyes, for even in her defeated state, she was still took his breath away.
She bowed her head. "Master."
"There's no need for formalities."
Kiara wiped away the smile and avoided eye contact, to show some respect to the new leader. Rex lifted her chin by the tip of his finger. He stared at Kiara's lips, although bruised and bloodied, her warm breath enticed him. Rex's lips brushed against hers but the slighted touch made them throb. He watched her wince in pain and pulled back until their noses touched instead.

"Race you back?" Kiara whispered.

Rex bolted toward the door and switched off the lights. Through the darkness he made out Kiara's eyes that glimmered with defeat. He moved aside and gave Kiara a head start.

By the time the pair made it back to the basement, Gabriel had arrived. Rex was bewildered by a coldness and the hairs on the back of his neck stand on end. He had to somehow explain everything from the broken office window, blood trails and scattered teeth across the basement floor. Gabriel stood in the doorway, arms crossed with the usual poker expression scribbled across his face. Rex limped through the basement and the clones parted for him.

"What the hell is going on around here? What have you lot been doing, you're covered in blood and the lab is a mess!" Harsh vodka slipped from his lips. He lifted the cellphone to his ear. "I need you both here, asap." He returned his gaze to the clones. "Well?"

The clones remained silent.

"I demand a response!"

"No, Gabriel." Rex tried to hide his angst but Gabriel saw his bottom lip quiver. "We can't stay locked down here forever."

"How many times are we going over this shit. You have no freedom. Now go upstairs!"

The clones shivered as Gabriel raised his voice. "It's alright," Rex said. "I'll go first."

A warm towel was placed over Rex's eyes to block out the lights. Gabriel sat beside him, tweezers in one hand a wet gauze in the other. He focused on the wound embedded in his right arm. Rex groaned as Gabriel was in full control, he toyed with the two ends of open flesh. The hook slipped through Rex's skin. A sharp pain radiated up and clenched his jaw. He spat beads of saliva toward the ceiling. "Tell me the goddamned truth of what happened last night before I let you clean yourself up."

"You wouldn't do that. I'll get an infection and I die."

"Don't be too damn sure."

"You should be thanking me." The needle looped through Rex's flesh again and he yelled in pain. The answer seemed farfetched but surely Gabriel would believe him after he saw the state of the office and basement. "We've been to the outside. It's thanks to me that my siblings stayed behind. I will lead them out of this lab and we will escape but I need your help," Rex mumbled through a clenched jaw.

Gabriel pressed the bandage against the fresh wound. He grinned, prided by the request for assistance. "My help?"

Rex didn't know what that meant but he took that as a no. Despite the pain, he drifted into the lull of sleep as Gabriel polished bandaged his arm. He was desperate for rest, even if only a few minutes.

Back inside the basement, everything seemed hopeless. Maybe they would never leave the but Rex wouldn't give up now, he promised it to the others. He clutched his bandaged wounds and dropped to the ground where Apollo sat beside him. "Don't happen to have a spare?"

Rex offered a cigarette to Apollo who proudly placed it between his teeth and gnawed at the body. The cigarette resisted and after some time the chewy exterior became soggy and grains of black filled his mouth. The tobacco soaked all moisture from his mouth and he spat the cigarette on the floor.

Rex laughed. "Maybe next time buddy. Don't worry, I'll teach you."

XXV

2010

After Gabriels' distress call, Oren and Halley ran for the basement. Their eyes almost bulged out of their sockets. It was a blood bath, all the clones limped and their injuries. Even Chino's hair was stained red and a purple bruise spread across his cheek. Halley crouched beside him. "Look at me."

He faced the ground.

She searched his face but found no apparent wounds. "What happened?"

Rex limped forward. He attempted to crouch down but his legs shook and he laid a hand on her shoulder instead. "It's okay."

Halley's jaw dropped open when she saw Rex's bloodshot busted eye.

"I know how this looks but everything is alright, I promise, but it's time for answers. We need to know who we are."

Halley pondered that thought, she could no longer ignore the pain, the agony, the fight, it was all in plain sight. She knew this day would come and was honestly surprised it wasn't sooner. The clones found their voice and had enough of the confinement of the basement. No matter how much time had passed, nothing prepared Halley for that day. She gazed around the room, over the clones with their expectant faces and eyes that pleaded for help. "Do you still have the letters?"

Rex nodded. He reached below the bed and pulled out a bundle of letters. The yellow-stained envelopes were pressed against his chest. The clones watched him, confused.

Kiara walked in stride. "You didn't tell me about this?"

"I was going to but then the leadership fight happened and there was no time."

"Oh really?"

"Not now."

"What are those?" Gabriel pointed.

Halley sat cross-legged on the floor and the clones circled her. Some sat on the bed and others sat on the floor. She laid the letters out. "I had the AncestryDNA test done when the clones were babies. I know the feeling of being an orphan and couldn't let them feel the same pain."

Gabriel strode forward. "You didn't say anything."

"You're not one to talk. Besides, there's no harm in this."

It was time or the truth to unfold. Halley's sweaty palms reached for the letter furthest to the right. It was crumpled and torn at the edges but the seal remained intact. Along one corner it read AncestryDNA and along the other was Halley's hand-writing. She toyed with the letter, maybe it would provide some comfort. It was addressed to Chino, who twiddled his thumbs and bowed his head. He was distracted by a thought about something but remained silent. Halley proceeded to rip the letter open and her heart raced but she couldn't understand why. She reached inside. The envelope was empty. This couldn't happen. Halley's heart almost stopped, it all made no sense. She turned to Rex. "How could you?"

He shook his head. "I had nothing to do with this."

She scoured his face for answers that never came. His head

shook back and forth. Halley breathed heavily, it was an error. There was no letter for Chino, somehow, he got missed.

"I'm sorry." She returned to Chino, lost for words. How could a company like this forget his letter. Was that even heard of? It didn't sit right with Halley. There was nothing to stop her from a new DNA test but the fact remained. Chino was an outcast and, for now, wouldn't know his origins.

He seemed unfazed and tossed the ordeal aside. "To be honest I don't really care where I came from. That doesn't help me but I do want to know why I'm albino?"

That answers seemed more treacherous than anything. Halley sighed, it was a flaw in the cloning process. There was no real answer to Chino's albanism. "It's just part of nature. It happen's, like a disease."

Chino frowned. "You said we were innovated to be disease free and a hybrid human species?"

"Yes, albanism isn't a disease, it's more of a malfunction."

Chino folded his arms and glared at the floor. More questions surged and no answers formulated. Halley opened her mouth to speak but realised she had nothing to say. Maybe it was a defective gene or a side-effect of the experiment. She reached forward but Chino retreated, he now understood she didn't have the answers.

"It's fine."

He crept into the shadow of the corner. His submissive eyes watched Halley from the darkness and somehow, she felt responsible. As if the albanism was her fault. A fragment of Halley's heart chipped away. She had to go on. "Kiara, you were

Mediterranean. From Israel, Turkey and Greece." Kiara absorbed the information. Her eyes darted back and forth to understand what that meant. Her mind ran a hundred miles an hour. She heard of those countries before in Oren's geography class and in movies. But didn't fully understand what that suggested.

Halley moved along the line of letters. Apollo was next. She opened the letter and reached inside. Apollo pressed his chin against her shoulder. She unfolded the letter. "Mexico, Germany, Australia and Spain. Your bloodline is quite direct."

A cheerful smile crossed his face. "Cool," Apollo seemed pleased with himself and twirled his spiked hair. Halley glanced at the final letter addressed to Cyrus and Rex. The twins gazed at her and awaited the final verdict. It seemed their entire life lead to this moment. Halley opened the letter. "Norwich, Great Britain. A descent of Henry Gilchrist." She frowned. "That's strange," Halley stumbled. She stared at the letter until her vision blurred and the words merged together.

"What's wrong?" Rex asked.

"His AncestryDNA test and had the same result. One of my family members descended from York."

"I guess it's rigged," Gabriel gestured. He shrugged his shoulders. "Sorry."

Halley ignored the comment and looked down at the letter. To say Rex and Cyrus both originated from Britain was fair enough but not the same town. Out of all the places, they also came from Norwich. Halley thought for a moment, she tried to remember the year from her own letter.

Oren clasped a hand on Halley's shoulder. He crouched down and whispered in her ear. "It's just a coincidence, that's all."

Halley searched for the right words but they never came. Her face tingled with a numb pain and iced chills ran down her back. Her ears were blocked from the outside world. It wasn't a coincidence. Oren missed the point. This was something more. It could be a false lead but Halley followed her gut instinct which said otherwise. The clones turned to the researchers for guidance but this time, there was none. Gabriel watched them beneath a frown. The silence made him impatient as he tried to understand it. Oren nodded at the clones. "It's okay." He tried to relax the atmosphere. Halley nodded at the thought. "It's all coming together."

"What is?" Oren asked.

"If I'm right about this, then … ," She twisted around and unfolded herself from where she sat. She clutched onto the letter and faced the clones. "Follow me." She headed out the door and climbed the stairs. Halley emerged onto L2 and ran toward the office. From behind she heard a crowd of footsteps. The clones and researchers shovelled each other aside, they tried to get close to Halley who led the way. She bit her lip and hoped she was right. If this fell through, she would look like a fool but her gut told her otherwise. Her fingers tightened around the letter.

"What's going on?" Oren asked. He grabbed Halley's arm and stopped in her tracks but she pulled away. "Trust me."

"I'm worried about you."

Halley leaned forward and pecked his cheek. Oren relaxed and walked in stride with Halley again. They reached the office and

Halley darted to the desk. She opened the top drawer and rummaged inside. She checked over files and sheets of paper.

"What's going on?" Rex leaned over the desk.

"You are from York. It was an old city in Great Britain." She raised a letter to her face and read the title. It wasn't what she was looked for and tossed it over her shoulder. "When I had my ancestry letter done-," She raised the letter to her face. Rex switched his gaze from the letter then to Halley. "This could be the answer to the puzzle."

She laid the letter over the table. Her eyes scanned the family tree, all two-hundred-and-eighty-nine-years of it. A descendant on the tree was from her mother's side. "York. Great Britain," she read. "Where's the laptop?"

"Here." Oren extracted the laptop from the third drawer. He tapped the keyboard and the screen flashed on.

"I need the coordinates for York." He slammed the keyboard and his fingers danced at incredible speed. "52.6 degrees North and 1.2 degrees East."

"Okay, what are the coordinates of Dob's Inn?"

"4 degrees North, 73.8 degrees West."

Halley grabbed a pen and scribbled the coordinates. She scribbled down the mathematical equation, where she added and subtracted the coordinates. "Almost four thousand miles."

"Gabriel. How far do mosquitos travel? How long do they live?"

"Twelve miles. Seven days."

Halley's fingers froze. There was a flaw to her plan. It didn't add. "Flying wouldn't be the mode of transport. It would be something else."

"I don't understand," Rex said. He looked at the equation and tried to make some sense of it.

He scratched his head in thought.

"The fossil was found along the edge of the cliff. It was near water. Water is the source. It would have to be continental drift." Halley panted. "I get it now."

Oren laid a hand on her shoulder. "Get what?"

Halley pointed to her AncestryDNA letter. "I originated from York, this letter dates it back to the early 1800s. So does Rex and Cyrus' letter."

"I'm looking but I don't see anything," Oren grew impatient.

"The coordinates of York are 52 degrees North and 1 degree East but we found the fossilised mosquito at Dob's Inn which is 41 degrees North, 73 degrees West. If mosquitos only travel up to twelve miles then that still leaves close to four thousand miles unexplained and I think it comes down to continental drift. The water pushed the fossilised mosquito further away and it makes sense because I found the mosquito by the rivers' edge." Halley gestured to Rex. "What was the name?"

He stared at her blankly.

"The name of the man in your ancestry letter?"

Rex peered down. "Henry Gilchrist."

"Call it a hunch but maybe … Maybe that's who I'm related to."

Gabriel broke out in laughter. "You can't be serious! Okay, you're both from the same background but that's a long shot."

"Hold on a second," Oren said. He scoured Halley's letter in one hand Rex's in the other. "They have the same bloodline. It's exactly the same until 1821 when Halley's branches off. Rex's bloodline stops at 1821, which makes sense because that's when he died. That's how old he was according to our calculations. Everything from there and back is the same. Halley is right."

"What does that mean?" Rex stepped forward.

"It means we're related. That some point in time, we were family." A tear dribbled down her chin. She looked from Cyrus and then to Rex. "We aren't orphans."

"Well," Oren began but said no more and embraced Halley with a heavy hug. She buried her face into his shoulders and wept. She cried away all the sleepless nights, the heartache and pain of never knowing her family. It had stood in-front of her the whole time. She tried to wrap her head around the concept. Oren held her close to his chest and pat her hair. His phone rung. "Sorry, honey." He flipped the Blackberry open. "Hello?"

Halley pulled away and turned towards Rex and Cyrus. They were gobsmacked. That moment took the room by surprise and a gush of emotions filled the atmosphere. Cyrus clasped Halley's shoulder. "We're family?" He pressed his head against hers and they cried together.

Rex sniffled. "What does that make me? I mean what title should I be given?"

Halley laughed. "You are both my historical uncles but age makes you my sons. So I don't really know!"

The joy in the office came to a stop. Suddenly Oren dropped to his knees and the phone slipped out of his hand. Halley ran over and fell beside him. "Oren? Oren?"

He was limp.

Gabriel emerged himself between Halley and Oren. His elbow

jabbed into Halley's abdomen and she fell aside. "He's fainted."
Gabriel tapped his cheek. "C'mon brother."
Oren's eyes flickered open. He searched around and sat upright.
His sight set on Halley. "It's Max. The school sent him to the
hospital."

XXVI

2010

It was that familiar scent of a musty hospital and sterilisation that made Halley's stomach churn and there was only one place on this damned Earth that could do that. She knew it all too well, the Royal Aberdeen Hospital for Sick Children. The hospital corridors boxed-in and filled with the sweet faces of nurses and doctors but their smiles were hideous. There was no happiness in a place like that. Max was in room ten, closest to the nurses' station and from the window in the door, they kept close watch. Halley saw them. She heard their whispers as the nurses' eyes locked on Max. Their upturned faces of sympathy.

"Not this shit again." Oren whispered from the chair opposite Max's bed.

"It's not his fault."

"I never said it was but I can't do this again."

"Not here, let's talk about this outside."

Halley pressed her heavy head against the wall. She watched as Oren paced an unlit cigarette in the corner of his mouth. She was about to ask where he got the cigarette from, for Oren never smoked, but she let the thought slide. It didn't matter. An elderly nurse approached him. "Excuse me sir, no smoking on the premise. You can go outside to the designated smoking area if you wish."

Oren faced the nurse. "Don't worry it's not lit."

"I suggest you take it outside, you're breaking the rules."

"It's not even lit!"

"Oren," Halley hissed. "Sorry, he will put it away."

Oren shovelled the cigarette into his pocket.

"We can't get ahead of ourselves. We have to wait," Halley said over the lump in her throat.

"Wait – wait? Our son is sick!"

"He doesn't know that, alright! Keep your voice down, I don't want him knowing about anything!"

"He's going to know now!" Oren exclaimed.

"No he won't. He's just a kid and let him be one."

"I don't understand, after all this time. After all these years, why now?"

"Keep it together. We just have to sit tight," Halley said.

The last thing Halley wanted to do was sit around all day but that was all she could do. No matter how many times she bombarded the nurses with questions there was no answers. To wait was the hardest part as Max suffered in that hospital bed. The same bed that some children walked out alive and others never saw daylight again. Countless tears had sunken into the mattress and desperate hands gripped the side rails. It was all the same in the end. Once they were discharged, the beds were wiped down and moved to another room. The children and families were forgotten, as Max would be.

The scent of old bricks seeped through the rooms of the Royal Aberdeen Hospital but the green garden outside the window compensated for its' rotten infrastructure. Halley glared out the window, across the grass plains and the endless string of cars that navigated through the city of Edinburgh. Each passenger was encapsulated by the realms of their own vehicle. Everyone went about their business and was oblivious to the sadness within bedspace ten.

Max rearranged himself in the bed with his eyes glued to the television screen. He was dressed in a pale blue gown and tucked into a jam sandwich. A cannula was planted in his left hand the translucent line of intravenous fluid trailed to a large bag that hung beside his bed. He chewed off another bite of the sandwich. "Mum I don't want anymore."

Halley peeked at the breakfast tray where an array of items lay untouched. Max had managed less than half a sandwich. She grinned and he turned back to the television. She rested her head against a balled fist and glanced down at her own bowl of soggy corn flakes. She tapped the cereal with the spoon and the milk squelched, it made her gag. She couldn't blame Max's lack of appetite when she hardly had one herself. She reached for the glass of water and as the rim pressed against her bottom lip, she took a child-size sip. The sensation of water made her throat swell and she forced it down.

There was a knock at the opened door and a young doctor dressed in a smart shirt, black tie and matching pants entered. He wore a smile too large for his teeth. "Good morning champ! How did we do? Have you given breakfast a go?"

"I'm not really hungry."

"That's okay Max, maybe later," he beamed. The doctor turned toward Halley. "Good morning, I haven't met you. I'm Niall, one of the doctors here for the morning."

"Halley, can I have a word with you please?"

The shoebox room was furnished with electric blue, red and green beanbags around the corners and a circle of metal chairs in the centre. Doctor Niall pressed his elbows atop his knees and watched Halley. He breathed heavily but maintained that professional smile. To the left was an oncologist and paediatrician, both of whom Halley had forgotten both names.

"Halley we have the test results back from yesterday." Doctor Niall paused. "The results of the CBC bloods found his white cell count to be at fifteen … The average is five. I'm sorry to tell you this but it looks like Max's Leukemia is back."

"Max is in remission."

"Was in remission. It doesn't look good but we caught it early. These kinds of diseases always have the potential to come back."

Halley tried to comprehend the news but it was too difficult to swallow. This couldn't be happening. "I don't understand."

Doctor Niall offered her a tissue box to which Halley accepted and dabbed the corner of her eyes. Doctor Niall gripped her forearm and she was surrounded by the lull of false hope. It almost felt as though he was the disease itself. Halley didn't care if she was angry at the wrong person, in that moment it was his fault. Bastard! Who was he to think a touch of her arm was enough to stop the cascade of tears or fingers that trembled? He couldn't stop Max's pain by that over-sized smile, could he? Even with whatever-years' experience in the field of haematology and cancer, he knew virtually nothing. All that knowledge and practice yet he probably hadn't saved more patients from his first day of med school. He would try his best but that wasn't good enough. Halley bit her tongue but another flood of tears poured down her face. If only she could take away Max's pain and carry the heavy load herself.

"I'll be in touch with Doctor Innley shortly. Is there anything I can do for you in the meantime?"

Halley shook her head. The professionals stood up and collected bundles of papers about to exit the room.

"Wait! I don't want my husband to find out. Please, I am Max's primary caregiver and that means I get to make that decision, right?"

"It's important his father finds out too."

"You asked me if there was anything you could do," Halley's lip trembled. "So do this for me then." The prospect of Oren succumbing to another alcoholic slumber was horrific. If she could hide reality from Oren, then she could prevent the depression and whiskey obsession. This wouldn't be like last time. Doctor Niall nodded. The meeting was adjourned and Halley was left with the offloaded mess from the doctors. She was all alone. Oren had no idea of the extent of the situation and neither did Max. Nobody would know about the Leukaemia except for Halley. She had to be strong for everyone.

XXVII

Rex is 9/18

Dawn brought with it a heavy breeze of emotions. The letter from the previous day was anything but forgotten and instead made things worse. Rex watched the clones from the corner of his eye, they awaited their freedom under his reign. Rex owed it to them but he had to be smart. The only way to survive the outside was to learn how to live in it. He needed insight into society and how it worked.

Rex stood face to face with Gabriel. Whose cold face conveyed nothing other than authority, he wanted to retreat. But stood his ground or what he wanted, or tried to.

The basement door knob twisted, then Halley and Oren emerged. Halley wore the same clothes as yesterday and her eyes were buggy as though she had cried. "What's going on?" She said nasally.

The stare-off continued until Gabriel broke away. He rubbed his freshly-shaven head but avoided eye contact. "The clones want freedom."

"No," Oren said.

"That's what I tried telling this idiotic bunch!"

Rex thrust an arm through the air. "Is it so hard to believe that we want equality too? That we are people. I want to know who I was before I died, before you fuckers brought me back to life. I want answers. We all do!"

"That's out of the bloody question so you can stop asking!"

Gabriel retorted.

"Then we will find a way if you don't help us."

"Didn't we just give you answers? We traced back your DNA and closed the big problem of not knowing where you came from. As if that's not enough."

"That's where you're wrong! Halley granted us that gift and I am eternally grateful but you on the other hand haven't done any favours."

Rex turned to Halley, his eyes pleaded with the smallest glimmer of hope. He knew it was a difficult battle but she was the last strand of redemption. Halley reached forward and stroked the fresh wound atop Rex's forehead. She traced her fingers down to the slice below his left-eye. Her touch was gentle, like a child, and Rex did not shy away.

"What's going on?"

"We had our chance at freedom the other night. We saw the storm when we broke out of the office. My siblings stayed because of me, I promised them freedom. If that was not the case, they would have not returned. They all stayed because of me and I know you will help us," Rex begged.

Gabriel shook his head. "So you speak to Halley but not me?"

"Back off," Rex hissed.

"Shut up!"

"Enough!" Halley shouted. "I've spent the entire night in the hospital without a wince of sleep. If the clones' seeing the outside is the only thing that keeps me going today then so be it! Let them have their way, Gabriel!"

Gabriel strode toward her. "Or what?"

Oren lunged forward and grabbed Gabriel's collar. "Watch how you speak to my wife. I won't hesitate to have a go at you."

Gabriel's face was still.

"Apologise."

Gabriel leant his head back and watched Halley from the corner of his eye. She stood her ground but his stare chilled her to the core.

Oren thrust a punch and Gabriel's nose snapped. He dropped to the floor. "Now that we have an apology, what were you saying honey?"

"If my son cannot enjoy a damned Friday morning like a normal child then these clones will! I won't hear another word and if they want to see the outside, they are going to see it." Halley turned to the clones. "Where do you want to go, all of you?"

"The beach," the clones said in unison. She nodded. "Chino, where do you want to go?"

He thought for a moment. "Somewhere safe."

"I promise you will be safe. I'll be there the entire time."

His face lit up. Halley turned back toward Gabriel, tears filled her eyes. "You heard them."

Gabriel made his way toward Halley and placed a hand on her shoulder. He sniffled and drew the blood back up his nose. "I'm truly sorry for your son. I had no idea but this isn't the way to go about it."

"I don't want your pity but they do." She pointed at the clones. Their faces shone with excitement like never before. At almost ten-years old, their life was still wrapped in cotton wool and shielded from life outside the lab.

"I'll grab my keys," Gabriel mumbled.

Rex tugged at the seatbelt that clasped around his thick neck and suffocated him. He tried to keep a straight face but he'd never seen anything like it. The outside was larger than he expected and there were people. So many people. "Apollo ...," Rex whispered. "How big do you think the outside it?"

"I think it goes on forever." His face was smooshed against the window until his eyes stung because to blink was to lose time.

Rex caught sight of Kiara in the backseat. Beams of sunlight caressed her hair as she glared out the window and her eyes darted from one sight to the next. Rex noticed her cheeks and forehead were now a red pigment from the sun's reflection. He should climb into the backseat and shadow her delicate skin from the outside but she enjoyed herself too much. Kiara caught sight of Rex and extended her hand so that it hung over the seat. He toyed with her fingers, they were still bruised and swollen from the leadership fight. She had scratches along her knuckles and her index finger was crooked. His heart sunk into his back, she should have never been forced to fight. She should have been excluded. Fucking Cyrus and his bright ideas.

Kiara rubbed Rex's bandaged hand with her thumb. She stared at the fresh blood that seeped through the dressing. All of a sudden, her face crumpled into a pitiful look. Rex pulled his hand away and blew her a kiss instead to which she blushed.

Beside her was Chino, who shut his eyes to keep the sunlight out. His mouth moved rhythmically, as if he was spoke to himself. Rex laughed on the inside, he'd be alright. Cyrus unlike the rest of the clones, focused himself on the road ahead. He watched the outside through the windshield of the van. His eyes daren't waver. "How are you holding up?" Rex asked.

To his surprise, Cyrus grinned. Enough said. He finally warmed up to Rex as leader.

The van pulled into a tar carpark and the team poured out. Rex moved in stride with the researchers and the clones walked at least a few feet behind him. They were too obedient. He glanced over his shoulder. "Walk in stride with me, everyone. This is you're doing too." The clones slowed their walk. "That's an order," Rex smiled.

Kiara bowed her head and stood beside Rex. He extended his hand, to which she accepted the offer. Her fingers slipped between his. "Come on."

The clones now walked in a straight line, with beaming open-mouthed smiles that grew with each step. They passed a red-and-white a sign that read, Sanista beach. Halley warned them to come bare-footed. She never explained why but said it was simply better that way. Rex felt the speckled gravel beneath his feet and a small pebble wedged itself into a cut. He grimaced but not for long, the outside took away all pain.

"We made it," Kiara whispered.

"We sure did."

Rex reached the end of the concrete footpath and inhaled and his nose filled with a saltiness, so bitter he scrunched his nose and sneezed. He watched where the sea met the shore and how a small crowd of people walked along it. A pair of children held onto tree branches that drew a line across the s and their parents held towels beneath their armpits. A dog chased a stick and an elderly couple sat on the sand entranced in conversation. Rex placed one foot forward and the grains of broken shells caved beneath his weight. Soon enough his foot was encapsulated by the warm sand. He winked at Apollo. "Race you!"

They ran for the ocean and their legs burned against the weight of the shore. Apollo tumbled head first, it slowed him down.

Rex burst with laughter. He tried to slow down but his feet slid across the s and he fell backwards and slammed against the shore. Ouch. How could the sand swallow his feet but also hurt if you fell on it? Not fair.

Rex was covered in a fine layer of sand, now stuck to his fingers. He tasted it. It was grainy and emitted a crunch.

The water seeped into his shorts and his hair stood on end from the cold. The clones surrounded Rex and dived into the ocean. Rex plunged beneath the water and he tried to breath but his lungs heaved against nothing. He pressed his feet against the floor and broke through the surface. This time, he breathed in a mouthful of air. He flicked his head sideways and beads of water shot against Cyrus' cheek. Rex cackled but was silenced when he saw a figure bolt towards him.

"Be careful! You can't swim!" Gabriel yelled.

Rex faced his siblings. "Hey, go under. Now." The clones submerged themselves beneath the water surface. Rex slipped his eyes open but they stung in agony. His ears were blocked with water and the odd sound of laugh emitted but it seemed seemed different. It was faded and muffled and came from all directions. Rex laughed inside his mouth but his lungs soon gasped for air and he broke through the surface.

"Look where we are," Cyrus said.

"I know," Rex replied.

"Freedom is that way," Cyrus titled his head toward the endless ocean. "Do you reckon we could swim all that way out?"

"I wonder how far it goes."

"Maybe forever."

"No. It must end somewhere. Everything has an end."

Kiara pulled up alongside her brothers. "If you boys paid attention to Oren's classes, water stops when something blocks it's path. You see that." She pointed to an island in the distance. "The water stops there but it would continue around whatever that is. So it does go on forever then." She turned to Cyrus and jumped onto him. The pair dropped into the ocean. Water splashed into Rex's face and a gluey film of prickled sand became entrapped beneath his eyelids. He cackled. Cyrus splashed water in Kiara's direction but she dodged the playful attack. Rex whipped around to see Chino stood by the waters edge. A pair of sunglasses protected his fragile eyes from the UV rays and he dipped his toe in the beach. Rex had an idea. He crept up and pretended to focus on. He inched his way back and then leapt from the water. Chino screamed as Rex threw him into the ocean. The clones cheered at the top of their lungs.

XXIX

Rex is 9/18

Rex dwelled on the beach trip and it consumed his every conversation. When he closed his eyes, he remembered the ocean and the bittersweet taste of sand. But the question still remained; did the beach end? It stretched for miles and even in movies, it seemed to continue far as the eye could see. That didn't give a definitive answer and Rex decided upon his own. The beach never ended.

Despite his triumph, Rex couldn't help but pity Halley. She didn't say much but the shadow of fear in her eyes screamed otherwise. Her son was in hospital and nothing else mattered. Not the beach, not the outside. Rex felt guilty for enjoying himself.

He fiddled with a cigarette, it was the last one. Since he saw the outside, the cigarette offered little entertainment and Rex offered it to Apollo. "You sure?"

"Yeah, it's yours."

Apollo exhaled a plume of smoke. "You keen for the trip today?"

"You bet."

The brothers sat in silence. Time moved but the promise of return to the beach was worth more than anything. Across the basement Kiara twisted her hair into a pony tail. It hung behind her ears and she examined her delicate face in the bathroom mirror. Rex watched her morning routine. She moved swiftly and it appeared a dance, one Rex memorised: first she attended her teeth, then moisturiser, hair and then she gazed at her reflection. She examined her face and reconciled with the stranger in the mirror. Although she never knew her real name or family, Kiara seemed satisfied with with more knowledge of where she came from.

Before long the researchers entered the basement and everyone clambered into Gabriel's van. The beach it was, again. The clones ran towards the ocean and dived in, with more confidence this time. The water engulfed their bodies and instinct told them when to resurface for air. It truly was freedom.

A few minutes from the shore of Sanista beach was a disheveled café. It was constructed of wooden planks with white paint that melted away. The barricaded round-tables were sheltered by umbrellas. The researchers and clones were sprawled across two four-seater tables amidst the sea of strange faces. Rex scooped another spoonful of mango ice-cream into his mouth. The cool sugar chilled his cheeks and began to melt.

"It's too damn cold." Apollo said whilst he placed the ice-cream on the corner of the table and allowed it to soak up the sun.

"What are you doing?" Chino wondered.

"Warming it up!"

Chino shrugged and plunged another spoonful of ice-cream into his mouth.

"Hurry it up everyone, we don't have much time left." Gabriel insisted as he held an empty cup that dripped with the residue of mint ice-cream. "It will be dusk soon and we need to get back home."

"Home?" Apollo asked. "I never heard you say that one before. This is new."

"Ugh!"

Apollo caught sight of Kiara. He leaned back into the chair and ran a hand through his hair.

"You look like a child when you make that pouty face, so please don't," Kiara said.

It was somewhat true, they were children. At only ten years old but eighteen-years corrected, the clones were at the tail-end of teenage-hood and the start of what it meant to be an adult. In Rex's eyes, they lost time as they aged so fast. The cafe was only half-filled with the faces of strangers, most of them were old and engaged in small talk. Rex stared at a wrinkled man, who relied on the aid of his walking stick. He'd never seen someone so old before, it was strange and he couldn't help but think in only a matter of years that would be him. The more he grew up, the more he doubled in age. There seemed a chance he would die before the researchers and a fragment of Rex's heart broke away. The excitement of freedom had its' consequences.

"Are you alright?" Kiara placed a hand his arm.

He cleared his throat. "Yeah, yeah."

Her eyes searched his face for answers. She knew him better than anyone but Rex gave nothing away. Instead, he leaned over and placed a kiss on her cheek. "Don't you worry about me, I'll be fine."

Kiara was about to speak when an ear-piercing cry sounded from somewhere near. It was a woman's voice. They peered around. Then Rex saw it. A woman watched them, with her face pressed against the glass doors. She pointed in their direction and spoke through the glass but it blocked her words. The woman ran outside, she shoved past customers and knocked over a chair or two. She wore waist-length auburn hair and an over-sized tank top. The small hand of a child no older than eleven held onto her. The boy had brown hair and a pair of glistening eyes appeared awfully familiar.

"Harry, it's me," the woman said through eyes filled with tears.

Halley whispered something in Oren's ear and the researchers engaged amongst themselves. Rex looked over the clones as if he was missed something but they appeared equally lost. He placed his ice-cream on the table and stared at the woman. It felt as though he should know her but didn't. The woman pointed and continued to cry.

"Apollo ... I think she is referring to you," Cyrus said.

"It's me, Casey!"

"I don't know you," Apollo replied. He straightened in the chair and stared at Casey. Their eyes met for some time. He was entranced by her presence but nothing else. He tried to remember, to think back but the answers didn't come. "Who are you?"

"What do you mean? Where have you been all these years?"

Apollo remained silent and looked over the cafe, as if the answers would be written on the walls or carved into the sand. Then his blank eyes returned to Casey and she understood he would gave nothing away.

"You better answer me right this because I am not walking away."

Rex's heart pounded. He stood upright, ready to lead his siblings into safety if it came to that.

"Who do you think I am?" Apollo asked.

"We met when we were children in middle school on the playground. Your mum didn't want you around me thinking you needed more male friends … You know this, come on."

Gabriel placed one hand on Casey's arm. "Who do you think he is?"

"I know who he is. Harry Westin. He died almost eleven years ago in a car crash. I never got to tell him this but a few days after he apparently died I found out I was pregnant. This is our son, he has your eyes."

The air stood still and Apollo's ice-cream splattered against the floor. Gasps from neighbouring tables spread like fire. This was too much to fathom. Apollo, subject E-250, was extracted from the DNA of a host who died approximately ten years ago. He was a boyfriend and father, he did have a family. The answers were about to unravel before him. "Help me. Please. Who am I?" He begged.

"We better get going." Oren stood up. He placed a hand on Rex's shoulder, who nodded at the clones and they huddled around the far side of the table. Casey watched the team back away from her like a virus.

"Why did you leave us if you're alive?" Casey begged. The boy hid behind her leg. He did have Apollo's eyes. The same deep brown warmth and a head of over-gelled hair.

"You're crazy. This guy, my friend right here his name is not Harry." Oren stared at Casey. "You have him mistaken for somebody else."

"Please!"

"Listen," Oren insisted. "I'm sorry for your loss but you are wrong. I can't help you."

The researchers ushered the clones away and they avoided eye contact with Casey, as she cried. Her small figure seemed as though it would collapse from the conversation she just witnessed. The clones followed the researchers and Rex was last to leave.

Casey reached forward and clawed at his forearm. "Help me, please."

Rex opened his mouth to speak but couldn't. He looked down at his feet, for the truth was too much to fathom. He wanted to help, he felt the raw pain and saw an ache burn inside Casey. Yet there was nothing he could say, it would only make matters worse.

"Rex!" Halley yelled.

"I'm sorry," he spun around.

"Don't walk away from me!" Casey slapped Rex's cheek and his face burned. Her eyes darted in all directions, she tried to make the connection.

"Talk to me," she demanded.

Apollo now stood by her side. 'I got this Rex, it's alright." Casey seemed to calm down at the sight of him. All the customers at the cafe watched the scene. Nobody moved and their meals grew cold. A man who wore a white apron appeared, he held a tea towel in hand. He jogged towards the scene. "Hey! What's going on over there!"

Rex spun around but tripped and fell onto a round table. His hands dropped into the plates of food. He jumped over the table and people threw their fists in the air and barked words of fury as their meals smashed to the floor. Rex leapt over the fence and bolted towards van, it was only a few metres away. "Come on!" Halley urged.

"Wait, where's Apollo?"

"Right here, go!"

Rex pushed Apollo inside and then himself. Casey wasn't far behind. As she reached for the door handle, the van sped off into the distance. That was a close one.

XXX

2010

A week passed since the incident at the beach and the upcoming spring was replaced by a storm. Halley gasped against the howl of the wind whilst she tackled the umbrella closed. After some time, she slammed the door shut against the breeze that tried to pry it open. Her face was mottled with contortion and her thick hair was plastered across her cheeks. She looked as though she had been lost at sea for days.

"GABRIEL!" she exclaimed and fumbled with the buttons on the coat.

Gabriel popped his head around the corner, attracted to the commotion. His face was scribbled with confusion as Halley straightened the coat over her shoulders.

"What's going on?" He asked.

"Oren called me, did you know about this?"

"About what?"

"The cop car in the parking lot. Oren saw it on his way in. I don't know what the hell is going on but I don't think they will take their time!"

Gabriel spat a mouthful of coffee all over Halley's coat. He dropped the mug to the floor and it shattered into a hundred pieces. The coffee seeped into the soles of their shoes and the mess grew larger than what they started with. "I just put that on!" She tore off the coat, almost ripping the buttons out.

"Are you sure?"

"Here!" Halley threw him a clean coat and he caught it by reflex.

Gabriel glanced at his watch. "Fuck, this can't be happening! Hal, we can't afford mistakes like this!"

"I didn't do anything."

"Where is Oren?"

The door swung open. Oren was followed by two figures dressed in navy suits. "I'm right here." His face was stricken with fear.

Halley's lab coat was drenched. Gabriel stared at the police wide-eyed with his own coat half-done up and chest exposed, practically shirtless.

"You need a hand or something?" The female officer blushed.

"Oh – ," Gabriel stumbled. "Excuse me, I'm Gabriel Vogelsov and this my colleague Halley Makillen."

"Ruby, police officer." She held up her badge. She had a brunette pixie cut, a thick layer of gluey mascara and a fitted uniform without a single crease. She attempted a half-smile. Next to her stood a tall and slender man with a bowl haircut. "I'm Marlin Sinclair." He extended his hand to Halley and then Gabriel who shook it in turns." We've come here following on from a report."

"Ah – huh?" Gabriel folded his arms to stop them from shaking. "A report… What report was that?"

"A woman informed us there was a clone, well, that's what he called himself. Said he lived in the laboratory, the one over the hill and as far I am concerned this is only lab for miles. So, mind if we have a look around?"

"That's strange. Who was this woman?" Oren asked.

"Casey Milford made the report."

"Well, I'm shocked. I've never heard of a clone before." Oren pressed a finger to his lips. "I'll show you around."

Marlin and Ruby took turns to ask questions and ticked off a mental checklist of the lab, they started with L2. Ruby reached inside her black tote bag and revealed a clipboard and pen for notes. She spun around and faced the researchers. "What kind of research do you do, exactly?"

"We are currently working on an anti-viral," Halley said.

"Shall we check out downstairs first?" Marlin agreed.

"NO!" Gabriel exclaimed. He realised his rude demeanour. "I mean no, you must see the laboratory first!" he laughed nervously. "I'll meet you up there."

"Gabriel, you're coming with us," Oren prompted.

"I'll meet you in the basement when you are finished," Gabriel said through gritted teeth.

The basement door flew open and Gabriel burst inside. He pressed his back against the door and held it closed. For the first time He appeared genuinely scared and it was a nice change to say the least.

"What's all this commotion about?" Cyrus asked.

"Shh! There isn't much time. Now all of you listen up."

"Again Gabriel? Don't you ever relax?"

Cyrus sat on the edge of the bed, he unravelled the bandage from his leg that covered the wounds from the leadership fight.

"The police are here and I don't know who or how but one of you gave us away! They're upstairs and we don't have much time!"

"Well I got an idea," Apollo winked.

"What's that top shot?"

Apollo's face dropped. He was caught off guard and didn't expect an actual answer, for Gabriel would normally shun him down. He scratched the top of his head in thought and stared at the ground.

"This is what we're going to do," Rex began. "We exit through the office window but we need to find a way to get there without being seen."

"The stairwell," Gabriel said.

Rex was first to make his way through the concrete stairwell. Although dim and he couldn't see a metre ahead, He sprinted up the stairs. He held onto the railing for guidance. The clones followed, with Gabriel at the end. Rex reached the final step and pressed through the fire exit door. They were on the top level and across the corridor was the office. He took a step forward but heard nearby voices. He slipped back behind the fire-door and slammed it shut. The voices grew distant. Rex tried again. He pried the door open and this time the coast was clear. He gestured for the clones to cross the corridor. Gabriel peered over the staircase but couldn't see any sign of the police officers. Rex wanted to retaliate. If they caught sight of Gabriel who snuck around, it would only make them more suspicious. Rex decided against it. He knew Gabriel would erupt into an argument and attract more attention. Cyrus held the door open.

Cyrus slammed the door and the shutters banged against the glass window. Shit. Gabriel gripped Cyrus' jumper and hauled him upwards until they were nose to nose. "Could you be any louder!"

"I'll try harder next time," Cyrus gasped for air.

Idiots, as if they would fight at a time like this. Rex pressed his ear against the door and listened. Footsteps, multiple. He squinted, as he tried to listen harder and then he heard voices. This was not good. He tried to determine whether they were coming or going but over the whispers, he couldn't make it out.

"I hear them," Rex whispered. "Stop fighting!"

Gabriel silenced and he too heard the voices, they were now closer than before.

"The window!" Kiara whispered.

"No I just fixed that!" Gabriel winged.

'Now's not the time," Rex said.

Gabriel and Rex fumbled with the screws that held the window in place. They twisted them clockwise and the screw turned slightly but beneath the rusted base got stuck.

"I got it, this one is almost out," Gabriel whispered.

"Mine's stuck!" Rex muttered. He pulled harder and the edge of the screw dug into the underside of his finger and a dot of blood emerged. He jolted back in pain but the window remained shut. The door handle jiggled. There was no time left, this was it. They would all go under.

Rex turned toward Kiara. He didn't know what to say or where the police would take them but it all would end there. The basement would be no more and he would, more than likely be separated from her. His face grew numb and all motivation drained through his feet.

"I got it," Gabriel dropped the screw to the ground. Within moments they all hung outside the window with their toes pressed against the gutter. Their faces were a red hot mess and everyone held their breath. Rex's heart beat inside his head and his jugular vein bulged from his neck. He switched his attention to the outside. Beyond the white picket fence of the lab. There were rows of houses and to the Clyde Arc bridge where a string of cars travelled. He wondered where they would travel to and if he could do the same. Rex was thrust from his thoughts when officer Marlin stuck his head out along the balcony.

"I thought I heard something," he mumbled. He grabbed hold of the window frame which creaked. "Alright, let's keep moving."

Rex gulped and his fingers trembled but he dare not make a sound. His heart throbbed within his chest and he eyed his siblings, they got the message.

After the officers left the building, a whir of questions erupted into the air. Gabriel stared at the clones within the office but they gave nothing away. Gabriel paced back and forth, frustration radiated from his eyes. The clones faced the floor. Then Rex turned to Cyrus. "Nice move there. You couldn't leave before so you tried again."

Cyrus folded his arms. "It wasn't me, I would have been more discrete."

"You tried to leave before so why not try again?"

"Because I got what I wanted. I got freedom and I got answers to who I am. I am satisfied, for now."

"Apollo," Rex mumbled. He turned around but he walked towards the door. He strode with confidence and a sense of dissociation. Gabriel extended his hand. "Not so fast."

Apollo raised his fist and punched Gabriel in the face. He dropped to the floor, clutched his nose and cried in pain. Apollo bolted out of the office and towards the main door. Rex glanced at the others who were equally as shocked.

"C'mon!" Rex yelled.

The clones ran after Apollo. They ran at incredible speed and shoved each other aside. Cyrus and Rex ran in sync, their legs kicked high.

The clones charged forward at tremendous speed, they ran side by side as if they pushed each other along. It was too late, Apollo swung the lab door open and sprinted outside. The door wavered against the wind of the storm.

"Gabriel!" Halley dropped to her knees and fussed over his nose that bled profusely. Gabriel pat her shoulder and clambered to his feet, as the blood from his nose dropped to the floor. They ran and gathered tufts of the lab coat. But Oren was faster and cut in-front. He pounced through the air as did Gabriel who splattered trails of dotted blood along the floor.

Outside the storm grew louder and the wind pushed the researchers sideways. Halley stood in the parking lot as everyone ran around. The sand turned into thick mud and the wooden fence barricade began to sink around the lab. Oren darted forward and she instinctively followed. They dodged around the back of the lab and there was Apollo, who ran with everything he head inside of him.

"Stop!" Oren charged towards him but Halley couldn't keep up and ran ten feet behind. The wind picked up and slammed bullets of rain against Halley's raw face. She felt her cheeks redden. A foggy haze circled her and she could hardly see.

Apollo reached the padlocked gate which he shook violently. It remained shut. In a fit of anxiety, Apollo's slippery fingers tugged at the lock but the metal chain remained threaded through the gate. He cussed beneath his breath. Apollo pressed his body against the gate but it wasn't enough to push it open.

Oren reached him first. He grabbed either side of the white shirt and slammed Apollo against the gate. "Let me go!"

"Not until you tell me what the hell is going on!"

Apollo leaned forward and head-butted Oren.

Smack! Oren flew off-guard. Apollo's fingers fumbled along the gate but as he felt the metal latch, Cyrus was by his side. They tackled to the ground and their bodies slammed into the mud. Apollo bent his knees to his chest and kicked Cyrus off.

Oren recollected himself and knelt atop Apollo's abdomen. He squinted through the thick mud but each time he blinked it away, the heavy rain seeped more dirt into his eyes.

"Talk right fuckin' now!"

"I don't have time!" Apollo's words morphed together, perhaps from fear or the numbness of the cold.

Oren grabbed Apollo's collar and pulled him forward until they were almost eye to eye. "What the hell have you done!"

Apollo spat in Oren's face. A weak move but it was enough. He clambered to his feet and ran sideways along the parked car but this time Halley lunged forward and thrust his head against the glass window. Did I really do that? Halley's confidence built and she reached for Apollo's shirt but he blocked her.

Oren got back on his feet and Halley moved out of the way as he slammed Apollo's body against the car door. This time he was prepared for any immediate moves. He punched him in the face and again. A trail of blood oozed from Apollo's right nostril and he scrunched his face into an ugly victim of pain. Oren pressed his forearm against Apollo's neck and securely held him in place. "What have you done?" Oren spat through gritted teeth.

"Don't you see? Casey told me more than any of you bloody would have! I died in the year 2004, I had a girlfriend and now a son. You hid my life from me and I never got the chance to live again. I'm not going to die in this hell-hole!"

Oren paused. "What did you do?" He flicked his head sideways and pellets of rain flew off his face.

"Casey knows I'm here, she knows," he bounced with a nervous laugh. "Casey and the police know I am being held captive here. You thought I didn't know where the lab was, there doesn't seem to be another lab over the hill of the River Clyde, is there? I'm going back to my old life and she is waiting for me, so let me go."

"What have you done?"

XXXI

2010

Halley was drenched in mud and rain when she entered her home that night. The moisture seeped into the couch and a mud puddle formed into the cream carpet around her boots. None of that mattered anymore. She left Gabriel to deal with the clones, she couldn't look at them after Apollo's betrayal. After all those years they fought for freedom, the answers to their ancestry and even trips to the outside, wasn't enough. Apollo took matters into his own hands and for that, Halley couldn't forgive him. No matter her efforts, they fell short of what the clones desired and in return, they gave her no appreciation or despair.

She picked at the Waitrose pre-packaged lasagna and dissected it layer by layer. The meal unfolded and soon turned into a mushed mess of cheese and mince. It appalled Halley and even the hot steam was too much to handle. She pushed the plate aside and glanced at the clock across the kitchen, it was almost 7pm. Max would catch up on his Ben-10 DVD at the hospital and probably have tucked into dessert already. A tear trailed down Halley's chin. She was broken. Torn between the clones and Max, she couldn't be at two places at once.
There seemed no point to tell Oren the truth about Max's Leukaemia. Since the drinking habit and depression that happened last time, it made more sense to not tell him. Not yet. There were other problems at hand. Halley's head hurt, it was all

too much to bare.

Everyone took the news of Leukemia differently. Oren shut off from the world and found happiness in an empty whiskey bottle. It was as if he existed as a mute and a cripple, for he hardly left the bedroom. His entire life focused on a cure. He tried to play God where he shouldn't and tried to cheat life. Halley understood it all, she really did but the ordeal consumed him into a dark and endless hole. She guessed it would be the same this time, or worse. Not this time would be different, Max was older and more capable. His body could withstand the disease. She thought about the phone call from Dr Niall earlier that evening. He wanted to discuss chemotherapy. A tear trickled down Halley's chin, it was too soon. She trashed the half-eaten meal and made her way into the living room. She leant her head against the doorway, as she watched Oren clutch a bottle of Hennessy whiskey. He stood in a pile of shattered glass. He took a step forward and crunched over the fragile shards, reached inside the cabinet and produced another glass. Then poured himself a shot of spirits. Oren swung back the whiskey.

"One shot for the curse upon our firstborn." He poured himself another glass and downed it. "Two shots for the experiment that never should have been and … Three shots for being cursed again." He turned to Halley. "Did we do something? Was it our fault for wanting a child? Well down the drain it all goes because now the authorities have caught wind and they will be closing in on us faster than you can say run."

"Oren. Put the whiskey down and let's talk."

"Talk about what, huh?" He splayed his arms open and faced

her.

"Please, I don't want it to be like last time."

Oren gulped down another shot of whiskey and barely flinched as the spirits scorched his throat. His fingers trembled as he scratched nervously.

"How could you let Gabriel keep those embryos. All those years ago."

Oren stared into the pit of the shot glass. He shook his head and furrowed his brow. "We have been through this before, I told you. I didn't know about the clones and when I did it was all too late." He clenched his jaw. "As long as I have you by my side, everything will be okay."

"Oren." Halley held his cheeks in her hands and looked him in the eye. "I can't handle it if you keep drinking."

"This is how I choose to cope." He paced back and forth across the short breadth of the room. He hunched forward and was in a non-verbal conversation with the cream carpet. Halley watched hopelessly. She pressed her head against the wall for leverage. It seemed overnight everything turned upside down and there was no way out.

"Is there any update for Max?" Oren asked.

"No, not yet."

"How much longer can it be? It's already been a week, the blood results should have been back." Oren turned to Halley and stood still. An insatiable hunger for answers cast over his face. "You know this time will be different, right? He's going to be okay this time. It won't be like the last." He cleared his throat. "Max isn't ill, he's coming home soon." He poured a last shot of spirits and tossed the glass over his shoulder. Halley released a breath she didn't know she held. Her lie worked, at least for now. She knew she couldn't hide the truth from Oren and not for long.

Oren ventured upstairs. Halley knew where he was headed and followed. She pressed her ear against the door to hear Oren's slurred words that were laced with beautiful intoxication. "Max, my son. Don't you worry about a thing, everything would be fine. I'll be here the whole time. I promise, you will get through this and live the longest life you can. Just you wait and see. Just wait."

Halley listened to the broken promise between Oren and the empty room. She made her way back to the bedroom and lay onto of the sheets, still dressed in a lab coat and mud boots.

Nausea awoke Halley before sunrise and she quietly emptied her guts into the toilet bowl. She forced herself to get ready and hardly spoke to Oren. They pulled into the parking lot of the lab and chills ran up Halley's arm. She glared at the lab, it was less than ten-meters away. It was home to yet another abundance of problems but Halley's ears were blocked. There was only so much she could fathom at once. Her fingers trembled and beads of sweat rolled down her forehead that stung her eyes with each blink. She slipped into another white coat and ventured into the office of L2. She shuddered beneath the air-vent that thrust fifty-degree Fahrenheit ice air in her direction. To no surprise, Oren's face was hidden behind the computer screen. A trail of cigarette smoke rose from the corner of his mouth and the room stunk of tobacco. Halley sat in the chair opposite the desk and pressed her elbows against the wooden table. Beside the computer was a bundle of scattered articles, paper clips and highlighters. The topmost printed document read *Leukemia: Signs and Symptoms in children.* Oren finally turned toward Halley and plucked the cigarette from his mouth. He tapped the end and a trickle of ash dropped onto the table. His eyes were numb and he appeared to have not showered in days. They sat there, lost in the captivity of each other's helpless face.

"So where do we start?" Halley's voice was faint.

"I think the question is, is this the start of the end? Or is it the start of the start?" Oren took another puff of the cigarette. "We need to know how sick Max really is."

Halley reached inside the pocket of her coat and extracted the plastic case, her fingers struggled to produce a singular pick from the small hole and when she did it snapped in half. It would have to do.

"Hal?"

She placed the broken pick between her teeth and toyed with it for some time. "You already know the answer."

"No, I don't."

"The Leukaemia is back."

"How long have you known?"

"Not long."

"There has to be another way that we can save him. I'm not going to sit back and leave the fate of our son in the hands of strangers. I won't do it, not again," Oren said. A familiar lump formed within Halley's throat, it seemed to expand by the second. She knew what Oren hinted at but it still caught her off guard. She fought off the offensive jabs. She wanted to yell at the top of her lungs that she was sorry she missed Max's fever and lethargy. Halley wanted to scream about the sickness that barricaded her in the bathroom that morning. If only Oren too could feel the pain from within her abdomen, that sliced her open from the inside out. He saw none of the mind-controlled pain that was an obligatory right for to wake each morning. How could he? Once again, Halley remained silent.

"I'm saying that maybe we are looking in all the wrong places. We could collect some blood samples ourselves and run a few experiments. We are scientists for crying out loud. If anyone can save our son it would be us," Oren's voice broke off.

"We should be home right now with our son. All you care about is finding the perfect doctor, the perfect team to keep our child in this little bubble and keep him safe!"

Oren bit his lower lip. "Do you think I want to be here right now? I would love to be with Max but what I want more than that is to come home to him every single night for the rest of my life and not have to wonder when will be his last. Tell me you don't think the same? He's only a child, a child dealt a tough card!" Oren said.

"I don't know what else to do! The best place for Max is hospital. What are you suggesting?"

Halley reached for the Leukaemia article from the desk and pretended to read it."Throw me some suggestions." She pinched the space between her eyes. She watched Oren from across the table but he remained speechless. There was no alternative. "Right." Halley left the office and headed toward the staircase. Then she heard a pair of faint voices but there was nobody around. She waited, with her back pressed the stairwell. Then the fire door swung open and she saw a shadow on the floor.

"See I told you there was nobody there," said Cyrus.

"This is what we're going to do." It almost sounded as if Cyrus spoke to himself but after sometime Halley figured it must have been Rex since the voice came from another direction.

"We leave in five more sleeps," Rex whispered.

"Wasnt it four? Anyway we need to keep the researchers distracted for the meantime. They can't suspect anything. We play it off that we are still mad at Apollo and nobody talk to him during the day."

"Right, what about the exit point?" Cyrus asked or maybe it was Rex.

"The window of the office, we've done it once before and we can do it again."

"We best get going, the researchers could walk in any minute."

"They don't visit before midday."

A hand clasped over Halley's shoulder and she spun around. It was Oren. "Honey what are you doing?"

"The clones were in here. I - I just heard them."

He glared at Halley with the confused stare of a parent whose child spoke of an imaginary friend. "Are you sure?"

"I heard them."

"What did they say?"

"That they were planning an escape through the office window in a few days."

"Where are they now then?"

Halley and Oren headed down the staircase. They swung the

door open to see Apollo coiled into a foetal position. His bruises appeared worse today, an abstract display of blue and purple marks across his weak body. On the other side of the room, Cyrus and Rex lay in bed, hands behind their head and eyes glued to the television. A David Attenborough documentary blared atop the milk crate. Kiara sat upright from the bed and rubbed her eyes beneath the messy splay of mattered hair. She squinted at Halley. "Everything alright?"

"Yeah."

Oren shut the door and glared at Halley with bewildered eyes as if she had seen a ghost. There was no explanation to how the clones reached the basement at such a fast speed but they did. "Let's go honey. Max will be waiting."

Behind the driver seat, Halley exhaled plumed of thick hot air between the sweat of her lips. Strands of hair clung around her neck and the unwelcome sun brought with it much frustration which was enhanced by the buzz of a fly. It whispered words of annoyance and she almost wanted to punch the wheel. She felt Oren watch her from the passenger seat, an attempt to spark conversation but one that was ignored. Halley focused on the road. Her thoughts raced faster than she could process. The toothpick danced around her lips at incredible speed. Oren figured she must have swallowed the wooden splinters, there's no way she hadn't totally destroyed the toothpick.

"Red light!" he yelled.

Halley slammed the car brakes. Both their bodies hurled forward.

"Let me drive."

"No. We are almost home."

"I know but we need to get there in one piece."

Halley sighed. "I know what I heard. We have to get to the bottom of this."

"We will. We need to tell Gabriel."

Halley clenched her jaw and a crunch sounded. The toothpick broke in half and she spat it out the window. Her head felt heavy, she knew Oren was right about Max but if she let those kind of thoughts into her mind they would both drown into an empty pit of darkness. Halley reached for the passenger seat and squeezed Oren's hand.

"Oren, the police are on our trail and we don't even know the extent of their knowledge. We have no idea how much Apollo said. We need to go to the cops ourselves."

"And tell them what?"

"I don't know but there has to be a way to fix this."

"Listen, our signatures are on those contracts, the ones the embryonic donors signed. We agreed to have full control over the clones and under our guise they have been kept alive. We promised the embryonic donors we would take good care of the experiment and that's what we will do."

"I'm loosing hope in us."

"Well I'm not. There will be a way to fix this but for now we need to talk to Gabriel. The three of us are in this together, okay? Honey, I know you're scared but now is not the time to lose it."

"Why are you defending him?" Halley asked.

"Because we're here now and he's our only ally! We have to

work together, getting angry with him will be no good to us. I won't let anything happen to you or Max and you know that don't you? I would turn myself in if that meant saving you both!"

"Okay, I'm sorry."

They pulled into the carpark of the Royal Aberdeen Hospital and reached level three. Oren knocked on the door of room ten. "Is there room for two more?"

Halley pulled the chair closer to the bed. She stroked Max's cheek. It was the first time in years she'd seen Max like this. There was a cannula in the crevice of his arm and a monitoring machine beside the bed. Since Halley nursed the clones as babies, she knew what the numbers meant. Everything was stable, his blood pressure was on the lower side but given Max's scrawny physique it was okay.

"Mum, will I go home soon? I don't want to be here much longer."

"Very soon, the doctors said you're doing so well."

Oren lowered the side rail of the bed and climbed in with Max. He sat beside his feet and high-fived him for the upmost bravery. Max looked like him, with a chiseled jawline, beady eyes and red hair. All Halley hoped for was that Max didn't inherit her poor eyesight.

An ache welled from within her abdomen. She had become the perfect liar nowadays. First she hid the illness from Oren, to concealing evidence from the police. Now to hiding the monsters beneath the bed from Max too. He wasn't well and chemotherapy would start in only a number of days but Halley didn't know how to tell Max the truth.

"Mum, are you okay?" Max reached forward, his cold fingers weaselled their way inside her hand. "So much better your here. How about I stop past the library and buy another book or comic?"

"Oh can you see if they have Marvel or Ben-10?"

"Or both?"

"Yes please!" Max almost leaped out of the bed.

Halley entered the WH-Smith on Forrest-hill road. The stationary shop was small and the walls stuffed with a messy display of stationary, books, cosmetics and along the back wall was a rack of magazines. Her eyes scoured the top shelf but it was mainly adult content, cars, farming, gardening and news. She crouched down and plucked a comic from the shelf and stuffed it under her arm. In the near distance the bell rung, another customer had entered the store. Halley found a magazine with cartooned aliens and picked it up.

A pair of young men dressed in a navy blue uniforms appeared. They wore identical vests and holsters around their waist. Police. Halley gulped and placed the magazine back on the shelf. Was that suspicious? Her mind was consumed by the clones and the conversation earlier. What if they had already escaped? What if the police had followed her all the way to the hospital and now WH-Smith? They were onto her and watched every move. The police probably analysed her face and checked if she matched the description given by the clones. Halley looked at the nearest officer, who met her eyes. Brown eyes. The police now knew she had brown eyes. That was another important detail they could jot down. Halley hid her eyes by the magazine. This was insane. If the police were after her they would come past the house or the hospital. She couldn't be weary of every single officer down the street. Halley checked the magazine cover again and noticed Max already had it at home. She placed it back on the shelf and realised next to her hand was another Ben-10 magazine. Along the letterhead it read, '2 giveaways inside!' Halley stuffed that magazine under her arm and headed toward the counter. She could feel the gaze of the police officers as she walked past. She slapped the magazines on the counter and paid with trembling fingers that trembled. The officer stood behind Halley as she made her way toward the glass doors.

"Excuse me, ma'am!" One of the officers called but Halley quickened her pace until their voices grew too faint to comprehend.

"You forgot your change! Ma'am!"

Halley now stood at the grand entrance of the Royal Aberdeen hospital and opened her hand. She was short three pound. She laughed at herself. This was insane.

XXXII

Rex is 9/18

There was a fine layer of square-shaped dust where the milk-crate that held the tv used to be. The basement was, for the first time, divided in two. To the right, was the bed and to the left was Apollo. He was shrouded by the halo of his own misery. In the span of twenty-four hours he had already lost weight and his limbs were speckled with scratches and bruises. A reminder the clones were apprehensive at the loss of their TV. Gabriel removed their only source of entertainment almost immediately after the argument. He said all of them were in quick-s and the floor was caved in until Apollo throws out a life-line. In simpler words, Gabriel was certain they would return sooner than anticipated. All Apollo admitted to was that Casey knew of his whereabouts but his silentness spoke of something else.

There Apollo was, to the corner in the left of the basement with a plate of cold dinner, slice of buttered bread, defrosted vegetables and half-cooked pasta. Rex slid down the wall beside him. Apollo shivered in his presence and kept his eyes on the floor.

"It's okay brother. It's only me," Rex said.

Apollo remained silent. He smelt of wet dog and his top was still damp. Rex opened his mouth but realised he had nothing to say and swallowed the absent words. He understood why Apollo did what he did and for that, Rex couldn't hold a grudge. He could still envision Apollo's son, those innocent brown eyes of the little boy and his pale skin. He looked exactly like Apollo.

"I'm dead Rex," Apollo finally said.

"What are you talking about?"

"I died over nine years ago. I have a son and a girlfriend. She waited for me. I had a life and it was not this."

"That means we all did."

"We clones but clones of the dead. We lived before. Does that not bother you?"

"Sometimes."

"Do you not want to go back outside?"

"Sometimes. I want to see the outside but we need to go about it with a plan. If someone recognises us again we could hand ourselves over to the police. Like Gabriel said, we could be experimented on, stuck in another basement or charged for being clones. Who knows what would happen. Anyway, I have a plan." That was a lie and Rex hoped Apollo wouldn't further question his idea.

"I have a plan too."

"Yeah brother and what's that?" Apollo grabbed the stale bread from the dinner plate and ripped it down the middle, he passed half to Rex. The butter tasted of an oily film atop a hardened biscuit but it would do.

"I'm leaving. I'm going to be with Casey," Apollo said through a full mouth.

"I think the researchers heard us talking about it, the other day in the stairwell. We might need rethink it."

Apollo faced Rex and ripped off another mouthful of bread. He chewed on the thought for some time. He stare at his leader who had no answers but a pitiful heart. Apollo opened is mouth still full of food. "I think we still stand a chance. Casey is coming and so are the police. We can all be free together."

"The police are coming again?"

"Yeah. They are going to take this place down. We are going to live again ... well for the first time."

"I'm not so sure I trust the police." Rex toyed with a pea and tossed it into his mouth.

"Don't be worried. They will help us."

"I hope you're right."

"Trust me, I know what I'm doing. In seven more sleeps I will be free."

A tear trickled down Rex's cheek, freedom was closer than it had ever been. The first place he would go is the beach. His heart pounded at the back of his throat, this was an opportunity not to be missed.

"I'll tell the others," Rex whispered.

"What do you think it will be like?"

"Like the beach. I could stay there and never leave."

"I want to go somewhere I haven't been. I want to meet people and explore cities, all of them. I would like to be a father but I don't know how. Is that a bad thing?"

"Of course not, you will learn."

"What if my son asks me where I came from, where I was all of this time?"

"You will be okay, brother, you will be okay. Also, thank's for losing the tv."

Apollo cackled. It was his fault after all but he took the jab lightly. The clones demolished the rest of the dinner in a cloud of small talk. There was no answers to their questions for neither of them had any idea what the outside really was. All they knew was that they were headed home.

XXXIII

2010

Halley washed her hands in the bathroom basin and cleaned her mouth from the morning sickness. The front door bell sounded. Damn it. She made do with a couple of Panadol and prepared three cups of tea. Gabriel arrived earlier than expected and they sat around the living room couch with the packet of biscuits in the middle of table. She nibbled along the edges of one, she had to eat something.

Gabriel reached for the cup. "I know you both didn't call me over here for no reason, so I'm listening."

"We have a problem," Oren said somewhat sarcastic, he attempted to cover up the size of the matter. "We may have nothing at all. Halley heard the clones talking yesterday."

Halley nodded. "I heard them from the fire exit."

She gnawed along the edge of the biscuit and crumbles trickled into her mouth. She pretended to chew longer than needed to avoid the topic at hand. "They are planning an escape. They mentioned something about seven sleeps until 'she' will come with the police."

"Whose she?"

"I don't know."

"How is this going down?"

"I don't know."

"Is there anything you do know?"

"I already told you!"

Gabriel raised his hands in defeat, lost for words. Then he surprised them both yet again. "I knew this day would come but not so soon. Bringing the clones into the world was never going to be an easy task. There is only one way out."

"Well, I suggested ending the experiment nine years ago but you two didn't listen to me," Halley retaliated.

"How many times do I have to tell you goldfish? Death isn't the answer! We know that. The police are already on our tail and things are going to start moving a little faster than I anticipated." Halley focused on a small scratch etched into the coffee table. The sunlight glinted off the two-centimetre long imperfection.

"Halley? Did you hear a word I said?" Gabriel asked.

"I must have missed the bit where you said you could fix this mess and make things go back to normal but please continue," she snarled. She pressed the mug against her lips and took a sip. The now cold tea filled Halley's mouth with something other than truthful words. Gabriel didn't seem to catch onto the dry humour or at least didn't care, after all things worked in his favour and everyone else around him were puppets in a play that never ended.

"Hurry along Gabriel, what's this plan of yours?" Oren interjected.

"As I was saying, you can consider yourselves lucky because I have already planned our next move. We are going to take the clones and relocate. Completely evacuate the lab and destroy any evidence of the experiment."

"Just like that," Oren snapped his fingers."We're going to disappear."

"Got another idea wise guy?"

"Do we start packing Max's bags?" Halley asked as she rubbed her bloodshot eyes.

"I don't think he should come with us," Gabriel said.

"That won't be up to you."

"As you please but I don't recommend it."

"Alright, let's get the ball rolling. What are our options?" Oren asked.

"We leave the country. Given the circumstances we have no other choice."

Halley opened her mouth to speak but Oren beat her to it and this time he didn't hold back. "Did you not hear me when I said that if the police truly have an idea of what's going on at that lab we are all in deep shit. Do you know the consequences for cloning a human? Five-years jail and another half-a-million dollar fine? If we leave the country it will only attract more attention. Think of all the airports, cops, security officers we will pass. We're all going down big time!"

"The authorities are the only ones who can help us now," Halley pleaded.

"There is no way around this. What are you going to do? Go to the police? Hand yourselves in? You'll be doing me a favour and giving me a head start on leaving that damned lab. They will have you both in custody and you'll be clueless on my whereabouts," Gabriel yelled.

"It's not fair. We can't just uproot our whole lives'! Leaving the country is extreme, we can find another hiding place for them. For us!" Halley yelled.

"You only have yourselves to blame Makillen, we all do. I am taking the clones, all five of them, they are coming with me. You have the option to join me or stay behind but you know the consequences. I needn't explain them," Gabriel said. He paused and allowed them to process the information. He watched from the opposite side of the table as Oren whispered into Halley's ear. She fought back tears from behind her eyes. "What would happen for Max?"

She wouldn't be there to tuck him into bed or kiss his bucked-tooth smile goodnight. She was the only one that knew he liked his morning banana cut diagonally, milk before the cereal, a cold hot-chocolate which was far different from an iced-chocolate. Only Halley knew that. "I think you're absolutely mad," Halley grit her teeth.

"A million pound fine between the three of us and five-years jail time," Oren nodded his head robotically.

"On second thought, you both can relocate wherever you want and I'll go with the subjects. At least that way if anything else goes wrong I'll be liable, you can never turn your back on the dead," Gabriel said staring at Oren.

"What is that supposed to mean?" Halley gasped.

"It means whatever you want it to mean!"

"Gabriel, you lying bastard! I'm not letting you relocate with the clones, they are our research too. Who bloody knows what you'll do next and again our names are against that experiment which you've tampered with so damn much!"

"Then come with me," Gabriel grinned.

They were stuck and there was no way out. If they stayed

behind, imprisonment was a much larger price to pay and one that would permanently keep Max away. Oren stood up and disappeared from the room then he reappeared with three glasses and a bottle of Hennessy whiskey. He poured himself the largest portion, almost a half glass. Oren swung back the bittersweet whiskey, cocked his head to the side and took another sip. He smacked his lips together in thought.

"Oren I need you to focus." Gabriel clicked his fingers. "I can't have you drinking right now. I need an answer from you, are you in or not?" Gabriel clicked his fingers before Oren's face now.

"You will get a bloody answer and probably the one you want if I drink enough of this shit." Oren sighed and flopped his hands over his knees. He faced the floor. He peered back up at Gabriel. "Where are you thinking of going?"

"We are going somewhere far away. Somewhere where it's cold, colder than any other continent, colder than any of you Scots have been. Some place safe. Antarctica."

Halley leant forward and spat the a mouthful of tea over Gabriel's face. Served him right.

"Antarctica! Who in their right mind would go there!" She yelled.

Oren wiped beads of sweat from his forehead beneath his beanie. "No, no, no."

"There is no other way. If you both stay here the police will come for you."

"Then let them come!" Halley yelled.

"I know it's a hard pill to swallow but this is the only way out," Gabriel said. It almost sounded as if he had a hint of sympathy in his voice. Gabriel continued, "if the police are truly closing in less than a week, then we better move fast. We leave in three days."

Oren raised his eyebrows and replenished his whiskey glass. "I'll definitely be needing more of this then." He swirled the glass in his hand watched as the caramel liquor danced clockwise. "Alright Gabriel, you want to go to Antarctica? Let's do it then."

"Really?"

"Yeah, lets' go to Antarctica with no fucking citizenship, permit or anything and set up another laboratory in three days! Let's fly or set sail or however the fuck you get onto the other side of the world with illegal clones tagging behind us and politely ask that nobody check their non-existent passports. If you get all that shit sorted out, then I'll go with you," Oren said and stood up.

"Leave it to me."

He squeezed Gabriel's shoulder and whispered into his ear. "One more thing, my wife is walking out of this unharmed. Do anything else beneath my nose and I'll snap your neck. You hear me?"

Gabriel nodded frantically and Oren raised his fist high in the air. He punched Gabriel between the eyes and a curdling crack sounded. Gabriel clutched his face and through bloody teeth he splattered. "Alright I deserved that. We even?"

"Somewhat."

After Gabriel left the house, Halley locked herself in the bathroom and hauled her stomach contents into the toilet again. She dragged her fingers through her hair fought back tears. She slapped the cardboard box against the sink and extracted a pregnancy test. Halley stared at it. One line appeared. She breathed a sigh of relief. She wasn't pregnant, that was one less worry in the endless string of chaos. She glimpsed at herself in the mirror, her hair was a tangled and she had black shadows beneath her eyes. It even hurt to smile. Halley ventured into the kitchen where Oren welcomed her with a kiss and mug of tea. "Oren, how did this happen?"

"Listen to me, I know things look bad right now but we have each other and we have Max. All three of us are going to get through this. Do you trust me?"

"I do trust you and no matter what whatever happens, I love you but I have something I need to ask. I can't help but wonder, did you have something to do with this?"

"No, no! Honey, of course not. How could I have known?" Oren clenched his jaw.

"I'm so scared of what's to come and I don't want to be alone through this."

"You won't be, I'm right here."

Halley felt guilty to question Oren's honesty. "Antarctica," her voice broke off. "How can Gabriel think that's a good idea. He played us. He's a two-faced lying prick and this is his fault."

Oren lowered his head and a tear ran down his cheek. "There is no way out. I hate to say this but I think that moving to Antarctica will be the best move."

"What?"

"We are facing five years imprisonment and a million pound fine. I don't think we have a choice."

"What about Max? I'm not leaving him behind."

"He can't come with us!"

"How dare you say that!"

"The best place for Max is the hospital. He hasn't finished his round of chemotherapy. He doesn't have the energy to travel to the other side of the world. Besides that, he can never know about the clones. He would never think of us the same. He might even let our secret out and then things would move even faster."

"I won't leave my son behind!"

"Then I'll go with Gabriel."

Halley thought for a moment. She could stay with Max and lie to him, yet again. Tell him that Oren went on a business trip and he wouldn't be there during the chemotherapy. Then that phased Oren out of the picture. "I won't leave you alone with Gabriel, I don't trust him." Halley stared into Oren's eyes. "If Max stays behind, he would be safe. He would finish his treatment and the hospital is the best place for him. Or is leaving him behind a big mistake? What if – "

"What? He dies? He dies in the next few weeks or months while we are gone to Antarctica? That's not going to happen, I tell you that right now. If you even think that for a minute then you're as stupid as Gabriel!"

"Oren," Halley gasped. "How can you say that? He's just a boy! He doesn't deserve any of this and I won't let him blame himself!"

"Then go and explain it to him. Do you think that this is what I want? I don't but there is no way I am taking our sick son to fucking Antarctica with Gabriel."

"Then we move somewhere else and leave Gabriel go by himself."

Oren pulled away and walked over to the glass doors that led to the backyard. He placed his hands on his hips and watched the world. "We can't do that."

"Why not?"

"Halley, we can't afford to have Gabriel run off with the product of our research. That would give him total control, he would be walking around with our signatures on those contracts and not to mention ground breaking research. I think the police would already have our names on paper. You have to come to terms sooner than later because we are leaving faster than anticipated. Are you listening to me?"

"Yeah Oren, I am." She raised her cup into the air and doused him with chilled tea. "That's what I think of this whole situation."

Halley clambered up the stairs and she felt Oren glare at her. There was nothing more to say, Max couldn't come and that tore Halley in two. She slipped into the bathroom and pressed her back against the door. Three days was all she had left. It felt like a death sentence. Max wouldn't cope without her by his side for chemo. Her stomach curdled and she raised a hand to her mouth. She felt bile at the back of her throat. She placed one hand on the basin and felt the pregnancy test press against the palm of her hand. Halley gasped. There it was, two lines. Two pink lines. Halley was pregnant.

XXXIV

Rex is 9/18

The library was cluttered with the three researchers and five clones. Halley folded her arms, she could not help but feel her privacy was interrogated. Nobody ever used the library, it was her safe place and now even that was at stake. She glanced at the bookshelf across the library. She could still see it, the red slither of the New Gulliver was wedged where it always was. She gulped, it was merely meters away. It made her sick.

The clones were a formation, an army that spoke in unison. Something was different about them but Halley couldn't figure it out. It seemed as though the clones were only permitted to speak when Rex did and move with him. Halley was too fatigued to question it but she noticed their bravery. Even Chino faced the researchers and it made her proud.

Gabriel arranged a series of pencils, rulers, books and an A3 page on the table. He was the only one that still dressed in the uniform coat and pretended to follow the guise of an innocent scientist but they all knew he was anything but that. He placed a cigarette in the corner of his mouth.

"Since when do you smoke?" Oren gestured his head toward Gabriel who blew a plume of smoke in his direction. Halley frowned. Gabriel always had a secret stash but never use them. It seemed the cigarettes existed as a fashion statement.

"Throw us one," Rex called.

Gabriel shrugged his shoulders and decided it would be good

entertainment to watch the clone choke on his own breath. He leaned across the table. "If you can have one puff without gagging, I'll owe you an entire pack."

Rex plucked a cigarette from the packet, extracted a lighter from his pocket and lit the end. He poised his elbow against the table and extended his hand, to which Gabriel accepted. "Deal."

Rex leaned back in his seat and beneath the black beanie, inhaled the tobacco. He blew out a series of circles, one enveloped the other. He winked, particularly pleased by his win.

"Since when do you smoke?" Gabriel asked confused.

"Who cares? You have our attention, so let's get started?" Halley exhaled.

Gabriel stared at Rex, who gave nothing away. He returned his attention back to the meeting. "Things are about to change here." Gabriel sneered in Apollo's direction. "We heard you all talking in the stairwell. I know you are all planning on leaving and not to mention the police."

The clones peered at each other but remained silent. Ah, shit. There goes that plan. Rex held the cigarette to his lips but paused. He toyed with that thought. He wasn't discrete enough. Damn it. He would find another way.

"Five more sleeps, does that ring a bell?"

The clones turned to Apollo and whispered harsh words into his ear. Apollo shrunk into the office chair. He deserved it in a way.

Gabriel clapped his hands, regaining their attention. "As I was saying, you've all done this to yourselves. So, the time has come that we must relocate."

Rex folded his arms and tilted his head to the side so to whisper

in Kiara's ear. "Great, finally moving to the first floor."
She chuckled.
"You're not that lucky. We are moving far away, to a place you probably haven't heard of before. It's over 21 hours from here, more than 10,400 miles. The southernmost continent on the planet. We are moving to Antarctica."
The clones stared at Gabriel confused, the word did not mean much but the large numbers did.
"It's cold and hardly any life can survive but we will be ready for it. Antarctica is the only place for us to go. It's the furthest from civilisation we will ever get. The entire continent is unregulated by the restrictions of government, laws, infrastructure, people ... The police."
"Get to the point," Halley interrupted.
"There are currently no laws against cloning, probably because it's not been successful in the past. If we go, there will be no base to prosecute us upon. Not to mention the cold is a major benefit to us. Things like petrol freezes the Antarctic winter breeze, so the population basically halves. It means we can move quicker."
"How do you know all this?" Oren asked.
"Some years ago I used to work at a research facility called ORG twenty-six at Shackleton Ice Shelf. It's around four-hundred miles East of the Antarctic Peninsula. It's been empty for years. We will be safe there." He inhaled a breath of tobacco whilst the others attempted to inhale the information. "We leave in three days, that will give us enough time to get everything together and Halley ... If you must return home to your son, I

suggest you stay behind."

Oren outstretched a hand Halley slipped her fingers inside and his sweaty palm. She thought for a moment. Max couldn't leave chemotherapy, it was his only chance at life. If she stayed behind, what would happen to Oren and the clones? She looked up at Gabriel. Max was safe and the clones might not be. They needed her and so did Oren. "I'm coming," she gulped.

"Very well." Gabriel leant over the A3 page and drew a circle and at the top wrote *Antarctica*. He tapped the page with the blunt end of the pen. He then sketched a smaller circle in the northern hemisphere and scribbled *Scotland*.

"As I've said, Antarctica is over ten-thousand miles from us and getting there will be no easy task, but I can pull a few strings. It can only be done in two trips. First we catch a plane and then we sail. We fly to Ushuaia, Argentina in the Tierra del Fuego archipelago. That's eight-thousand miles."

Gabriel drew a dotted line across the page and scribbled another circle, titled *Argentina*.

"If we leave at eight-in-the-evening we can account for the time zone difference. We can't fly, since the clones aren't registered citizens, so we'll use my friend's private jet. The flight will be over twenty-seven hours so that cuts our time short by an entire day. I've got the flight organised and already sent him a small deposit. Two-thousand pounds and I shall pay the remaining six before the flight."

"Eight-thousand pounds!" Oren exclaimed.

"Don't worry about that for now, I have it covered. According to my calculations we arrive in Ushuaia before midnight and catch a boat that will take us South. We will sail through the Mar de Hoces, also known as the Drake Passage. It's the only connecting ocean from Cape Horn of South America and it reaches South-East of the Atlantic Ocean. From Ushuaia to Antarctica the journey is three-thousand miles. That trip will take four days and I expect we will arrive in Antarctica at approximately five in the evening."

Gabriel continued the dotted line from Marc de Horces to Antarctica and drew a small arrow at the end. He peered around the table at their blank faces. "I probably should mention that the Drake passage is where three ocean currents meet. The Atlantic, Pacific and the Southern Sea. Without any land-masses separating them, it's a raging mess when these currents mix. It is highly dangerous but so long as the weather permits we shouldn't manage anything more than a spilled glass of chardonnay."

Halley clutched her belly. There was an extra passenger on board this voyage and she was responsible for its' safety a. Halley tightened her fingers around Oren's. Now was not the time to tell him about the baby, it would have to wait. Gabriel turned back to the sheet of paper and drew an Asterix along the top of the large Antarctic circle. "This is the Antarctic Peninsula and from there we shall make our own way down to the Shackleton Ice Shelf."

He continued a dotted line and another small circle along the edge of the Antarctic circle, toward the Eastern hemisphere. "We have a huge advantage at the moment. It's July and although it is summer here, the Antarctic is the opposite. With the winds reaching minus fifty-degrees Fahrenheit, I expect the population to drop from three-hundred to almost one-hundred-sixty people. No-one wants to be in Antarctica at such a time." He puffed the cigarette and enjoyed the sweet-bitter taste. Halley stared at the abstract X's and circles which would soon be reality. The plan to venture into Antarctica was in motion and there was no going back now. She turned to the clones. Rex blew a mouthful of tobacco smoke to the ceiling. He titled his head back and basked at the prospect of freedom. His wavy hair reached past his shoulders and he surrendered to the moment. Then he drew his head center again and glanced a Halley. A wide smile grew across his face.

Everyone disintegrated from the library, the clones took to the basement and the researchers went home. Max was discharged from hospital and relished in his own home. Halley stood in the kitchen and diced the last few strawberries. The red liquid drained between her fingers and she was entranced in her own mind. There was no easy way to break the news to Max, so instead Halley granted his every wish and broke her own rules that night. She allowed him to stay up late and watch The Gremlins. She plated another lot of pancakes and decorated them with ice-cream, a thick layer of strawberries and chocolate chips. She balanced the three plates and made her way to the living room.

"Why am I allowed to stay up late and watch horror movies?" Max asked, as he took the plate with both hands.

"Do you not want to then?" Halley replied.

Max caught on and quickly diced the pancake into small cubes before greedily shovelled the creamy desert into his mouth. A trail of melted ice-cream dribbled down his chin whilst he looked up at the television, he didn't want to miss a single minute of The Gremlins. He was wise beyond his years and inquisitive, perhaps too much sometimes. "Does it taste good?" Halley asked.

Max tried to speak but through a full mouth his words became muffled in translation and instead gave a thumbs up. Halley reached over and ruffled his hair. She paused and drew her hand close to her face. Strands of the autumn ginger hair lay in her palm. The chemotherapy had worked its' job and there was a bald patch behind Max's head. Halley toyed with the pancake and the boiling rage, from having missed his first chemo session was hot enough to melt the ice-cream. Max's fell from his receding hairline but he was too entranced by the green goblins to notice. Oren clasped a hand over Max's shoulders. "You look like you're old man you know that?"

"I do?"

"You're smarter than me though. Listen, there's something your mother and I wanted to tell you." He cleared his throat and looked over at Halley. "We have to ... We have to go on a work trip and will be gone for a couple of weeks."

"What?"

"I promise we will be back."

"I'm coming too, right?"

Oren shook his head. "No, not this time. I'll explain it all when you're older."

"No! That's not fair. You always do that! You always leave for work, what about what I want?"

"I know, I know," Halley pulled Max towards into her lap and rocked them their bodies in symphony. "It's going to be okay," she whispered.

Max's eyes were glazed with a film of tears. He planted his face into Halley's jumper. "I need you to be strong. Tomorrow morning we will drop you off at gran's."

"I don't want you to go."

Halley nuzzled her lips next to his head. She brushed aside his hair and whispered into his ear. "I'm coming back for you, you hear me? I'm coming back."

They all sunk into the couch, encapsulated in each others' embrace. Halley looked over at Oren and despite his warm gaze, there was a fear that grew from within. Oren was scared and for some reason, it reassured Halley. She wasn't the only one that wondered what the trip would entail or feared the Antarctic. She liked nothing about the cold or the unknown. Halley would never desire to venture into such a place. Without a word, she felt the same reaction from Oren. They were in this together. Her hand crept along her belly and shielded the foetus from the stressors of the outside world. For the first time they were a family of four.

The following morning came around quickly and it was time for goodbye. Halley held Max's hand as the crossed the farmyard. The trees bowed before dawn and the only sound was their boots over the dirt road. She crouched beside Max. "You know I love you right?" She bit her tongue and her eyes clouded with tears. She bit down harder.

A halo of sunrise glistened around Max's face that was almost pale as the clouds in the sky behind the freckles that dotted his nose. Halley pushed his fringe aside and saw a new balding patch along his hairline. She didn't want to remember Max this way and instead focused on his strength. Halley lifted Max's chin by the tip of her finger. He held his head high and a pair of golden eagles flew above. That's the image Halley would remember.

"I'm coming back for you, I promise. I don't want you to worry about anything, okay?"

Max kicked the dirt. Then he switched his gaze to the red sedan parked along the metal gate. Oren sat in the driver seat, peering out the window and bitting his knuckles. He pulled the grey beanie down and shrunk into the seat until he was just a beanie above the steering wheel. "Did you say goodbye to your father?"

"Yeah, he came into my room this morning."

Oren couldn't bare the thought of goodbyes. It bothered Halley but there was nothing she could do. She took Max's word and was somewhat content to know the conversation was exchanged. Max bent his foot and used the toe of his boot to upturn a rock on the ground. He kicked at it and a bundle of dirt stuck to the grass. Halley took a deep breath and continued. "You're going to be fine and gran will be with you the whole time you have chemotherapy, she isn't going to leave your side. Not once."

She reached forward and wiped away a tear from Max's cheek. "By the time I come home, you will be all finished with the treatments."

"You promise?" Max finally uplifted the rock and kicked it

aside.

"I promise."

"Mum, what's wrong with me?"

"Nothing is wrong with you." Halley thought for the right words before she would continue. "The cells in your blood are malfunctioning. The same happened when you were a baby and you got through it. You are going to do even better this time."

"What's malfunctioning?"

"It means when something doesn't work quite right." Halley bit her tongue again. She faced the cottage, a stream of warm light seeped from behind the thick curtained windows and the scent of baked cinnamon buns wafted through the air. The warmth petrified Halley and she wanted to run across the farmyard, through the paddocked gate and into the empty distance with Max. Somewhere nobody could find them and where he would be safe. Halley snapped back into reality.

Her mouth filled with the metallic taste of blood. She'd forgotten to release her teeth around from her tongue. She pressed the doorbell and felt hundreds of swords pierce her abdomen. The front door swung open and in its frame was her mother who bore a gracious smile. Her white bobbed hair was in disarray and strands of hair stood on end. She reached forward but Halley's fingers stiffened.

"Hello Max," she whispered.

Halley clenched her jaw.

"Don't look so glum, Hal. You're only going for a short while."

"Yeah. I should be back in a week or two." She wasn't sure if she was fooling her mother, herself or anyone for that matter.

There was no telling how long the trip would be.

"America, right?"

Halley nodded. She pressed her lips against Max's tender ear. "I - I," she sobbed.

"Halley, you're going to upset him. Come inside Max."

The pair disappeared and Halley was alone. Her legs gave out and she dropped to the floor. She wailed silently. She was too damned caught up in her own emotions to make Max a promise. Like an idiot, she could hardly speak. Halley swore to herself she would come back for him. Although Max didn't hear it, the promise was still there. It would have to be enough.

XXXV

2010

Halley trailed her fingers along the white walls for the last time. She never envisioned she would leave the lab, let alone flee from fear of prosecution. It was home and was now that would disappear, all too soon. She felt Gabriel's eyes upon her and refocused her attention to the task at hand. He pointed to a large suitcase. "I've packed that one with snow gear. It's got everything, shoes, goggles, gloves, walkie talkies, spare rope." He heaved a black bag onto the table. "This one is for the paperwork, we need to bring the contracts of the cloning experiment with us."

"Shouldn't we destroy them?" Halley asked.

"No. The safest place is with us."

Halley fumbled her way through the drawer of paper documents and finally extracted the contracts and somewhere in the pile was Diane Thomson's. The Butterly earrings crossed Halley's mind. Their elegance and grace matched Diane Thomson's. She only wanted to help science, she never would have wanted any part of this. A weight lifted from Halley's shoulders. Once they hid the clones in Shackleton Ice Shelf and returned when everything blew over, it would all be normal again. Diane Thomson would be free of this experiment, not that she knew about it but Halley did. The only way she could reverse the damage was to set things right. "It's time to destroy this lab. Are you ready for that?"

Gabriel pressed his buttocks against the edge of the table beside Halley and they stood there in silence. "No but if it means concealing evidence from the cops then, yes. I'll do what I have to. I think the others have already begun."

He glanced around the lab and locked his eyes on the bench along the far wall. The microscope was covered in a plastic case and pressed into a corner. A layer of dust coated the metal bench where the clones first came to life. In those five petri-dishes they grew. So much had happened in the lab.

"It's still not too late for you to change your mind," Gabriel said. "You don't have to come with us."

"Im coming."

He nodded his head and placed a cigarette in the corner of his mouth. "Did you keep the story straight? I need to hear you say it," he said through a cloud of smoke.

"I said we're going to America. The hardest part was telling Max."

There was no point to tell Gabriel how hard it all was. It's not like he would understand. He knew nothing about love. Gabriel looked out for himself and everybody else was his paparazzi. "Anyway, I better go." Halley stepped forward when Gabriel grabbed her wrist. He stood up, extended his arms and engulfed Halley in an awkward hug. He patted her back out of rhythm. Halley was tense and not sure how to react. This had never happened before. She forced her head against his chest and beneath the crease-less lab coat and she heard the paced beat of his heart. It melted Halley, she loosened her arms and reciprocated the hug. She dug her fingers into his back. "I need to tell you something."

Gabriel leaned back and beneath a furrowed brow. He looked deep into her eyes. "What is it?"

His cold exterior returned but along the skirts of his eyes was serious concern. He really did care. It probably wasn't all the time but he did feel emotion. A tear trickled down Halley's cheek. She wanted to tell Gabriel the truth. She wanted to scream at the top of her lungs that she was pregnant. Maybe He would travel carefully if he knew. The baby needed protection on the trip and she couldn't do it alone. She opened her mouth to speak but was choked by the words. "It's nothing. Excuse me."

Halley made her way down the corridor of L2E, all the while she clutched at the innocent life from within her abdomen. Now was the time, she had to tell Oren before they left. She couldn't venture into Antarctica and be the only one responsible for the baby. She walked across the corridor and as she neared the office, vibrations danced through the floor. Her ears filled with the blared words of Jon Bon Jovi's *It's my life*. The music played until the words morphed together and sounded static. Halley rubbed her belly, it was too much noise for the baby. Inside the office, Oren was shirtless with a leather jacket draped over his shoulders and his pale pecks protruded from beneath. His hands danced above his head, as he held a whiskey bottle. Oren turned on the spot, he beat his head in tune to the music. His hair was, for first the first time in years, gel free and tossed with each movement. He guzzled down the liquor and twisted on the spot until he kicked over the plant. He danced as if no-one was watched. His arms beat with the music and he moved towards the bookshelf. His mouth moved but the words were drowned out by Bon Jovi. He spun around and smashed the rear-end of the bottle against the shelf. Glass rained over him and the textbooks slammed against the floor but his dance remained calm. Halley sighed, clearly now was not the time to tell him he would be a father again.

She headed toward the staircase, held onto the rail for support and placed her feet in-between the chemical spills and unravelled bandages. She reached L1 and took one step forward when Kiara slammed against the wall. Rex held her in place by the neck of her jumper. They watched each other, nose to nose and lost in the depth of each others' eyes. Then Kiara swung her leg outward and knocked Rex behind his knees. The pair tumbled to the ground and Kiara eloquently poised herself atop him. "I win, again."

"Only because I let you," Rex taunted.

Halley stepped aside and emerged onto L1N. She slipped into the library and shut the door. Beneath the hexagonal window was Chino. His face was covered by an open book but his snow white hair protruded over the top. Halley squinted at the crimson book covert wasn't *The New Gulliver.* She breathed a sigh of relief. "I need to be alone, Chino."

"It's too loud and bright out there." Chino curled his toes inwards. She strode forward and crouched down. "What are you reading?"

Chino checked the front cover. "Battle Royale." He searched

Halleys face and began to laugh. They both knew that was a fib, Chino never read anything besides fantasy or comics. The book was a cover and he blew it. Halley stroked his arm. "It's going to be alright."

Chino glanced around the library. His eyes shot upright but was blinded by the light that he blinked away. He glanced at the endless string of books. "How many books are in here?"

"Around five hundred." Halley sat beside Chino.

He almost drooled at the thought. "Have you read them all?"

"No. There's only one book in here that I like."

Chino scoured the titles along the side of the books. He was entranced by the endless adventures that surrounded him. Then Halley realised. Chino didn't really want to see the outside, he wanted to explore it in a different light.

"How about you choose a book to bring with you," Halley offered.

Chino's eyes widened. "You'll let me do that?"

"Yeah if it makes you feel better." She extended her hand. "But on one condition, you need to leave the library now."

Chino thought for a moment before he sealed the deal with a handshake. He past the row of books along the back wall and touched each one by his index finger. Halley watched him. She had a soft spot for Chino, he was so gentle natured and offered more than this world deserved. He extracted a book and although the title was hidden by his hand, the front cover was white and displayed a vibrant picture of a man who rode a horse. She nodded. "You better go."

Chino dodged out the door.

Halley was alone with nothing but the endless stream of stories. She ventured over to her usual spot, two-hundred-sixty-five books to the right and a hundred-eighty books to the left, as she had done so many times before. Only this time was different for it would be the last. She stroked the crimson cover of *The New Gulliver.*

A tears ran down Halley's cheeks and soaked the paperback book. She opened the red cover and ran over the letters, where their crumpled edges drank up her salty tears. A part of Halley died with the letters that day. She made all of those letters for Max and now it seemed he would never read them. If the lab would be destroyed, then so would the letters. She was leaving Max behind to endure chemo. This was the only way she could punish herself. She pushed the *New Gulliver* off the edge of the table and the letters flew to the floor, they tore in half. Halley stood up and the words of Bon Jovi rang louder this time. Her head bobbed in tune and her breath moved in sync with the music. This was it. The lab would be no more. A surge of rage filled her core and she plunged forward. She ripped the books from the shelves and the stories inside were sprawled across the floor that was now a mess of colourful images. Halley twisted her feet awkwardly and somewhat danced to the corner of the back wall. She paused before she extracted a book and tossed it over her shoulder. This time she tipped the books off the shelf by her finger. Tears ran down her cheeks and she exhaled a gust of fear. Life would not be the same, not for a while, and there would be no letters to write. The books piled up, they engulfed each other. Then the door swung open. Apollo stood in the frame and smoothly danced into the library. His bare feet stepped on the books and made his way over to the *New Gulliver.* Halley's heart chipped away, she still wanted to protect the letters and the book that housed them. The paper wrinkled beneath Apollo's foot. He peered down and noticed he was stood in a bundle of envelopes. He reached down.

"No, leave it," Halley said.

Apollo spun around and danced towards her. He extended a hand, to which Halley accepted and twirled her around on the spot. Apollo bounced to the rhythm but his gel spiked hair didn't move.

"May I do the honours?" He asked and without a response, pushed the bookshelf down. The wooden case clattered over the floor and the hundreds of stories rained across the library. He seemed proud of himself and Halley headed for the door. The library was forever gone.

The lights in the lab were smashed out and in the shadows, the truth of the clones remained hidden. The clones were loaded into Gabriel's van whilst Halley and Oren detoured home.

They collected the last pieces of clothing for the trip. Halley slipped into a white puffer jacket and black jeans with boots. She pulled the furred hood over her head and walked out of the bedroom.

"Honey," Oren called. She ignored him and ventured into Max's room. She looked over the navy blue carpet that matched the thick curtains and the Ben-10 quilt. A series of posters were plastered against the wall atop Max's bed. He was a collector. Halley eyes were pink and swollen, she had no tears left to cry but the heartache seemed to never end. It was time. "Come on, they're waiting." Oren clasped a hand around Halley's shoulder and they ventured downstairs. She stood on the front porch and although she was dressed in three layers of clothing, she felt utterly naked. As if the outside world could see the mistake she made, to have kept the clones alive. As if they knew what happened. She glared at the van, with Gabriel in the driver seat and all five clones piled in the back.

"We need to go," Oren said and kissed her cheek. The private jet was due to depart in two hours. Halley slipped her sweaty hand into Oren's and they walked forward. She inhaled the last few breaths of free Scottish air. The air in Argentina would be different. It wouldn't be home.

"Are you ready?" Gabriel asked a hint of enthusiasm in his voice.

"Not quite," Halley said above the lump in her throat.

"There may be the smallest part of me that wants to see Antarctica again," Gabriel said. "We are headed to Edinburgh, so get comfortable. It will be a bit of a drive."

Halley snuck one hand beneath her jumper and her cold fingertips traced her belly and encircled the foetus within. She would protect the baby at all costs, if it was the last thing she would do. Her head rocked with each bump in the road, it made her dizzy. The car ride was mostly silent apart from small talk and the clones whispered among themselves. Halley caught wind of a few words and enough to know that Casey and the police were due to show up that night. They left just in time. Once the police raided the lab it would be empty, filled with nothing other than the messy splay of chemicals, books and smashed glass. Everything of importance was within the van. The clones, the contracts, the researchers and Halley's unborn child. Everyone was there apart from Max. It was too late for regrets now, the plan was in motion.

Halley reclined her seat and pulled the hood over her eyes. She longed for sleep, to forget the world even for a short while.

In the backseat, Rex passed a cigarette to each of the clones. Their enthusiasm enveloped the van as they fought over the lighter. Rex was shoved in every direction as hands reached over his biceps to extract the lighter from his grasp.

"Easy, easy, ladies first," Rex held two cigarette that were poised between his teeth. He winked at Kiara and suddenly spun around.

"Cyrus, you're first," he taunted. Kiara covered her mouth to giggle the faintest laugh of pure triumph that seeped through Rex's ears. Cyrus bit down against the cigarette which bent in half. He muttered beneath his breath. He leant forward and allowed Rex to light the end. The van was soon filled the claustrophobic smoke of tobacco and it hazed the air, which made it incredibly to see past the dash. "Roll down your windows, that's enough partying back there," he called.

Rex now held a cigarette in each hand. "Don't be sour you lost the deal, Gabriel. There's always next time." He drew a puff from the cigarette in his right hand before he continued. "I mean, you might win some back," he laughed and then inhaled the cigarette from his left hand.

"I hate to break it to you but there is no tobacco sold in

Antarctica. I have a stash but only enough for one person. I guess this will be your last cigarette for a long time."

Kiara blew a circle of smoke. Rex smirked, she learnt fast. He exhaled a larger circle that encased hers' and the pair chuckled at their victory. Gabriel watched the clones from the rearview mirror and fine lines appeared on either side of his eyes.

"Don't worry, I'll teach you some moves," Rex winked and placed both cigarettes into his mouth. Gabriel rolled his eyes and inserted a CD into the slot and surely enough, Russian music echoed through the van. It would be a long drive. Even so, Halley drifted into sleep.

A sudden jolt forced Halley awake. The van rounded a corner and sped through a pair of rusted gates. Through the darkness Halley couldn't see past the headlights but the sheep whined and the clamber of hooves suggested they were in farmland. The van tilted sideways. The front wheel dipped into a pothole and then flipped back into place. Halley glanced over her shoulder at the clones, they all held onto the seat in-front or beside them and the residue trail of cigarette smoke wafted through the air. Chino clutched the novel from the library, a small piece of the lab came with them and Halley grinned. She pressed her head against Oren's shoulder, to which he rubbed her cheek by his scarred thumb. The imperfect indentations reminded Halley of home and the bucktooth smile from Max that would await her return. Eventually they reached an old barn, where the timber frame was lop-sided and the hinges were loose. Gabriel parked the van inside the barn and glanced over at the researchers. His face was unreadable, pale and stiff. He seemed focused and probably calculated the amount of time until the plane left. "We're here."

"Where exactly is here?" Oren asked.

"This is my friends' farm, we can leave the van here and use his jet." Gabriel grinned and swung open the door.

Oren turned to Halley. "Are you okay?"

"Just a little dizzy," she forced a smile. Oren tried to kiss her although his barely moved. Instead, he brushed his chapped lips against hers. A heavy wave cast over Halley and she allowed her head to press against Oren's. The warmth of his pale skin was a soothing embrace and although on borrowed time, they enjoyed the moment.

"Let's go!" Gabriel called.

"I'll be alright," Halley nodded as she peeled away.

Oren jumped down and opened the door for Halley. He slipped one hand beneath her armpit. She stood up straight but her vision was fuzzy.

"I am okay, let's do this."

The warehouse was constructed of timber and the interior roof overflowed with hay. A range of barrels and threaded bags lined the walls which surrounded a mini jet. The barn smelt smelt of steel and manure. The clones emerged into the foreign barn and stood side-by-side. Rex stuffed the used cigarettes into his jumper pocket, perhaps he could relight them in Antarctica unless Gabriel was the sharing the kind, which he wasn't. Rex slipped his hand around Kiara's waist and she leant into his embrace. He had to be strong for her, regardless of what was to come. He puckered his lips and placed a feeble kiss against her head when the sweet smell of Victoria's Secret perfume sweetly encompassed his body. Rex checked over the clones but someone was be missing. "Where's Cyrus?"

"I - I don't know," Kiara stuttered.

"Wait here, I'll be right back."

Rex crouched down and snuck out the front entrance of the barn. He emerged into the night, where the endless hills and wind whispered words of freedom. His mouth slipped open and he almost appeared to drool at the sight. Rex looked into the distance and listened to the heavy breaths beside him. "What are you doing?" Rex asked.

"Brother. You see it, you smell it. Look all around you. Let's go and be free, we can end this nightmare for once and for all," Cyrus said.

"Let's play out that scenario. We run off into the distance with no food. After a couple of days the chances are that we will die of starvation and dehydration. As far as I can see, there's no civilisation for miles, so what good would freedom be?"

"Maybe so but I'm not going to stand aside and believe everything the researchers tell say. I think they are full of shit."

"Brother, we are about to embark on the greatest journey of all. We are travelling to Antarctica and not many people can say they have been there. We got our freedom. If we stick with the researchers, they will show us a new life and we will never have to worry about being caught by the police or experimented on by other scientists. You and I, my twin, will live like we should have. They are the only ones who can help us now."

"I don't trust them," Cyrus said.

"Well I do. If anything, do this for Halley. She fought for our freedom and now we have to fight for her. If she hides, then so do we. We must keep her safe."

Cyrus pulled the hood over his head as his brunette hair blew in the gust of wind. A piece of hair clung to his lower lip and quivered against the breeze. He turned towards Rex. There was a mutual understanding as Cyrus scoured his face. "Do this for Halley," Rex said. "We owe her for all she has done."

"Deal." Cyrus pushed past Rex and knocked his shoulder. When the clones re-entered the warehouse there was an unfamiliar man engaged in a conversation with Gabriel. He slapped a thick bundle of cash into his hand. The man stood aside and presented the short staircase to the jet. The paint peeled off from the wings and the underside was spotted with grey tarnish. They climbed inside, the last of whom was the bald-headed man, that Rex presumed was the captain. The interior of the jet was small, two-seats separated by a narrow walkway, circular windows and a cubicle toilet at the back. Rex sat beside Kiara. He tucked her side-fringe behind her ear and admired the doll-like face. Rex peered around and realised that along the tail-end of the plan Chino was curled up over two seats.

"Psst! I think little brother may need me," Rex gestured down the walkway.

Kiara leant across the chair and watched Chino hug his knees and clutch the seatbelt until his knuckles almost popped out of his hand. "Go," she whispered. The moment Rex left Kiara's side, she dug her nails into her own seatbelt and panted.

Rex slipped into the window seat beside Chino. "You sure you don't want to check out the view?"

Chino shook his head. His fringe flopped from side to side and for the first time Rex noticed it reached halfway down his nose. "Listen, there's no shame in being scared."

"Alright!" The captain called in a Russian accent. "Everyone keep your seatbelts on, we are about to depart." He turned his head enough for Halley to notice, that he was blind in one eye. "Stay seated, we are about to take off." He sat in his allocated seat and the jet's engine roared to life, it head out of the warehouse and along the gravel road. The engine blared louder and the jet sped forward. Suddenly, it shot straight up into the air and Rex's stomach smacked into his lower back and his head was forced against the pillow by the pull of gravity. He swore could feel his brain hit the other side of his skull. He dug his nails into the armrest, and tried to find stability. Chino cowered further into his own seat and shrunk into his jumper. He grabbed the drawstrings and tightened the hood.

After what seemed like hours, the jet travelled across the sky. Rex curiously peered out the window and watched the city lights shrink into fireflies and the warehouse faded into a disintegrated square complex. The plane shifted and Rex's stomach dropped forward this time.

Gabriel sat upright by his elbows and spoke in Russian to the pilot, the foreign conversation lasted for some time. The pilot's voice sounded awfully familiar but Halley couldn't put her finger on it. Then Gabriel unbuckled his seatbelt and pressed his hand into the headrest of his chair and eyeballed the clones. "In approximately twenty-six hours we will be landing at the Beagle Channel of Argentina. Stay in your seats, it's going to be a bumpy ride."

As if on cue, the jet convulsed with turbulence. Rex locked his jaw, he could've sworn that any second they would be flies splattered against the wall. He waited for the jet to tip over but it didn't. He couldn't sleep or distract himself. There was nothing other than the thumb-twiddling silence for the twenty-six hour flight ahead. Gabriel stumbled down the hallway and grabbed hold of Rex's headrest for support. He eventually made it to the back of the plane and rummaged through the bag. Moments later he re-appeared with his arms filled with cans of assorted soups and tossed one to each of the clones. The front label read *'Hearty Chicken and pea soup.'* The description made Rex's mouth water but his stomach seemed twisted with fear and uncertainty. He glanced at Apollo who already devoured the contents. Rex couldn't hold back and he ravenously sliced the lid off and gulped down the soup. He disregarded the use of the plastic spoon. Rex scooped out the remains with his fingers and turned to Chino. "You feeling alright?"

"For lack of a better word, yeah, I'm alright."

Rex folded his hands and allowed his eyes to slip shut. With over twenty hours of the flight remaining, he would rather not remember it all. His mind began to drift when the plane shuddered. It rocked abruptly and the turbulence was a constant reminder of his newfound hate for planes.

Suddenly, a cry pierced through the jet. Rex spun around to see Apollo slumped forward with his face hidden by a paper bag. Then Cyrus pulled it from his hands and he too threw up the soup contents. Something wasn't right, Rex unbuckled his seatbelt, when Halley beat him to it. "Stay seated," she pointed to him.

"Hal, that goes for you too. There's too much turbulence, it's dangerous," Oren said firmly. His eyes didn't waver.

"They need my help."

She knew the pain all too well, a solemn reminder of the lonely morning sickness that greeted her each morning. Halley tumbled down the hallway and crouched beside the clones. The jet shuddered again and she held onto the armrests for support. "It's okay boys, its' only motion sickness. Now breathe. Deep breaths."

Apollo huffed and gulped down air, then he forced it out of his lungs at an incredible speed. He leaned into the bag and once again was sick.

"Apollo, nice and slow, copy me." Halley demonstrated slow breaths that even calmed her own nerves. The clones copied her technique. "That's good, very good," she prompted.

Cyrus' face grew pale and he planted his face into the paper bag again. Halley gagged at the site and covered her mouth. She stumbled with the turbulence. Gabriel made his way over but she was too fatigued for any of his nonsense. To Halley's surprise, he extended one hand to which she held onto for balance. Gabriel guided her into her seat and Halley shut her eyes. "How much longer?"

"We are just about to land," the pilot called.

XXXVI

2010

It was almost midnight when the jet descended toward the mountains of Argentina. It shot downward at an angle but this time their stomachs were plastered forward. Rex decided gravity was a shit thing when flying. The jet bounded along the grass runway of Beagle Channel, Argentina. The overgrown weeds whiplashed its' wings and the jet swivelled to a halt.

"We're right on time." Halley bowed her head and whispered to her belly. "I don't know if that's a good thing or not."

After all they had been through, Halley was beyond exhausted but the triumph of Argentina was exhilarating. Then she realised, the clones were far from safety for the trip had only just begun. Worse yet, there was no guarantee they wouldn't get caught yet. Halley thought about loosing the clones, the tight metal handcuffs around her wrists as authorities lead her into a prison cell. She could smell the stench of cigarettes and alcohol from their uniforms and the unsanitary toilets she would be forced to share. In her cell would be a palm-sized photograph of Max, a reminder of the treasure she lost. "Do you think this is going to work?"

Gabriel dabbed at the trail of sweat from his forehead. "Of course it will, we are almost there."

Nobody in Argentina knew who the researchers or where they were headed. Everything was going to be okay. In a few weeks Halley would be home and this nightmare would end.

Beagle Channel of Tierra Del Fuego was an unwelcome place, with a rocky ground that was broken up by sunburnt shrubs. Their stems were black and although the ocean loomed nearby, a gust of hot air blew through Argentina. The researches and clones walked in a narrow line down the corridor and upon departure, a gust of hot air blew into their face. Cyrus and Apollo were last to exit and they held onto the handrails, they followed Rex's lead. "Brothers."

Apollo watched him from the corner of his eye. "I can't walk … My body hurts."

Rex crouched down and looked into their eyes. "I'm right here with you. I won't let you behind, take your time."

Halley pulled up alongside Rex. "Here." She stoop beside Cyrus, slipped a hand around his waist and tucked her shoulder beneath his. She carefully extended her torso and Cyrus winced. He bit his lower lip and exhaled a gust of saliva. "One small step at a time, Cyrus. You go this," she whispered.

Halley took one step forward and then another. Cyrus' eyes were half-shut and a trail of saliva drooled down his chin. His feet barely dragged and Halley pulled him over the pot-holes. Oren supported Apollo and the four of them moved at a gentle pace. They followed the tobacco trail from Gabriel's cigarette as he headed for the wharf.

"Now is probably a good time to tell you that no matter what happens from here on out, we cannot account for any mistakes. We stick together as if our lives depend on it because they do," Gabriel said.

A plume of smoke circled Halley and when mixed with the hot

Argentinian air, she broke into a sweat. Her fingers slipped from Cyrus' arm which dangled over her shoulder. She tightened her grip. "I thought that was the plan all along."

"Argentina isn't like Scotland, which permitted therapeutic cloning. We functioned under the ideology that the clones were produced to find treatments for premature neonates. Argentina, however, however, isn't like that. Cloning is banned both therapeutically and reproductively. If we get caught, that's it."

"What's our plan B?"

Gabriel took another long puff from the cigar and winked at Halley. Then she realised, there was no option B. This was it. The researchers would be in deeper shit than they expected and prosecution in Argentina would prove far worse. She looked at Oren who stared at her wide-eyed. So much for Gabriel's plan but they couldn't turn back now. They headed along the East hemisphere of the coast and found wharf 13, where a thin layer of fog floated around a white ship. Fluid white writing along the side read the *White Seal*. The dock was busy with a crowd of people who minded their own business. The line leading up to the White Seal must have been twenty-people long and at the front end was a security guard. "This is going to take too long," Gabriel whispered.

"Well, we don't have a choice," Oren said.

"Listen, we need to secure a place on that ship and soon. If it fills up too fast we won't get on."

"What the hell are you talking about? I thought you organised everything. Don't we have tickets or something?"

"No. There wasn't enough time." Gabriel lowered his head and spoke to Cyrus and Apollo. "Boys, I know it's tough but I need you to act normal. Walk for yourself."

"Gabriel, they can't do it!" Halley hissed. She tightened her grip around Cyrus' waist as he wobbled in her grasp.

"I don't have time to give a shit, just do as I say!"

"How are you going to get us on that fucking ship?" Oren snapped

Gabriel reached inside his pocket and revealed a plastic bag full of cash.

"You've got to be kidding me." Oren nervously turned toward the clones. "Cyrus, Apollo, you know what to do."

"He's right," Rex muttered. "C'mon, brothers, on your feet."

The clones stumbled and walked at an angle. Each footstep was more painful than the last but after a while pain turned numb for the prospect of freedom was worth every ache. Apollo's foot twisted inward as he tried to remember how to walk.

Gabriel pushed towards the front of the line and ignored the crowd of strangers who shouted in Spanish. A guard appeared, at least six-foot tall, with a pair of black sunglasses despite the night-sky and a bulky build. He ushered Gabriel aside. The man spoke in Spanish and Gabriel glared at him. "English? You speak English?"

The guard crossed his arms and pointed to the back of the line. They understood each other, it was mutual and Gabriel sighed. He reached inside his jacket, extracted a small plastic bag and revealed a handful of cash. The guard peered over Gabriel's shoulder at his entourage and shook his head. He bore a set of ugly yellow teeth and tapped his foot, impatiently. The guard raised an eyebrow.

Gabriel reached inside his jacket. Two bundles. The guard pressed his chest against Gabriel's arm and slipped the money into his pocket. He then ushered them to the front of the line.

Halley walked over the narrow steel ledge that connected Beagle Channel to the White Seal.

From beneath the hood of Rex's jumper, he peered around at the White Seal, a six-levelled voyage. The ceiling was at least eight times Rex's height with a mesmerising glass chandelier and the cream walls were decorated with eloquent trances of gold. He now realised how the ship could hold over one-hundred-thirty passengers, two dining rooms and an observation deck. He was entranced by its' size but all the while contemplated whether it welcomed him with fear or peace and tranquility. A stubby man pushed past Rex's shoulder, he trudged a large suitcase at his feet and grumbled. The voyage was filled with the banter of hundreds of voices that came from all directions. Rex had never seen so many people before. "Move it. Don't look at anyone!" Gabriel snarled. He smacked the back of Rex's head. "Go right. The guard said room 101."

Rex cocked his head to the side but couldn't see Gabriel past his hood. "You speak Spanish now?" Rex followed the instructions before he got another slap to the back of his head.

The brass door handle led to room 101. It was a spacious two bedder, furnished with a mini bar, entertainment section, velvet furniture and red accents. The researchers divided everyone between two rooms. Room 101 would host Halley, Oren, Apollo and Kiara. The alternative was room 420, three levels up where

Gabriel, Cyrus, Rex and Chino would be. The ship shifted almost ninety-degrees and the chairs gritted across the floor.

Halley walked across the breadth of room 101 and flopped her backpack on the bed. She trailed her fingers along through her hair. The voyage seemed farfetched and with no escape. Oren emerged into the bedroom, hands tucked into his pockets.

"It's nice in here." He watched Halley from the other side of the bed.

Oren looked so much like Max and it was painful. The last image of Max flashed across Halley's face. He stood in the farmyard with the natural glow of sunrise around his head and eagles soared above. He was so strong. She would have to see Max in Oren's face that entire trip, a constant reminder he was left behind. Halley felt as though she deserved the punishment. She couldn't stand the sight of Oren anymore and left the master bedroom.

The room was silent apart from the pitter-patter of small feet and the occasional screams of joy from the other side of the door. A squeaked giggle filled the air and Halley's trembled hands faltered at the door handle. She peered down the corridor to see three small children danced around a woman. The hems of their pink dresses floated as they moved. The girls ran along the emerald floral carpet and revealed the woman which they encircled. Halley could now see in full view as the lady reached toward a baby dressed in a onesie, who crawled across the floor. Her chubby fingers flew upward, wavered mid-air and slammed hard against the ground. Her knees scuffled along the floor and the woman towered over the little girl. She scooped the infant into her arms walked in the direction of the older children. Halley clutched her belly, the foetus listened to the world around. She closed the door and pressed her forehead against it. She felt the cold on her face and her heart throbbed in her mouth. Halley balled a fist and gently punched the door. And again. A cascade of tears trailed down her cheeks as she cried into the empty wooden door. The laughter of the little girls echoed down the hallway and each one burned its way through Halley's ears, like a blazed trail of fire. She peeled her forehead off the door.

Halley slumped into the couch and switched on the television, where the volume was cranked to the maximum and actors yelled so loud that it sounded static. She bit into the her jumper sleeve that was now stained with black mascara and tears. Her hand was covered by the wet and sticky jumper sleeve and she pinched the tip of her nose.

Inside room 420, Rex poised himself by the circular window of the bedroom and his fingers coiled along the metal frame. A spotlight illuminated the water and the waves danced before his eyes, one engulfed the other. The ocean would be his home for now.

The room was white, all white. White walls, white sheets, white pillows, white towels made him nervous. Rex crept along the carpet that was soft and nothing like the basement concrete floor. In a strange way he missed the basement, the stench of rotten vegetables, the hard dusty floor and television held up by a milk crate. It was home and this ship was anything but that. It seemed too perfect. Rex's thoughts were interrupted as a voice erupted over the loudspeaker but he could not find where it came from. The voice spoke in Spanish and then silenced. A few seconds later it resounded in English. "Hello everyone and welcome aboard the White Seal. I'm captain Rodriguez and we shall endure this voyage together over the next four days. Please remain seated, we are about to depart and make our way towards Antarctica. For those of you who have sailed before with us, it's a pleasure to have you here again and for those of you who are first timers, welcome aboard." Captain Rodriguez continued his speech for a few more minutes but inside room 420, the crew lost engagement.

Gabriel cupped his hands beneath the tap and washed away the perilous journey from his face. He watched the clones through the water that dripped down his eyelashes. Cyrus stood up from the couch and made his way toward the alcohol cabinet. Gabriel raised his wet hand in the air but it was ignored.

"I'd say let's enjoy the most of this trip. Whiskey anyone?"

"How do you know what that is?" Gabriel hissed.

"One here," Kiara said.

"Sister," he pointed "and you brothers?"

Apollo and Rex agreed. Cyrus plucked a fresh bottle of whiskey from the shelf, it had an expensive price tag stuck on it but before Gabriel could attest, the lid was already ripped off. "Bit young aren't you buddy?" Gabriel demanded.

"Not when you've been dead."

"Nice try, but you can't use the 'dead and came back' to life excuse. Besides Apollo and you were viably ill on the plane. I wouldn't do that if I were you."

"All the more reason to cast out the demons from our hungry bellies," Cyrus beamed with triumph.

"Don't come begging for my help when you're sick again." Gabriel pointed a finger.

Cyrus handed out the glasses of whiskey. "Don't worry, we wont."

The clones raised their glasses in the air and once Gabriel left the room, Rex turned to Cyrus. "A toast to freedom."

"To freedom."

Rex tilt his head and slurped the whiskey. He cringed. It was nothing like beer but the taste was warm and fuzzy. Maybe it wasn't so bad after all.

The day seemed long with nothing to do other than pace the room but Rex occupied himself with the view of the ocean, the waves appeared calmer today. From all the oceanology classes with Halley, Rex knew the ocean was inhabited by an abundance of marine life but he was yet to spot anything more than limp seaweed. His knees cramped up and Rex readjusted on the bed. He switched his attention to the alarm clock on the bedside table. 5pm.

Cyrus entered the bedroom, followed by Apollo. He held a glass of water in hand strode towards Rex. "I know something you don't." Cyrus lay along the bed and sunk his muddy boots into the white sheets.

Rex cackled. "What do you know brother?"

"That the researchers are going to dinner tonight. They are eating in the foyer from 6pm."

"We're all alone," Rex's eyes widened.

"Drinking time?" Apollo couldn't hold back his glee.

Rex thought for a moment. "No. I have a better idea. Cyrus, go to room 101, three levels up and to your left. Bring the other clones down here. This is going to be fun."

Rex wiped away the fine layer of condensation from the bathroom mirror and glared at his reflection but felt as though he was watched a stranger. It was something Rex always knew, but suppressed. He was the face of a man who died before. He lived an entire life and there wasn't much in life that was certain but he knew this much was true. He stared at his lime green eyes. They were from Norwich, Great Britain although he couldn't be certain what they saw in his past or how he died but Rex was related to Halley. Even with the odds stacked against him, it came to be. Rex wiped his face with a towel and his hair was a mattered mess. He grabbed Apollo's comb and raked it through but residue balls of gel clung to his head. Rex examined his face, although the bruises from the leadership fight healed, a scar remained, along his chin.

A knock at the door sounded. "Coming."

The clones followed Rex back inside the bathroom. He reached for the fresh hand-towel slumped over the basin and caught sight of Kiara's reflection as she entered the room. He flattened his black hair and the curled ends licked his shoulders. "So?" Rex asked.

"I think she brought it." Behind the certainty in Kiara's voice was the subtlest hint of fear and for some odd reason it made Rex's stomach flutter. Kiara had a way about her, she pretended to know what she was doing but the truth was, she made it up as she went along. Rex turned around and stroked the side of her face, to which, Kiara closed her eyes.

Cyrus sat atop the toilet lid. "Did you stick to the plan Kiara?"

"Yes, I think they believed me."

"You think or you know?"

"I can't be certain … I stuck to the plan, alright?"

Cyrus cackled.

"What's so funny?"

"If we're going to be smart about this then I suggest you better start acting it."

"We need to be discreet, we mustn't draw any attention to ourselves," Rex hissed.

Cyrus' face was blank but after some consideration he nodded. "Alright, you heard the master. What do we do next?"

"It's time for a bit of fun. We've complied with the researchers all this time but now it's our turn to live. The whiskey, I want all the bottles opened in ten. Then we make our way around this joint and check it out. I want to see what the ship is like, I want to see the people but on one condition, nobody sees our faces."

Cyrus folded his arms. "Boring." He tucked his hair behind his ears and turned to Rex. "I have a better idea. I want bargaining power with the researchers. I want to walk in stride with them and make decisions too. I say, we send them a message and something that says 'we can have our freedom but we would rather be considered important.' That means no more bossing us around or concealing information. I want in."

Kiara raised an eyebrow and smirked, the petite dimples

emerged on either side of her cheeks. Cyrus wasn't wrong, the clones should be involved in the decisions and navigation of this trip too, they weren't kids anymore.

"We need a plan though but nothing too drastic," Rex said.

"I like the latter option. We need to make a statement. Scare them a little, prove we are powerful too."

"No," Rex breathed.

"Yes," Apollo implored.

Cyrus cackled. "We need to show we have rights and if the researchers don't buy it, we make a proposition. We replace ourselves with someone else. Five children to take our place in Antarctica. After all we are in the middle of nowhere and nobody knows who we are."

Rex spun around. "No. We won't do it."

"Do you want me to comply with your leadership? Then listen to me first. We must work together."

The clones rhythmically turned to Rex and awaited his confirmation. Rex lowered his hands to his knees and glared at Cyrus. Sneaky bastard was always up to something.

\He always had to take matters into his own hands.

"I'm not trying anything funny," Cyrus taunted. "No one gets hurt and everyone gets what they want. Now, I'm leaving this room and getting this plan into action."

"No you're not. I will do it. I will fulfil this proposition, that way nobody gets hurt."

Cyrus leaned in closer. "Fine." He glared at Rex from beneath the strands of hair that shadowed half of his face.

"The researchers are at dinner now, so we must move onto phase two of the plan," Rex said.

"They have been gone almost twenty-three minutes. We have time but how much, I can't be sure."

Kiara had a worried look scribbled across her face. She brushed past Rex and allowed his fingertips, warm as honey, to glide along the circumference of her waist. Kiara bowed her head, to which Rex did the same. He pressed his lips close to her ear. "If anyone is walking off this ship unharmed it was going to be you. I promise you."

"Always."

Inside the living area, Apollo snapped open a lid from a fresh bottle of Hibiki whiskey. He poured five shots, clumsily spilled the liquor along the bench and licked the excess from his fingers. Rex gave attention to the radio. He managed to switch it on and clicked through the channels, until he finally stopped on the one English Channel where RNB blared and he cranked up the volume. "This is what I'm talking about."

Rex spun around and took Kiara's hand in his own. He twirled her on the spot and they danced rhythmically to the beat of *Wall to Wall*. Shots were thrust in their direction and the clones clinked their glasses. They cheered at the top of their lungs and from the level above, someone stomped feet attempted to quieten the ruckus. Cyrus clasped his hands over his mouth and sung louder than before. To everyone's surprise, Chino bounced his head to the tunes and already swung back two shots. "Can someone dim the lights!" Rex pointed his finger and continued his fluid dance. Chino gladly did the honours and the party continued until everyone's speech was a slurred mess and the floor was sticky. Rex was three shots in when he focused on Kiara. Her slender physique hypnotised him like a serpent and her moves appeared well thought out. She guided another shot to her lips but missed and the whiskey cascaded along her curved hips. Her confidence grew and Kiara untied her hair and tossed the luscious locks from side-to-side. Rex slid across the floor and danced before her face. Kiara nuzzled her nose against his but when Rex leaned in, she drew back. She bore a cheeky smile, one that was guided by the whispers of an alcohol hypnosis. What a tease. She bit her lower rose-tinted lip and Rex leaned in. Her sweet lips were glossed with alcohol and they virtually melted in his mouth. Rex spoke to Kiara's tongue that glistened with temptation. "It's time, my love. It's time for phase two."

XXXVII

2010

The circular tables were hardly a meter apart within the confinement of the curtained walls. Intricate vintage detailed borders match the ceiling and floor which, frankly, made Halley dizzy. The downlight above the table shone brightly and she was temporarily dazed. The seafood linguine before her appeared mushy dog-food, she'd bit one morsel of the meal which made her gag and forced it down her throat with water. She upturned her face at the wine on the table. Something Halley had never quite enjoyed, especially now she was pregnant, but Gabriel and Oren had a particular nose for it. Across the table Oren leant back into the chair and laughed into the napkin at something hysterical Gabriel said. Halley check the room, where apparently nobody listened in on the conversation. To her surprise, each huddle of people were engaged with their meals or conversation. "The chief baker himself survived from the purity of alcohol alone," Gabriel twisted the glass and the cranberry wine danced clockwise. "This stuff made the baker so calm that he swam until daylight, when he got rescued." He turned to Halley. "One of the few survivors of the great, historical, Titanic." He smacked his lips together. "Anyway, back to the clones. They think there's this new age around, drinking whiskey and have you noticed them acting differently? I think Rex is the leader these days."

"In all seriousness Gabriel, I think we shouldn't speak of the clones at a place like this," Oren gestured.

"Nonsense, nobody around here speaks English too well."

Oren gnawed on that thought. He lifted his glass. "Does anyone want another glass?"

"Shall we pour a glass for the clones too?" Halley asked.

"They may fancy it," Gabriel said in a lucid stare.

"They may, considering it will help them float to stay alive." Halley leaned across and bit her tongue to stop the words tumbling out of her mouth. Gabriel raised an eyebrow. "So tell me about this lab we are going toward?"

"It's a research facility actually, called ORG-26. It's on the top of a rock formation."

"That's an odd name."

"It's the registration number." Gabriel downed the wine.

"According to Captain Rodriguez, we are headed for the Drake Passage. Brace yourselves," Oren interjected.

"I doubt we should feel anything, Oren. We are too modern day for this ship to go down … That's probably what they said about the titanic too, come to think of it."

"I think we should head back to the room before it gets bumpy," Halley added.

Inside room 101 Halley entered, followed by Oren. The lights were dim and it seemed quiet. Halley made her way over to the clones' bedroom, where she twisted the door knob and a figure emerged from the dark room. "Hal – Don't come in, Kiara has been sick all evening," Apollo whispered.

"Then, step aside and let me in. I can help."

"No. She is finally sleeping."

"I'll be here if you need me."

The White Seal rocked to the lullaby of the ocean current and the floor danced with it. Halley walked into the living room where the atmosphere was silent apart from the rain that pelted down. It thudded from somewhere nearby and a chilled breeze gushed through the room. She shivered and saw the living room curtains flap in the wind as the rain immersed itself into the carpet. She walked toward the curtains that shadowed the balcony and the fabric licked her goose-bump laden skin. Through the translucency of the wet fabric was a silhouette. Oren was hunched over the metal railing, perked up by his elbows. Halley stepped around the curtain until she too was a silhouette. She smelt the pleasant aroma of cinnamon spice, it was Oren's Versace cologne that he only wear on special occasions. She followed the scent and it reminded her of home.

Oren lifted his elbows from the rails, the rain soaked his clothes and numbed his skin. He extended one arm and Halley nuzzled her face into his bed of chest hair that protruded over the top.

"Oren, you know amidst all the fighting and stress ... I hate to admit but it almost seems I've forgotten our love. We've been so pre-occupied with the clones, and Max," she paused, it was best to leave out Oren's drunken habits. Halley would rather not see him drown his sorrows in a drunken fit.

"Hal. Whatever happens in Antarctica, I love you and always will."

The rain intertwined with the spicy cologne, which stung Halley's eye.

"What do you think Max is doing right now?" Oren asked.

Halley paused. The question caught her off guard, neither of them mentioned Max since they left Scotland. They both succumbed to the internal pain in solidarity and it seemed to make them stronger. "It's past his bedtime so he's probably laying in bed wishing we were there, by his side for chemotherapy tomorrow."

"You know what I think he's doing? I think he's dreaming. Max is having a dream where he is Spiderman or Ben-10, his own hero."

Halley couldn't hold back the tears and they poured down. She gasped for air as the rain slammed into her face and dripped down her backside. Oren shifted his body to shield her from the storm and he now took the brunt of it. His coat was weighted down with the heavy rain. "He's a strong kid, like you," Oren rubbed her arm.

"But what if he's not? What if this time he isn't strong enough because we aren't there?"

Oren clasped both hands around Halleys face. There they stood, face to face and glued together by the storm. Neither of them looked away. Oren breathed heavily and appeared to want to say something but he toyed with the idea before he spoke. "Halley, there's something that I need to tell you." He paused and tried to catch his breath but every time he did his mouth was filled with splutters of rain. Halley searched his face for answers but only saw pain in his eyes.

"I - "

WHACK.

Out of nowhere a thud vibrated through the balcony and laid flat on the deck was a petite body. The young boy must have been about thirteen years old and he scurried to his feet. He took one look at the couple and yelled at the top of his lungs all the while he scuffled backwards. The rain washed a trail of blood drained down his face and along his cream shirt.

Halley dropped to her knees and yelled above the thunder. "What happened? Are you alright?"

"Don't! Please! Help!"

The boy moved backwards, he was headed for the balcony rail. His cry was riddled with absolute fear. Halley kept still to stop him from making any panicked moves but the boy only moved faster. His arm knocked against the rail but he didn't seem to realise. He pushed his body against the balcony edge. Fuck. He was going to fall over.

Halley instinctively thrust herself across the deck. She grabbed hold of the boy's forearm as he fell beneath the rails. He dangled over the edge of the ship, the back of his shoes kicked against the window pane of the room below. His legs thrust in every way and his arms flailed.

"OREN!"

Oren grabbed Halley's jumper and supported them both by the rail with his free hand. But the cold metal was wet and Oren's hand slipped forward. Halley felt herself fall forward and her arms began to burn. She tightened her grip until her fingers grew numb and the only way she knew she held the child was to she look down. She screamed loud against the storm. She knew the boy would plummet to his death if she didn't pull him up soon.

Time was short.

The boy bellowed whilst his body flopped against the side of the White Seal like a fish out of water. The more he thrashed about, the more difficult it was for Halley to hold onto him. She swung her head over her shoulder and nodded at Oren. He pulled them up when a black silhouette dashed past. Halley squinted against the storm, there was someone there. A figure or maybe two. She was hauled closer to the safety of the deck and her vision cleared. There were two people on the deck. Halley twisted around.

"What is it?" Oren asked puzzled.

She lay on her back and caught sight of two figures a few levels above her. They were dressed in a black and grey hooded jumper. They swooped around and disappeared from sight.

"The top deck."

Oren scooped the boy into his arms and the three of them darted inside without further thought. The boy dropped to the couch and Halley fussed over him, checked his head abrasions and searched for any other wounds. "Are you alright? Are you hurt?" The boy shook his head, tears streamed down his face. "Are you sure? Show me your arms!"

The White Seal dipped leftwards and Halley was thrust off the couch. She tumbled across the living room and suffered a carpet burn. The curtains flapped above and the furious rain devoured Halley's body. She lifted her head off the floor and clambered across the living room. The ship tilted again and Halley reached for the vase beside the television but it dropped beneath her hand shattered over the floor. The ceramic clashed and the echo tore through Halley's eardrums. She stumbled across the floor and swayed to the rock of the ship. She braced herself against the wall for support. She walked along the hallway and her stomach dropped with the rise and fall of the ground. Halley thrust the door of the clone's room open and peered inside. The blankets were strewn across the floor and the room was empty. The clones were gone. "Stay with the boy, I'll be right back!" Oren barked from beside her.

"NO! I'm coming with you!"

"I can't let you get hurt! Stay here and call Gabriel!"

"You're not doing this alone! I'm coming with you!"

XXXIIX

Rex is 9/18

The boy fell over the edge of top deck. That wasn't part of the plan. Kiara was meant use him as a warn signal. Rex watched the boy disappear inside the room, he was alive. Good. He swung around and pushed Kiara away from the edge. A fury boiled from within his stomach, all she had to do was stick to the plan. "What the hell are you doing? I told you not to be seen!"

Kiara raised her shaking hands before her face and curled her fingers into crippled fists. Her confidence faded and she bore the persona of a frightened child. "Kiara … Kiara, I'm sorry. I – I'm not going to hurt you."

"They saw me, they saw us. We – gotta go. Now!"

Rex's eyes pleaded for forgiveness but there was no time. They had to move fast. They pulled the hoods over their heads and ran across the top deck. Kiara skidded along the rain covered cement when Rex entered the stairwell of the fire exit. "Ready for phase three?"

Before she could respond, Rex disappeared into the empty blackness and descended the stairs. He panted, this was going to be harder than he anticipated. They must have descended twenty or thirty steps and then they heard it. Voices, familiar and close. Shit. Between the whir of fear and the alcoholic dizziness, Rex couldn't focus. Nothing went as planned. He peered around but the sound echoed from all directions. "Run," Rex whispered.

They climbed five steps above and burst through a random door.

They entered one of the levels of the White Seal where there was a row of doors and the familiar metal railing encircled the deck. Rex pushed through the alcoholic hypnosis. They were in the open and would be easy to spot. He feared they were on level four, where room 420 would be and the chance of the researchers stood guard, was likely. Kiara knocked her elbow into Rex's abdomen. She held the hood over her head and Rex copied. The next few seconds would be crucial. They must not drop their guard, no matter what happened, their hoods couldn't reveal their identity but on a vessel with countless civilians, anything could was possible.

"What do we do?" Kiara whispered, she tried to disguise the desperation in her voice although Rex saw her teeth chattered.

"Follow your instinct."

Kiara lead the way, she walked too close to the door knobs on the left and her bony elbow knocked against them each in turn. A gust of wind pushed her back and the rain smacked against his cheek. She blindly reached for a nearby pillar.

"Hey, is everything okay here?" A man dressed in a black suit with a top-hat asked. His presence took Rex by surprise. He continued to speak but the words appeared a static mumble. "Sir?"

Rex was confused by his English tongue but there was no time for questions. "We're fine," he said.

"What are you doing out here, it's too dangerous." The man yelled above the roar of the waves and thunder.

"I said go away!"

Before the strange man said another word, Rex ran off but Kiara was nowhere in sight. There was no time to spare. Rex took off, unsure which way to turn. For all he knew, he could run into the arms of the researchers but it was a risk he would have to take. A civilian had already heard his voice, the voice of a clone. That was one slip up. He darted across the balcony but the tides seem to have changed and the ship rocked rightward. A coffee table dragged along the deck. Rex leaped over and stumbled along the deck. Then he noticed one of the doors ajar. The ship lifted and the door flapped open. Kiara was in there, he knew it. As he slipped one foot inside the room, the angry shriek of thunder warned Rex not to enter. He ignored the sign and emerged into room 213. Similar to the design of room 420, there was a television with a couch and thick curtains covered the window. It was quiet, almost too quiet and for a moment Rex suspected he'd chosen the wrong room. He crept around and his boots squelched over the carpet. A bolt of lightning illuminated the room and for a quick moment Rex saw another door was left open down the corridor. He gently placed one foot before the other. A dull pain radiated through Rex's foot. He glanced at the ground to see a silicone spiked ball. It flashed shades of neon blue, red, yellow and green. Rex kicked it and the ball knocked against a messy splay of coloured picture books. He tilted his head to the side, *The Very Hungry Caterpillar.* Kiara followed the plan better than expected. Rex's eardrums filled with the vibrations of his own heart that raced faster than ever. Phase three was now in progress and a chill racked his spine.

XXXIX

2010

The Drake Passage teased the White Seal and threatened to rid every civilian of their life. The sky was dark as the ocean depths and the storm blurred the sight together. Oren leaned over top-deck and peered at the levels below. They were empty, for nobody dared set foot into the cold front of the storm. He watched the waves reach five-feet high and then collapse. Heavy raindrops clung to Oren's eyelids but every time he wiped them away, a slimy film coated them again. Halley kept watch of the fire-exit and clutched a kitchen knife, although it was too blunt even to cut an apple, she wasn't about to take any chances. "Oren, they're not here!"

He released a distorted yell. "Come out Rex! I know you're there!"

"Oren ... Oren," Halley muttered.

"What!" He spun around, his shoulders heaved, they rose and fall in sync with his breath. His face distorted with trauma and Halley hardly recognised him. "They're not here. We need to move on!"

"I knew it. I said we should have gone through every level of that damned stair-well!" Oren barked.

"There's no time to argue now! We don't have any time to waste!"

"What do you think they're going to do?"

Halley thought none of it made any sense, it didn't add up. The clones got their damned freedom and they got to see the outside like they asked. Why did they run? Why did that little boy fall off the roof top?

"Call Gabriel," Halley's broken voice said.

Oren rummaged through his jean pockets and shook his head, he didn't have his phone. Halley pulled out her own cellphone and dialled a series of numbers but amidst her despair, she could only hope to get the combination right. The line rang and then it went dead. Halley dialled the number again but this time the line didn't ring at all. She checked the screen and wiped away the raindrops with her hand but were replaced by more. The time read 3:05 am … or 8:05. The numbers morphed together and time was almost senseless at that point. She squeezed the phone in the palm of her hand but it made no difference. The storm interfered with their reception. Fuck. Halley used every tendon of her body to not slam it on the concrete. Gabriel was the last person on the entire ship that could help them now. It was useless. This was the beginning of the end.

"Any luck?" Oren yelled.

The screen darkened. Halley pressed the keyboard but the phone was officially dead. She threw the cell against the floor and the screen smashed.

Oren and Halley plummeted down the staircase, they followed a blind path of hope. Time was against them with with six-levels, a kitchen and basement, the White Seal was great in size and even greater with civilians. To find the clones was almost impossible. Halley followed Oren down the fire exit, where the metal stairwell was tight and over-heated.

"What if they are back in room 101? They know we won't check there," Halley exclaimed in short-sentences that were broken up by the huff of the stairs.

"No, they wouldn't run toward us. They are stronger in numbers."

"This was a bad idea, coming here altogether was a terrible idea."

"Don't you ever say that!" Oren yelled. He spun around and leant toward Halley. "Don't you ever say that again. Don't you see?"

"See what, Oren? What am I supposed to see?"

"Shh!"

"Excuse me?"

Oren pressed two fingers against her lips in silence. He peered around the stairwell, his eyes darted. "This way ... I think."

He backtracked the way they came down. He reached one of the exits and pushed it open. Halley followed close behind for the fear of being alone taunted her, more than a wrong turn. They emerged onto one of the levels. Oren disappeared down the balcony, hunched forward. Out of nowhere, a bald man dressed in black slammed into her shoulder. "Oh – I – I'm so sorry miss," he muttered.

"Don't be."

"Don't go that way miss! Turn the other way, there's some kind of weird man that way. You need to be careful!" He warned and pointed an unwavering finger in her face.

"What do you mean?" Halley asked.

"I'm going to alert the security. Come with me, please!"

"Don't tell a single soul what you saw."

They stood at the door of room 213 where a muffled cry emitted but instead of relief it sent chills down Halley's spine. The clones were close, almost too close. She pressed her body against the wall and slipped inside room 213 and almost as if on cue, a loud wail pierced the air. It seemed to come from the corridor. The fear-riddled screech sounded again. They narrowed in on the screams and burst through one of the bedroom doors and there was Kiara and Rex were hunched over a cot with two toddlers inside. Kiara's arms were wrapped around one while Rex was only meters away. A part of Halley wished to not have found the clones. A fragment of her heart died and she began to lose hope in the clones' humanity.

Oren shuffled forward and pat the air. "Let her go."

Kiara's arms tightened around the little girl's waist and the tuft of messy blonde hair shook. Her legs kicked off against Kiara's core.

"What are you doing? Where are their parents?" Oren asked.

"This – this is phase three," Rex said groggily.

Halley shifted her gaze to Rex, who stared at the floor behind the jailed bars of his mattered black hair. A wave of selfish pity crossed Rex's face but he said nothing. He encircled the crib with heavy footsteps.

"This isn't you Rex, I know who you are," Halley pleaded.

"Get away from him right now, he's dangerous!" Oren yelled. The children squealed and tears cascaded down their cheeks. Halley locked her sight onto the small girl caught in crossfire, her bewildered eyes desperately searched for hope. She looked much like Max did, scared but still brave. Halley forced a grin between her shaken lips and the girl relaxed momentarily. Halley switched her gaze to Rex. "You're not really going to hurt those children. Tell me I'm right ," she whispered but Rex's eyes were that of a stranger.

Beneath the mask of this new-found authoritative exterior, his humanity dwindled but it was still there. Halley spoke to the innocent clone she raised, to his conscience. In a normal world Rex would never harm the children but nothing about him was normal and never would be. Intoxication clouded his mind and Rex embraced the sweet surrender. His vision was hazy and his mind almost thoughtless. It was a pleasantry he'd not yet experienced. He raised his head and looked Halley in the eyes. "Have you forgotten the other half of who I am?"

Drool hung from his bottom lip and the foul smell of garbage on a summers' day drugged the air. The stench almost made it too hard for Halley to breathe.

"Have you both forgotten the other half of who we all are? Man on the outside but-," Rex raised an open hand "there is another side to us. We are half human and half science. There's a part that's missing. We want answers beyond what you can provide. There is a truth you are hindering and I can feel it. You haven't been honest about why we were brought back to life. There is more to the story, I just know it."

Rex circled Halley, he whispered the blood-curdled words into her ear. She followed his voice but avoided eye-contact for the truth would be far too difficult to comprehend. Rex was right.

He was cloned for science and in an a twist of events, lived longer than proposed. He should only have lived to the fourteenth day. Halley's jaw jittered. She never wanted his life to continue, it wasn't right.

"I'm offering you a proposition," Rex whispered.

"Whatever it is, I know this isn't you."

"The kids in exchange for us."

Halley peered out the window at the waves which roared, almost as if it lectured Halley for the stupidity of the clones', the deceased's resurrection, and to have brought to life something that was not human but science. The experiment became more than what it should have. Now the lives of these two children hung in the balance, should they die, their death would be in vain. Rex walked towards the crib, where the two toddlers shrieked at his presence. His shadow blocked out the lightening that illuminated the room and Rex appeared larger than his physicality. For the first time since his resurrection, he was almost unrecognisable as the man he once was. A darkness lingered around him and a burn for hunger yearned from within. "In exchange for our freedom, take the children instead. Nobody out here knows we are clones, let us be free. Once and for all."

"That's a lie, Rex. You had your chance to escape, the night when you broke out of the office but you led yourselves right back to us. So what is it you really want?" Halley glared into Rex's empty eyes. "The children will never take your place, you were not meant to be reborn, I understand but here you are and I wouldn't change this adventure for the world."

Suddenly, a distant stampede of footsteps sounded and began to close in on them. Muffled voices yelled from all directions and the walls banged with insatiable rage. Time slowed and Rex heard his heart pound within his skull. "There's no time left, we failed." He glanced over at Oren, his eyes filled with the brokenness of defeat. He shook his head and almost as if snapped back into reality, dropped to his knees. "What's wrong with me?" Rex pleaded. He hunched over and clutched his abdomen. "You must understand this was not my doing but Cyrus. He threatened to harm the children, to kill them, if I didn't make a peace offering. Cyrus will avenge my leadership led by a new testimony, should I not provide any answers. He will avenge freedom and is stronger than me. Cyrus mustn't know that you found us." Rex headed toward Kiara. "Leave them alone. That's an order."

An entourage of flashlights darted across the hallway and the children screamed as foreign voices stormed down the corridor. Halley scooped up the infant boy and his fear-stricken arms clung to her neck. Oren cradled the girl, who encased his waist with her stubby legs and buried her face into the fabric of his dining jacket. She cried hysterically.

"Leave, now! Go back to the room," Oren demanded.

Kiara's face dropped and spoke of a thousand words. Cyrus would challenge for the title of leader once more. She was too fatigued to endure another leadership fight but for Rex, she would do anything. Rex gestured towards the window and thrust his fist through the glass. He grimaced as shards rained over his arm and the window collapsed into itself. The ruby curtains twisted against the rage off the wind and contorted into abstract shapes. Rex allowed Kiara to climb outside and she skidded across the balcony. Her body was hidden by the contorted curtains and she disappeared into the dark of the storm. Rex watched as the abrupt wind blew hair over his shoulders. He leant forward, ready to jump, when the storm changed direction and the curtains encased his body. He fought the fabric but became entrapped inside its' body.

"Shit," Oren muttered.

He darted across the room, the girl in his arms and slammed against the door. He took hold of the door handle and it jiggled from the other side. Halley leapt into action and pressed her back against the door as countless hands beat from the other side. She tired, all too soon. Her feet slipped forward. The door creaked open. Halley grit her teeth and slammed her head back against the wooden door. Across the room, Rex battled his way out of the curtains. He emerged from a slit and pushed his way out until his entire head was visible. The door pushed forward and this time stayed ajar as Oren and Halley gave out. The children clung to their chests but it weighted them down. Halley clenched her jaw and watched as Oren was thrown to the ground.

The door burst open and a group of people entered. A combination of security guards, middle aged men and a women with dirty blonde hair, who crouched down. The children threw their petite bodies into her arms. Halley's heart beat in her mouth but as she turned towards the window. Rex had vanished and all that remained was the limp curtain, the only bystander of the clone's existence.

A security guard pulled Halley's arm and spoke in Spanish. She stared at him dazed and he annoyedly acknowledged her confusion. She couldn't speak Spanish. "Come with me," he said in English.

In the security office, Halley cupped her hands around the mug of tea but despite the warmth, she continued to shake. A blanket was draped over her shoulders and pressed the wet clothes against her body.

"Misses Makillen, I need more information than that. Is there not anything more that you can tell me? Even if it seems insignificant," Security officer Fernandez said as he dropped back into his seat. A blind light reflected off the top of his head, surrounded by a U-shape of receded hair. For the past ten minutes he avoided eye contact with Halley and Oren.

Instead, he focused on the box of unopened donuts halfway across the room. She could practically hear the watered smack of his lips with each sentence and the frustration that laced his voice was probably not because he didn't get answers he wanted but due to something else.

"I already told you officer, the room was dark. Far too dark for me to see," Halley replied.

"This ship docks tomorrow and I need more of an answer before I release everyone." His face flushed bright red. "Fine. Was he tall or short? What did his voice sound like?"

Oren kicked Halley's ankle beneath the table. He knew that if she made one small mistake, the officer would warrant a room search.

"I never said it was a man," Halley drew a long sip from the tea that scorched the back of her throat but she figured it was less painful than the truth.

"If we remember anything, anything at all," Oren paused dramatically before he continued, "we will be sure to give you a call, we have your number." Oren raised a paper card in the air, the one that was handed them earlier. Fernandez scratched his head, glanced from Oren then to the sugar-glazed donuts. His foot tapped against the floor.

"Alright, get on your way!" He threw his hands in the air. He pointed one chubby finger in their direction. "I'm watching you, make note of that."

Oren and Halley scurried their way out of the basement, led by another security officer. He eyeballed them but the stare was not reciprocated. Oren gripped Halley's hand as they walked away. That was a close one. The clones had to stay under the radar for the next twenty-four hours.

XL

Rex is 9/18

Rex pressed his back against the window pane and relished in the comfort of a full belly. Although the hearty meal may be his last as Rex pondered what Antarctica entailed. There was no fresh veggies and he already missed the aroma of poached eggs on a Sunday morning. He had food withdrawals, if that were even possible. Apollo demolished his meal until his eyes rolled into his head with ultimate pleasure and he fell lopsided. His head hit against Rex's knee and then he slumped to the floor. "You right there buddy?" Rex asked.

"I've never been better."

Rex uncoiled himself and walked toward Kiara. Her hair was plastered beneath the freshly applied bandage around her head that was spotted with blood. He feebly traced his fingers along the bandage and sighed. Everything that happened was his fault and this time, he didn't do enough to protect Kiara. He offered the remains of his dinner but Kiara politely declined. From the opposite side of the room, a pair of jealous eyes glimmered. It was Cyrus, who toyed with the fish carcass in his mouth, he drooled and then his jaw snapped shut. He chomped down on the skull that shattered bones across the floor. A warning but Rex scoffed at the remark. "Too much for you to handle?"

"More than you can," Cyrus replied.

Gabriel plucked a glass and bottle of vodka from the alcohol cabinet. He slammed the items against the granite island with such force that Halley awaited the glass to break but it didn't. Gabriel hunched over the glass of whiskey as if hypnotised by its' drunken grace. He swirled the glass and watched the caramel liquor rotate on a clockwise axis before he swung back the drink. "Halley, did you do this?"

"What are you talking about?"

"Put on a whole show to get the clones exposed so we can go back home? Why not throw them over the edge of this bloody ship? It would've been much more discreet. It's how I would've done it anyway."

A fire spurred within Halley's stomach for the sincere accusation in his voice was beyond comprehension. She leant across the isl and was about to start an argument but Oren squeezed her waist. Halley shot him an uncertain glance to which he ignored. Instead she swallowed her words. She knew Oren was right, she couldn't fight Gabriel, not if she wanted to make it across Antarctica in one piece. He was the only one who knew how to get to ORG-26.

"All of you are so damn lucky I got to that room before the security guards did. We would all be under interrogation this moment," Gabriel snapped.

"Let me guess, you bribed the guards like you did to get us onto this damned boat?" Halley retorted.

"No. I cleaned up the mess Rex and Kiara left behind." He produced a yellow-lined specimen jar with a few strands of hairsinside. Gabriel was right, if the security guards got their hands on any evidence, the clones would be one step closer to exposure.

"None of this is my fault. I was at dinner with you, how could have we known?" Halley muttered. Oren obviously shared her frustrations as he paced back and forth, he fastened his step. He pointed a finger at Gabriel.

"Don't you dare involve my wife in any of this again!"

"Or what?" Gabriel yelled back, his arms splayed far apart ready to tackle Oren. The only thing that held him back was the precious glass of whiskey in his hand.

"I'll show you what happens next time, back down!"

Gabriel threw the glass, and the whiskey splattered against the wall. "Makillen, don't forget the whole reason we are here!" He trudged past the clones and headed toward the bedrooms to drown his sorrows in solitude.

Halley turned to Oren. "What does he mean?"

"I have no idea and I'm not about to find out."

"Check it out!" Kiara said dazed as she leapt toward the glass window. A slither of white light shone through the crevice of the curtains and she thrust them open. The clones rearranged themselves into a straight line, they sat on their haunches like children in the school room. They were mesmerised by the spectacular view. Oren and Halley made their way over and their jaws dropped. The view was dim and endless mountains welcomed the White Seal. Icebergs reached toward the heavens, one closer than the next. Some remained fully intact and others hollowed at the core, which formed nooks that would house the hungry mouths of wild beasts. Shards of over-sized ice chunks drifted through the ocean. "Well, well, would you look at that," Cyrus was astounded.

The loud speaker sounded across the White Seal and Captain Rodriguez conducted the long awaited announcement. "Good morning everybody, it's now six O'clock in the morning but nonetheless the Antarctic Peninsula welcomes the White Seal yet again. Welcome to Antarctica."

XLI

2010

The arctic winds were -81 degrees Fahrenheit and the choppy waves of the Southern Ocean slammed into the icebergs. The landscape was shrouded by a shadow of winter for was no sunrise or sunset. The thing about the Antarctic is that there's no rise or fall of the sun. Everything appeared the same, you could be circle yourself or have walked miles and wouldn't know the difference. They followed the arrow of Gabriel's compass and continued toward the Eastern hemisphere of Antarctica, toward Shackleton Ice Shelf. It was approximately 1 hour into the journey when 62 miles remained. Halley peered over her shoulder and watched the clones plow through the snow. Each of them were indistinguishable from the next, apart from the colours of their shell parkers. Everyone was dressed in a three-tiered layer system; a base layer that clung to every crevice of their body, then was a mid-insulation layer, followed by the shell. Halley sport a blue shell, Oren next to her was in coral red and Gabriel wore black and their faces was shielded by balaclavas. Halley only recognised the clones when they spoke. She focused on the trudge of her heavy footsteps which broke through tufts of snow and all the while prayed not to take a wrong step, where she would plummet through a frozen floor. Oren nudged his elbow into Halley's arm and she stumbled sideways, he seemed to have had no idea the force exerted through the restrictive layers of clothing. She grinned but instantly felt ridiculous. Oren couldn't see her face. She was met by his black-balaclava and buggy goggles. "How far are we?" Halley asked although unsure of how loud a pitch was required to transmit a message through the knitted balaclava.

"Let me ask." Oren made his way toward the front of the line and sparked a conversation with Gabriel. The pair walked almost in unison and for the first time, Halley realised they de-bulked some their luggage. She couldn't be sure when but now Gabriel only carried the small backpack slumped over his shoulder. She peered over her shoulder and saw the endless chalk landscapes. The luggage had disappeared in the ice plains. Someone emerged to Halley's right and their knees reached chest-high before they slammed into the snow. The figure glanced at Halley and waved.

"How are you holding up?" Halley tried to figure out who it was.

"Not too bad," it was Kiara. She glanced over her shoulder stumbled through the snow. "They might need a hand back there. I better slow down."

"No, you keep up." Halley allowed herself to fall to the back of the line where a clone dressed in an orange shell stumbled through the snow and was held up by the shoulders of two others. The three clones moved in a waddled motion and were too entranced in their own difficulty to notice Halley's presence. "Do you need a break?"

The clone in the middle lifted his head. "If you don't mind," Chino responded, his muffled voice was barely audible over the balaclava.

"I think we should all do with a break," Rex agreed whilst Chino who rested on his shoulder.

Halley cupped her hands over mouth and yelled at the top of her lungs. "Wait!"

Oren and Gabriel must have been almost twenty feet away and sound seemed to travelled differently, for they barely flinched. She whistled and was sure someone else would have heard the call but nobody was nearby. Gabriel spun around so the backpack flopped against his shoulder.

"They need a break!" Halley yelled.

"No. Keep moving."

"They can't do it, they will never make it if we keep going at this pace."

"It's getting late and the animals will be about. Now move!"

"You can't say that for sure. You don't have any idea what time it is around here!"

"Move." Gabriel's tone reassured the clones that they would all be left behind if they stopped for a moment longer.

This was insane, Chino would not make it, much less the rest of them. Halley shovelled Rex aside and assumed his place next to Chino. She tucked her shoulder beneath Chino's armpit and plowed through the snow. She stomped one foot in front of the other and tried to ignore the sting from her knees. She puffed breathlessly and fog blurred the non-reflective goggles. By that point, Halley moved robotically for the more she allowed thoughts inside her mind, the more crude the trek became. She took her place behind the researchers and amongst the clones. She peered over her shoulder to which Rex raised his hand in the air, a tender reassurance he was alright. Although none of them spoke, an eerie feeling vibrated through the air. Unfathomable fear.

Halley knew the only way to survive this suicide-riddled trip through the Antarctic glaciers was to remain quiet. Everyone fed off Gabriel's fake confidence, which by that point, was the only source of hope. Halley's throat became narrow and her despise for fitness began to show as she fought through the knee-high snow. She stumbled backwards, something blocked her trail. Halley looked up and realised Oren stood still. He stood still and watched Gabriel plough through the snow in solitude. Halley stroked his arm and whispered words of encouragement but he remained still. His mind was adrift the Southern ocean.

"Gabriel, I think it's time now," Oren called.

Halley held her breath, something wasn't right. Gabriel was a few meters ahead when he turned around.

"We best be on our way," Oren encouraged.

"Ah – yes!" Gabriel caught his breath. "Of course, Makillen." He swung his right shoulder down and the backpack slapped into his chest. "There is one last thing before you go."

He rummaged inside the backpack and then his hand ceased movement. Gabriel raised his goggles to reveal his squished face beneath the tight balaclava. Oren pushed Halley behind him and she watched the scene about to unfold from his shoulder. Gabriel dropped the bag and now held something black and cold in his hand. It was a gun.

He clicked the barrel and pointed the gun directly at Halley. "Last chance Oren!"

"What's going on?" Halley's distorted voice cried.

"This wasn't part of the plan. We are going to take what's ours and be on our way."

"I can't let you do that. This is your final warning." Gabriel tilted his head and his voice was laced with a combination of sarcasm and seriousness. Despite his tone, Halley knew he was serious.

"What's he talking about?" She wailed and a stream of tears seeped through the base protective layer and stung her cheeks. She looked over at the clones, each of them remained speechless and still. The gun riddled them with fear and nobody attested Gabriel's patience. Chino lifted his head and his knees bent, which drew him closer to the ground.

"We had a deal. I stuck to my half, now stick to yours!" Oren exclaimed. He raised a hand to his face and ripped off his goggles.

"C'mon Oren! Did you really think I was going to let you both get away with this? You really are dumber than you look."

"What the fuck is he talking about?" Halley backed away, she felt abandoned by Oren. She clutched her belly, the baby was the only one that wouldn't double-cross her. The two of them were alone in Antarctica for Oren was a traitor himself.

"G'on Makillen, tell her why we are really here!" Gabriel laughed. He stepped forward and now clasped both hands around the barrel of the handgun and his finger wavered against the trigger. The slightest wrong move and Gabriel would click the gun, they would all be murdered. Halley fought the urge to back away and instead prayed internally, all the while she shielded the baby with her hands. Oren turned toward around. His eyes shadowed by a cloud of pity but it was not reciprocated. Halley was petrified of him and stumbled backwards.

"Honey, I … I agreed that we would help Gabriel transport the clones to wherever he needed and in exchange, he would help me save Max."

"Save Max? What the hell could Gabriel do, he's not a doctor?"

"Think Halley!" Gabriel spluttered. "I'm no doctor but a scientist and there is so much more I could do for your boy. I can save him."

"I don't understand," Halley panted. Her hands shook before her belly and she knew the foetus would sense her insecurities. It no longer felt safe. Halley failed the child before it was even born.

"The other half of the deal was to extract Max's DNA and clone him. A clone that had the same genetic makeup, with replicated DNA, bone marrow, organs. Someone rather close in age. It would be the best way of giving our son a future and all we have to do is return to Scotland, kill the clone and harvest it's organs. The only way to save Max would be a donor with the same genetic makeup."

Halley could hardly believe her ears, it was all too much to fathom. She shook her head. "So you're going to make a clone and use them to save Max?"

"No Halley, I already made one," Oren said particularly fond of himself.

"When?" Halley's jaw dropped open and her teeth chattered.

"Nine years ago and that clone has walked by our side the entire time. It was a coincidence the Leukemia came back and what good timing it turned out to be because everything has worked out so well."

"No!" Halley yelled. She couldn't comprehend a single word. She no longer cared.

"I can't sit back and watch our son wither away into nothing! I won't let him die like you will! He's a boy, an innocent boy and I have this - this gift to save him! Don't you see how much good we could do?" Oren shouted.

Gabriel stepped forward and the ice crunched beneath him. He held the gun at chest-level. "I warned Oren it would be those eyes. The damned eyes would be a give away but he never listens," Gabriel exclaimed with a hateful taste that coated his tongue.

Halley furrowed her brow. Eyes. The remark sent her three steps back. The truth was far more complicated than she anticipated and it was didn't make sense. Halley looked over the clones. She envisioned their innocent faces as they too, heard the painful reason for their existence. Then she realised and it all made sense. Halley turned around and her chest convulsed with pain. She gagged against the lump that rapidly grew within her throat. Against all odds, she hoped she was wrong. Halley opened her mouth to speak but it was too difficult. The clone born of Max's DNA had been amongst them the entire time.

"That's right, it's Chino," Oren said.

"Chino," Halley muttered and burst into a firework of tears.

"You're favourite part of your mother was always her eyes. You always spoke about Max's grey eyes, and I made sure Chino

291

would have them. He was made from a syringe of Max's blood, not a mosquito, this is our son. Of course, I stole Chino's AncestryDNA envelope and destroyed the letter inside. I couldn't have you find out he was related to us too soon because I know you wouldn't want any part of it."

Halley dropped to her knees and wailed the most ungodly shriek. Before her were the five clones, the same ones that have walked by their side and yet she was foolish to not recognise those eyes. The truth was right before her every day and she missed it.

"You knew about this and you didn't tell me?" Halley turned to Oren.

Chino heard the violent truth and raised his head. Although too fatigued to even speak, his pant was enough to know he heard it all.

"Put the gun down," Oren said.

"Did you really think I was going to let you both return with Chino?" Gabriel laughed. "I mean, maybe it crossed my mind once but I can't let anyone know about my research. I can't afford to go to jail and have my precious clones running around the city. It all ends here. I'm taking the clones and Oren you can come with me or die with Halley. The choice is yours."

Gabriel levelled the gun, the barrel was focused on Halley's forehead, and he closed one eye. Halley stood her ground for all the clones awaited her next move. Regardless of what was about to unfold, she remained by their side. If she was going down, then she was surrounded by family. Nothing else mattered.

"Don't do this," Oren whispered. "Let us go and you can have the rest of the clones," Oren snuck his hand behind his back and felt for Halley.

Her teeth sunk into her bottom lip and forced herself to stop slapping him away. Tears evaporated into the balaclava and her mind clouded with confusion. Oren did all of this for Max, he tried to save him but in the most inhumane way and it all made sense; the clones alive, Chino's missing ancestry letter, all of it. Halley straightened her back, perhaps death was the only way out of this ordeal.

"One ..."

"You cheating fucking bastard! Take all the other clones, give me this one. That was the deal you fuck-wit," Oren's voice echoed through Antarctica and his frustration encircled all of them. The truth was revealed and the gruesome words propelled into their mind of the clones.

"They want to kill us," Cyrus growled.

"Don't hurt them, we will never find a way out of here," Rex hissed.

"It's our turn. We walked in stride with the researchers, we trusted them and now they are going to kill us all."

"Two," Gabriel said cooly.

"Be smart, Cyrus. If we do something stupid now we will be eternally lost. There will be no way out, we must get to safety first," Rex urged. He switched his focus to Chino. There were no words to express what he must have thought for he, amongst all of them shouldn't have lived.

Halley shut her eyes and covered her ears.

"Three," Gabriel grinned.

BANG.

BANG.

The snow crunched like the grind of teeth and there was a gasp from somewhere near. For a moment Antarctica was silent as the gunshot echoed across the open plains. Halley's hands pulled away from her ears. She panted against the cold air. She knew she shouldn't be able to breathe. Her hands searched her face and felt every indentation and for some reason, she wasn't hurt. Halley opened her eyes and saw everyone stood in their positions. Although confused, her heart jolted with triumph, Gabriel missed and nobody got hurt. The snow crackled like the scrape of chalk on a chalkboard and Halley's world crashed down.

Oren dropped to his knees and began to face-plant towards the snow. Halley threw herself down and every joint of her body locked. She awkwardly guided Oren into her lap like a guardian angel. Her fingers trembled across his chest and her gloved hands were soon coated with thick blood. "Oren, you have to get up!" Halley wailed until her throat raked with agony and she screamed until her lungs gave out. She pressed her forehead atop Oren's and mumbled an incomprehensible plea. She begged him to stay with her but blood spurted from the hole in his chest.

The clones watched the sight unfold and Kiara ploughed towards Rex. She wailed for Oren, who was now a remnant of the steep price of freedom. Instantly, Kiara regretted every time she pushed to see the outside and wished she could take it all back. She turned to Rex and without a word, he knew her intent. "Don't do it," Rex whispered.

Kiara tugged on his and whimpered, she wasn't ready for anything like this.

Gabriel charged forward with the gun raised high in the air and fired another shot into the silent innocence of the sky. His sight was locked on Halley.

"Now!" Kiara roared.

"No!' Rex barked.

It was too late.

The fight had begun.

Apollo was first, he rammed into Gabriel and they both slammed to the ground. Apollo thrust his fist through the air and smacked Gabriel's face sidewards. He locked his knees on either side of Gabriel's waist and fought with everything inside of him. They battled across the snow and the clones ran towards the scene. Rex was frozen stiff and thought before he moved. He switched his gaze from the Halley and then to fight. He watched Gabriel elbow Kiara in the face and she fell backwards. Rex instantly dropped Chino to the ground and ran towards the scene. Gabriel loaded the gun and aimed it at Cyrus. He clicked the trigger but missed. Rex slid across the ice and rammed into Apollo's abdomen and pushed him to safety. Rex shielded his face, prepared for the attack, as Gabriel thrust countless punches in his direction.

"I'm not trying to hurt you," Rex roared. "Leave them alone and help us get out of here!"

Gabriel climbed atop Rex and smacked the gun against his head. The heavy blow forced him to lower his guard but not for long. Rex elbowed Gabriel in the throat and the gun dropped out of reach. Rex stared at the gun, it was half hidden by the snow but the handle stuck out. He reached over and his fingers licked the metal, he closed his hand grabbed nothing but air. Rex knocked the gun further away and grunted beneath the weight of Gabriel's knee atop his abdomen. A blunt force pain radiated from Rex's jaw as Gabriel punched him and dragged himself towards the gun.

Rex suffocated against Gabriel's cladded shell that covered his mouth. Then, Apollo sprung into action and stomped on Gabriel's hand grabbed the gun. He pointed the barrel towards Gabriel but his hands shook, he had no idea what he was doing.

"I have to do this, he was going to kill Chino," Apollo said in a broken voice.

"Don't do it," Rex wailed. "If you kill Gabriel we will never make it the research station. He's the only one that can lead us there."

"Kill him!" Cyrus yelled.

"Back down," Rex bellowed.

"Do it!"

"Don't do it, that's an order!"

The twin brothers opposed the words of each other. Their voices sounded the same. Apollo couldn't tell who spoke. He lost track of his Rex's orders and tightened his grip around the gun. Apollo's mind clouded with uncertainty and either way, it was a losing battle. He closed his eyes and his hands fumbled uncontrollably.

BAM.

A puddle of blood oozed from Gabriel's balaclava. It drained down his head and he shuddered. He gagged on his own blood which dripped into Rex's face. Gabriel tried to speak but choked on his own blood and saliva. He dropped forward and convulsed atop Rex. His eyes dilated.

"You killed him," Rex gasped.

"I had to."

Cyrus swung forward and clasped one hand over Apollo's shoulder. He raised his bothers' hand in the air and they yelled with victory. Cyrus' beamed with an insatiable hunger and they all knew what that meant. Rex was no longer leader, the birth of the new leader had arisen. It was Cyrus.

The sky grew darker as Halley fussed over Oren's body limp. He bore a gash along his forehead and two gunshot wounds. One to the right side of his chest and the other in his arm. Halley clung to his neck as if her life depended on it. She rocked their bodies in sync and her warm tears united them. She pressed her ear against his mouth, he still breathed but his chest bled profusely and would soon enough loose heat.

"Oren," Halley wailed. "Please don't leave me."

She reached for the zipper along Oren's neck and untied the tight thermal wear. She removed his balaclava, and cried into his face, it was the warmest part. "Open your eyes."

Halley checked over his wounds, the bullet hole was to the right side, it would have missed his heart. "Keep your eyes open," Halley whispered.

With each criying breath, her words became incomprehensible. She forced her hands down on Oren's chest where they were coated in a pool of blood. The blood didn't stop, it spurted out.

Oren looked up at Halley with glazed eyes.

"I – I – I'm sorry," he whimpered. "I tried save Max," he choked on the blood in his mouth. Oren inhaled deeply, which made it harder to breathe.

Halley shook her head, she needed to relax him but didn't know how. She was totally helpless.

"Shhh." She pleaded for him to stop his speech.

Halley forced her hands harder against his chest but her vision blurred as the tears came poured down. Oren's mouth moved as if he tried to talk and she placed her index finger on his chapped lips. She leaned forward and pressed her forehead against his. "I need you. We need you," she said but her words broke off she cried inconsolably. "You're going to be a father," Halley dragged Oren's cold and bloodied hand over her belly. His eyes widened. Halley tried to kiss his forehead but couldn't help but cry.

She raised her gaze and peered around at the bloodbath. She caught sight of Gabriel's deformed body, he didn't move and the horrific smell of blood curdled the air. Halley returned her attention to Oren and slipped one hand beneath his arm. "On my count. One … Two … Th -"

His face crumpled as Halley manoeuvred his weak body until she carried him atop her back. Oren grizzled with pain and the slippery blood along his chest gravitated him further down her back. Halley clutched onto his arms that dangled around her neck, she screamed in agony and pulled him further up, desperate not to let go. Oren's cheek was warm against her own. There was hope and that gave Halley strength.

Cyrus made his way over and bowed his head. "I am sorry for

what I am about to do but I'm sure you have the same apology for us. None of this would've happened if we were never reborn and Oren would still be with us. I avenged Gabriel in exchange for Oren's life. I gave you justice but now I must do what is right for us."

"He's still alive and I won't let him die," Halley spat. "We have to get to the lab."

Cyrus scoffed. "We are not in this together anymore. I gave you the gift of revenge and now we part ways." He bowed and turned away.

Rex stepped forward. "She's right, we are stronger if we stick together!"

"I don't need you. You are the weak link." Cyrus leapt over Gabriel's carcass.

"Halley and Oren come with us. We have no idea where the fuck we are. They are our only hope of getting to the research station. Especially now with Gabriel gone."

"I will lead this pack to safety. Don't challenge me."

"You wont be getting far without this," Rex produced Gabriel's compass and dangled it mid-air. "I'm not handing it over unless we stick together."

"Fine. The three of you can come with us but if you fall behind, you're on your own. Now move, we will follow the compass to Shackleton ice shelf."

Rex fell behind the clones and took his place beside Halley, who carried the heaviest load.

XLII

2010

Halley watched Chino walk in front of her, he limped through the snow but dared not wine about the obvious pain. He was home, for Antarctica was cold and dim, a place where he could embrace his albinism. Halley couldn't help but think that Chino was cloned from Max and in some profound way that made him her son. He was a blessing in disguise, for no matter how feral Chino would become and however much he changed, Halley was home. She thought of his grey eyes, she smelt the burnt cinnamon buns on a Sunday evening and the French vanilla perfume her mother always wore. Halley was torn in twos halves that couldn't find common ground. Chino was her child but also the saving grace she prayed for. He was the only one that could promise eternal life for Max and a decision needed to be made. Oren was too weak to speak and Halley was forced to comprise an answer. She could either embrace Chino as a second son or to harvest his organs for the purpose of Max's preservation. Oren was right that, it would be the only promise that could save Max but would cast Halley a murderer and either way she would lose a son. There would be no happy ending.
Should she explain the ordeal to Max, that his brother died for him, was there even the slightest moral compass behind that?
Halley stumbled and the weight of Oren rocked atop her back. Rex reached over but she ignored the gesture and instead tilted her head to feel Oren's skin against hers. He was cold but she

could still hear his breath. "Hang in there."

Perhaps it was love or the pure guilt that the bullet was meant for her but either way Halley held onto Oren with everything she had. She wouldn't give up on him now. She felt Rex's stare and nodded her head, the silent remark was enough to reassure him not to offer again. Halley was sure her body would collapse but she was determined to reach the research station. They ploughed on, somewhere between the Antarctic Peninsula and Shackleton Ice Shelf. Another hour had passed, or maybe two, time was no longer essential in the Antarctic plains. Rex checked the compass and the arrow pointed North when they should have been headed East. "Hal, we're going the wrong way. Shackleton Ice Shelf is that way." He pointed in the opposite direction.

"I don't care. I need to keep moving," she puffed. As long as she walked, it was progress and enough to maintain her sanity.

"It'll take longer, you can't keep going like this. Hang on, I'll be right back," Rex snarled with his eyes set on Cyrus. "Brother, we need a break. Halley can't do it."

"Tough. She can stay here for all I care, that's none of my concern, now move it or I'll break your legs."

"Not if I break yours first," Rex whispered.

"What did you say?"

Rex spat into Cyrus' eye and the saliva drooled down his goggles. He began to walk away but Cyrus grabbed him by the shoulders and thrust him to the ground. Rex was quick on his feet and he punched back. Cyrus gripped Rex's neck and pulled him in close. "You know, we wouldn't be here if it weren't for you. You trusted those researchers and I believed you!"

The brothers tackled each other over the frosted ground and the clones cheered in a circle. Their feet stamped and balled fists were thrust into the sky. Halley watched the fight unfold and focused on Rex, from beneath his balaclava a trail of blood dribbled into his merciful eyes.

Slam.

He collided into the floor. The clones battled until they were an abstract mess of each others' saliva and blood. Halley watched the blood fall and her vision grew hazy. She swayed on the spot and as she lost concentration, Oren tumbled off her back. He smacked against the ice and moaned defencelessly. Halley reached below Oren's armpits and dragged him backward with a heavy thrust. He wailed a blood-curdled scream and Halley pulled him away from the fight. His wounds were stretched open with every pull. "Hang in there."

Beneath Halley's foot the ice cracked and the loud split ripped through the air. Her hands froze still and she wiped snow away by her foot which revealed a translucent glass film. The sight almost made Halley's heart stopped. They were atop a frozen river. "STOP! Don't move, the ice will break!"

The clones peered down at the frosted floor. They remained still as Rex pulled his knees to his chest and pushed away. Cyrus landed on his ass and the ground split.

Crack.

The ground was instantly covered with slits that zig-zagged every way. Rex placed both hands across his chest and coiled his knees, he was defenceless and awaited the pain to come. The ice collapsed.

Halley plummeted into the ocean that was unbearably cold. An army of swords jabbed her from all angles. Now, below the glass-frosted surface, she realised at some point she let go of Oren. She looked around and the water felt like sand particles raked across her eyes. She had to find Oren before it was too late. She pushed through the pain and dived further into the water, her body was tossed in every direction as the cold tried to force her eyes shut. Halley looked down to see a red matter sink toward the bottom of the ocean. It was a long shot but Halley felt it was Oren. She thrust her arms forward and swam awkwardly beneath the heavy clothes. Halley was fatigued but the familiar red shell was at arms' length now. She clasped her stiff fingers around it and swam toward the surface which must've been three meters ahead. She pushed through the water but every time she did, Oren's body felt heavier and the surface teased further away. The current dragged her away from the surface. There was only one way out. Halley fumbled with the zipper of Oren's shell. She tugged at the sleeves but the shell was resistant from the weight of the water. Halley pulled and Oren's arm released. She clenched her jaw and attended the other side but it proved harder to remove.

Fuck it!

Halley paddled her way to the surface with Oren clutched beneath her arm and the shell filled with water that tried to drown him. Halley burst into the open and shards of ice thumped against her forehead. She screamed as her face stung but there was no time for pain. She realised Oren was still beneath the surface so she arched her back and tried to pull him up. "Rex,"

Halley wailed.

Through the fatigue she couldn't manage another word and her head dropped beneath the surface.

From the edge of the ice, Rex jumped to his feet but slipped and tumbled backwards. He slammed against the floor and slithered until he reached the ledge. Then he took a deep breath and dived in. Apollo followed close behind and the clones disappeared beneath the surface. Halley felt the vibrations through the water as the clones zoned in on her. Then a strong tug forced Oren from her arms. Rex burst through the surface, his hands clamped around Oren's waist and he paddled toward the edge. Apollo heaved Halley onto his shoulders and swam for safety.

Along the frozen ground, Apollo slapped Halley's face, which forced her awake. She sat forward and realised what had happened. A few feet away the clones sat around Oren and Halley scrambled across the ice and clambered atop him. He was limp and his lips were a sinister blue. Now that his shell had been ripped open, the wounds were obvious and Halley's numb hands fumbled with her own shell. She instinctively tore it from her shoulders and began to guide Oren's hand through the sleeve when she felt the scar along his thumb. Halley froze and the tender indentation reminded her of home. She wept uncontrollably, for she couldn't be strong this time.

"Let him go, Hal. He's been through enough," Rex whispered. His eyes trailed over the gunshot wounds which were worse than anticipated for it penetrated through the other side of his chest.

"He's still breathing," she said through the lump against her throat. Oren's chest rose and fell but his breathing was light and uneven.

"Move aside," Cyrus said. He lowered himself and dragged Oren's limp body atop his back. "Oren looked after us for nine years. He doesn't deserve to be left behind."

Halley opened her mouth to speak but Cyrus' eyes warned her not to question him. He carried Oren to the front of the line. Halley shuddered, without the protection of her shell she was weak but would have it no other way. She took a step forward and almost fell to the ground. Her body was broken. Chino pulled up alongside her and knelt down. Halley allowed him to slip his hands behind her knees and she pressed her heavy head against his chest. She was coiled into a ball as Chino carried her. Halley's eyes closed and drifted into the numbed unconsciousness as her son carried her to safety.

Nobody knew how much time had passed but at some point Cyrus sniffed the air and was welcomed by a metal scent. They were close but amidst the darkness, the research station was out of sight. He forced another step forward and huffed beneath the weight of Oren. "Are you good there, pal?" Cyrus panted.

No reply. Cyrus paused, he thought he heard Oren breathe and realised the life drained from him, they were on borrowed time. He didn't know if Oren was alive or not but carried him for Halley's sake. "Hold in there," Cyrus muttered. "He doesn't have much time left!"

"He doesn't need it," Rex called back. "We're here."

For the first time in hours, Cyrus cast his gaze upward and was confronted by a leveraged pillar of magmatic rocks. They stood at the base of an uneven staircase. It was carved into the rock that circled toward a levelled surface and there it was. A small grey complex with a red roof and capital writing that displayed the registration number. ORG-26. Through gritted teeth and stone-cold bones, the clones and researchers somehow managed their way towards ORG-26. It was protected by spot-lights along the perimeter of the roof and a metal fence. Rex stood still as the clones walked around him. Their shoulders knocked against his with a linger of arrogance, they were exhausted.

"Are you coming?" Kiara's meek voice emerged.

She removed her balaclava and Rex realised that she looked different; her cheeks sunken in, lips chapped and skin mottled. Her face was encased by greasy hair plastered across her lifeless brown eyes. Rex had almost forgotten her face before this entire ordeal. A fragment of his heart broke off, he wished he could have protected her. They had all lost a part of themselves but the journey had come to an end now. They had made it to ORG-26 and the metallic scent was stronger than ever. They were safe.

XLIII

ORG-26

Warm ripe pumpkin soup filled the air but Halley was ignorant for her bones throbbed and the sorrow would never be a remnant of the past. Chino lowered Halley and she clambered out of his arms. The wooden interior of ORG-26 was a neat fit with an eloquent hide-rug, orange couch and curtained windows.

It appeared a homely cottage rather than a research station. The clones began to slip out of the balaclavas and everyone's battle scars became obvious, each worse than the next. One thing was consistent, they were all exhausted, from their corpse-like eyes to the flesh sunken in-between the bony prominences.

Cyrus laid Oren over the couch where Halley crouched beside and slipped her fingers through his hand. She found the old scar along his thumb scar and she rubbed it like a genie in a bottle, she hoped he would feel her presence. "Oren. We made it," she whispered.

Halley stroked his hair that was coated with sticky blood. She smiled and although it hurt, it felt good. She drew Oren's hand over her belly and flinched as the cold penetrated through her skin. "He's cold. Someone get me a warm cloth and some bandages."

The gunshot wound to Oren's chest was no longer bled but Halley pressed her fingers into the depths of the crusted wound and applied pressure. "Don't stand there, somebody help me!"

She touched his Oren's wet face. "Oren. Honey … Open your

eyes."

Oren's eyes didn't waver and his purple lip remained shut. "Oren. C'mon we made it!"

Rex clasped his hands around Halley's waist and eased her off but she buckled and struck Rex with a rear-ended head-butt to the nose. Halley thrust her hands around Oren's neck and stared into the shallow depths of his face. "You have to wake up."

Cyrus crouched beside Halley, his sour breath in her ear whispered, "look at his chest. Halley, look at his chest."

Oren's chest didn't move. He didn't breathe.

"Rex, Cyrus, help me."

Halley kneeled beside Oren and pushed her hands into his chest. She had never performed CPR but still her shoulders heaved back and forth and she plunged her body forward.

Crack. A rib broke. Halley fell onto his chest as her spirit broke. They were supposed to be safe.

Oren was dead.

The clones encircled their fallen ally and Cyrus cupped his hands around his mouth. He screamed to the god-forsaken heavens above. The clones copied. The room was filled with trembling hands coated in blood and cried a tearful symphony of pain. They cried louder, they cried together. The harrowed howl for their lost friends. Halley joined in and cried louder than them all. She wailed until her voice gave out. They may have begun the devoted cry of symphony in memory of Oren but it ended with Gabriel's death and the uncertainty of their own future.

Unexpected footsteps silenced them all and in the doorway stood a strange figure disguised by the fur-trimmed hood. He pulled off his gloves and unveiled his face. Halley almost dropped to the floor. The man was bold, blind in one eye and spoke in a Russian accent. "I'm glad to see you all made it here."

"Sebastian," Halley whispered.

Sebastian glanced from one clone to the next and ignorant of the deceased body in the room. He threw the gloves onto the coffee table and mumbled something with his gaze fixated on Chino. "Where is Gabriel?"

"W – what are you doing here?" Halley stammered.

"Did you expect this place to be empty?"

"It was you, wasn't it? You were the plumber back home and you flew us here."

"Where is Gabriel?"

"He didn't make it."

The blood drained from Sebastian's face and he was speechless. He showed no remorse, instead he appeared stunned. Sebastian folded his arms and from the corner of his eye checked the clock on the wall. "It's after five and according to my calculations there will be a blizzard tonight. It's best you stay here."

Halley gulped. Something wasn't quite right about Sebastian and she didn't trust him to say the least but there was no way out. There was no reception, no town or people around. It was her and the ice plains. Halley pinched the space between her eyes. "Fine. We stay here but only for tonight."

"Where do we go tomorrow? I mean where even are we?" Kiara interjected.

"I don't know but we will figure something out."

The clones made their way to their allocated bedrooms but Halley stayed in the living room.

She clung to the curtain and made eye contact with the crescent moon from atop the iceberg. She tried to relax, tried to forget but knew there would be no such thing. She bit into the sleeve of her jumper and twisted it in her mouth. Halley's teeth shook with rage and her jaw locked in place. Her eyes were too swollen to cry anymore.

"It's beautiful, isn't it."

Halley spun around. She was over-shadowed by Sebastian who glared out the window from behind her. "I can't say I know how you feel because I don't but I am truly sorry for your loss."

Halley placed a swollen hand on her belly. "It's just the two of us now. I think it's a girl but I guess you never know this early."

Sebastian's jaw dropped. "Did Oren know about her?"

Halley ignored the redundant question and glanced out the window.

"I need you to listen to me carefully." Sebastian crouched beside her and spoke in all seriousness. "There's a Chinese ship docking along the Antarctic Peninsula in five days. I can take you there and help you get home."

"We can all go home?"

"Only you can leave. I'm giving you a way out of this. You were not supposed to come here, it should have only been Gabriel and the clones, nobody else."

"What happens to the clones?"

"The clones' future was always to be in the hands of Gabriel and myself. Forget about them and think about your baby, she needs you."

Halley bowed her head. Sebastian was right, she had already lost too much on the trip. First she left Max behind, then Oren and Gabriel. She stroked her belly, the baby needed her but the thought of the clones' abandonment was unbearable. Halley looked at Sebastian. "They are my family. They carried Oren and I when we couldn't keep going. I would have died if it weren't for the clones. What will you do with them? I need to be sure they are well taken care of."

"I will teach them how to hunt, to survive in the hopes that one day, they shall live away from civilisation. You and I both know they cannot be found by the world. Nobody would be ready."

Sebastian lifted Halley's chin by his index finger. "I promise they will be happy. At the end of the day these clones are still children and don't let the accelerated growth fool you. They need guidance to learn the ropes of life and they have so far learned the hard way."

"Gabriel shot him, he killed Oren but it was supposed to be me." Sebastian's pitiful eyes screamed a thousand sorrows, he really didn't know what happened out there. He raced across the room and leant his head over the sink, he would be viably ill. He hacked and clutched the wooden bench for support. Halley unfolded the details of Oren's death, she couldn't stop the words that tumbled out of her mouth and Sebastian listened. He shook his head in disbelief and tried to come to terms with the fact that his friend was a cold-blooded murderer. Sebastian eventually re-collected himself and crouched before Halley. He placed his hands over her belly and tears streamed down his face. "I know this isn't the time but … We can't have a dead body in here. The animals will smell it out."

"Let me have one last moment, won't you?"

Oren's Scottish complexion was replaced by that of death, something Halley had never seen before. His cheeks were dehydrated and ginger hair was dull. Halley's fingers trailed along his etched jawline, she circled up to his blue lips which were soon coated in her own salty tears. She reached forward and attempted to kiss them but all she could do was cry into Oren's mouth. Her hand fumbled inside his breast pocket when a gooey sensation chilled her fingers. She closed her eyes, it was the gunshot wound. She rummaged her hands through the inner pockets of Oren's jacket and extracted a soggy piece of folded paper that disintegrated in her hand. Halley tossed it on the floor and it began to melt before the heater. She found a mini flashlight and the blackberry cellphone. Halley laughed, she hated that damned phone but given Oren's stubbornness to upgrade it was something she loved most about him. Halley placed the phone in her back pocket and coiled her body around Oren. She nuzzled her head into his neck and brought her knees to her chest, they throbbed even more. She cried until she fell asleep. Oren had suffered so much in his final moments but Halley was too pre-occupied by her own pain as she carried him to the station that she didn't even notice when he died. Oren died alone and she cried for she could never forgive herself.

A warm breeze awoke Halley. "It's time," Sebastian's voice whispered.

There they stood, along the ledge of ORG-26 and Halley felt the snow burn her face with frostbite. She shut her eyes and prayed to the deaf ears of Antarctica to please, take care of Oren. Halley held onto one end of the carpet and Sebastian the other. Oren's body was wrapped inside and it was the closest representation of a casket. "On my count … One," Halley whispered.

"Two."

They stood in the middle of nowhere and she clutched onto hope. She listened for Oren's voice and hoped he would move again. But it never happened.

"Three."

She let go.

Oren tumbled over the edge. His body bounced off the rocky formations and shards of ice came down with him. He slammed against the ground and the sky cried tears of snow. Halley reached into her pocket and extracted six origami flowers constructed from book pages. Endless words trailed across the petals. She twisted them in her hand Sebastian leant over.

"Let them go," he ushered.

Halley dropped the origami flowers which twirled as they descended onto Oren's grave. He was now a memory and his body would be lost within the mystery of Antarctica.

Forever.

XLIV

ORG-26

At the base of ORG-26, Cyrus held a spear over his shoulder. He demonstrated a lunge pierced the spear through the air whilst the clones watched. Impressive.

Cyrus tapped his neck with the spear. He marched across the Antarctic plains and the clones followed. Rex trudged through the snow but his wounds ached. His body appeared one big bruise beneath the protective gear. He glanced over at Kiara and slipped his hand behind her back. Beneath the thick gloves, he still felt her skin.

He lowered himself to the ground and locked his sight on the seal that waddled across the ice. He placed one foot before the other and slowed his breath in tune to the southern ocean. Round two of the hunt had begun. Kiara nudged him and from beneath the furred hood he spoke words of encouragement.

"You got this Rex. Now... Run!"

Rex took off and Kiara jogged alongside. The clones followed the target.

Rex closed in on the seal. It flopped against the ice and grunted, as it scuffled away. The Weddell seal was headed toward a crack in the ice but Rex wasn't about to lose sight of his round of the hunt. He revved up his speed and took longer strides. The seal's tail was now between his feet. Rex reached forward and the blubber slipped between his fingers. He scratched its' back and the seal changed directions. Dammit. A blunt force pushed Rex over. He tumbled along the ice. His legs fell over his head. Then he outstretched a foot and slowed down.

"Follow your own trail," Cyrus snarled.

Rex attempted to stand up but was met by another kick from Cyrus. Slam. Rex hit the ice. His head pounded and his vision blurred. Rex must have passed out for when he regained consciousness Kiara pounced through the air and her hands clasped around the seal's body. She pulled a hand-knife from her pocket and plunged it into the seal's abdomen. It flopped against the ice with Kiara poised above it. The hunt was over.

Inside the dining area of ORG-26, the table was covered with buttered bread rolls and a silver platter of seal liver which the clones devoured, seemingly proud of their hunt. Halley tapped the pumpkin soup with her spoon but refused another bite.

"You need to eat for the baby, she needs you," Sebastian encouraged.

Halley nodded and managed to eat without chewing, she did it for Max and the baby. Her mind was set on going home.

Sebastian rested his head atop a balled fist. "I saw you all hunting today. Everyone, well done but you must work as a team, it's your strong point especially considering how many of you there are. You all have different strengths."

"Like what?" Chino asked.

"Chino you are a child of snow. You can move quiet and swift, more than the others. Cyrus and Rex, you attack and fight much the same. Fast and fearless but you must learn to savour your energy because you are tiring at the vital moments. Then, Kiara you think on your feet, something the others can learn from. I suggest that next time you head right for the jugular vein," Sebastian tapped his neck. "Kills them faster and Apollo, you think faster than you can move. Slow down but you are a great runner."

"So tell me, how much longer are we staying here?" Cyrus leaned back in his chair and slapped his boots against the table.

"For as long as possible. Gabriel and I wanted you here for protection but the only way to do that is by teaching you how to survive."

"Where's the bathroom?" Rex interrupted.

"Second door to your left."

Rex excused himself from the table. He wasn't about to listen to the same speech about being protected from the rest of the world. He knew about death, how to fight and source food, there couldn't be much more that Sebastian could teach him. He wandered down the wooden corridor and was about to enter the bathroom when something caught his eye. On the other side of the corridor was a door with hand-painted writing. It read HAR8378. Rex twisted for the handle but it was locked. Strange, none of the rooms here were locked. He peered through the keyhole but was met with nothing other than blackness. Back in the dining room everyone had polished off their dinner and now lounged about the couches. Rex looked around. "Where's Kiara?"

Cyrus gestured to the front door.

"What's she doing out there?" Rex grabbed his gloves and jogged toward the door. He pulled his hood up and emerged into the cold where snowflakes planted themselves into his shell. He rubbed his hands together and strode forward. Up ahead was Kiara who sat cross-legged. Rex crouched down beside her.

"We're home," Kiara sighed. "But I don't recognise this place. I miss the brick walls, the television held up by a milk-crate and our window that was covered by a sheet."

Rex couldn't deny it, she was right. "One thing is for sure though. After all those years trying to look for the outside, all those times that we scratched the masking tape from the window, it paid off. We got to see the outside, Kiara and - and it's not what I expected to be honest."

A tear trickled down his balaclava and he promised to never forget the basement. No matter how much they had all changed, he would always remember Kiara as that little girl that dreamt of the outside. There they were, not quite sure who they had become or what was to come but life had a new meaning. Rex listened to Kiara's light breaths and knew he was home.

"We killed Gabriel. Does that mean we are no better than him?"

"You didn't kill him but I did and that makes me no better than him. I am the monster," Kiara said.

Rex kissed the top of Kiara's balaclava. "You want to know what I think? I think that given all we have been through, you are the sanest of our brothers. You did nothing wrong."

Rex brushed the tip of his nose against Kiara's and although neither of them could feel it through their clothing, they were together. Rex was choked by a pain he could not describe and it sucked the air from his lungs. A pain he never endured before. He spoke to the top of Kiara's shell.

"It's as if we shouldn't have pushed to see the outside because this was all harder than I ever anticipated. But I got to do it with you and for that reason, I'd live it all again. Let's go inside though, it's too cold out here."

Almost twenty-four hours later, the sun didn't shift and the darkness didn't grow darker but stayed the same. Halley felt as though she was caught in a time loop. Her head was pressed against the pillow which was rock-hard and smelt of old socks. The thin blankets were drawn up to her shoulders and she shivered. From across the room, she watched the window that was frosted over and somewhere out there was Oren. She could still feel the weight of his body atop her back and the warmth of his cheek against her own, whilst they ploughed through Antarctica. The unstoppable tears poured down. Her throat scratched up and she was a mess. She couldn't be strong without him.

Halley made her way into the kitchen and flicked the light-switch on. Sprawled along the couch was Cyrus, who hauled himself upright. "Hal?"

"I didn't mean to wake you."

"I came here because I couldn't sleep with Chino pressed against my back and shaking all night long. He's scared of his own shadow in the dark."

Halley managed a half-smile. "I can imagine. Don't mind me, I'll be gone before you know it." Halley entered the kitchen and searched the cupboards. She squinted inside at the clean array of stacked cans and long life milk. Her swollen eyes made it hard to see.

"Can I help?" Cyrus asked.

"You don't happen to have a pen and paper do you?" Halley pulled open another cupboard, to no surprise it was empty and the next one was lined with perfectly stacked cans of soups. She looked in all the wrong places.

"How's the baby?" Beneath the fierce eyes was something else tonight. A slither of warmth or maybe it was pain. Cyrus actually cared.

Halley peered down at her belly. "I can still feel her."

Heavy footsteps broke the conversation and in the doorway was Sebastian with his elbow poised against the doorframe. He shielded his eyes against the blinding light. "What's going on?"

"I was looking for some paper. Sorry, I shouldn't search around in the middle of the night but I ... "

"Wait here," Sebastian yawned. He disappeared down the hallway and emerged with a paperback novel and pencil in hand. He bent the back cover over and tore it off. Sebastian turned the book in his hand then he ripped off the front cover. "The magician's hand, I never liked it anyway. I have a small library in my room so let me know if you need more paper."

Halley accepted the pencil, front and back book covers.

"I rip off the covers all the time, you get sick of reading the same books but if I don't know which is which, then it makes the story all the more interesting."

Halley curled into bed with the blank side of the book-cover pressed against her thigh and with the pencil in hand, she began to write:

To my son and daughter,

There is no way for me to put this lightly but I think so long as the truth comes out in the English language, you will understand. Your father and I made a decision to venture into Antarctica. Someday I shall explain it to you, the white landscapes and the dark sky. The reason we came here is for another time because there is something you should know first.

Halley paused as her vision blurred by a gust of tears. She gulped against the lump in her throat and tried not to dampen the page. Halley forced herself to write the letter with a broken heart. It was the kind of pain that one would not dream of re-living. She turned back to the page.

Your father and I had a friend. She crossed out the final word, *bad man. To my daughter, I made sure your father knew you existed before he died. I know he heard me because even though he was in a lot of pain, he smiled. To my son, your father is now an angel up above and watches over you whilst you sleep.*
Until we meet again.

Halley folded the letter and slipped it into the breast pocket of her jumper, right beside Oren's blackberry phone. She coiled beneath the covers and cried until her head throbbed and she blacked out.

XLV

ORG-26

Halley nursed a mug of tea and leant her head against the window pane. She peered down at Oren's Blackberry that lay in her lap. She pressed the power button but the screen remained blank. A tear trickled down the corner of her cheek. She pressed the button again but it was no use. The phone was dead. Halley stroked the metal device and her fingers traced over it. Someone knocked on the door but Halley didn't have the strength to speak. The knock sounded again. Seconds later Rex entered the room, he was dressed in an over-sized jumper that Halley assumed wasn't his. He sat on the opposite edge of the window and hung his elbows over his knees. His vision was focused on the frosted window as he tried to forget about the hunger that debilitated his body. They sat in silence for some time, each entranced in their own pain. Rex turned towards Halley and for the first time she noticed a scratch over his right eye. It was fresh and reached from his brow to his cheek. Halley offered her tea to Rex but he shook his head.

"I made a mistake. I never told Oren that he was going to be a father, every time I tried there was a problem. One thing after the other and he found out too late. I regret it, every second."

"May I?"

Halley nodded. Rex reached forward and placed his hand on her belly. His warm fingers encompassed the foetus. He tilted his head and a glum demeanour cast over his face. Halley was about to ask what was on his mind but decided against it. "It's not safe for me to stay here, not with the baby on the way. There's a ship docking in three days and I'm leaving with it."

"So you're going to leave us?"

"I can't stay here."

This would to be more difficult than Halley anticipated but her mind was made-up and there was no going back. She dismissed stood up and the Blackberry dropped to the ground. She couldn't look Rex in the eye and reached for the bedroom door. It slammed shut as Rex pressed his face close to Halley.

"Look at me," Rex clicked his fingers before her eyes. "We don't even get a choice in what happens anymore? We have to stay here and that's it."

Halley placed the mug of tea onto of the drawers. She raked her fingers through her hair. "What do you want me to say?"

"That this wouldn't be permanent." Rex clenched his jaw. "Have you decided what happens to Chino?"

"He stays behind."

Rex dragged his fingers through his hair and glared at Halley. "Are you going to forget about us and move on with your life, like nothing ever happened? Is that it? Nine years we spent together, you raised us. Does that not mean something?"

"Of course it does but I have to think of the baby now. Come and sit down so we can talk."

Halley picked the Blackberry off the floor and sat on the window ledge with Rex opposite her. This time there was an invisible wall was between them.

"Have you realised this place is bit odd?" Rex asked.

Halley looked at him confused. Sure, there was nothing normal about this situation but they were safe. Halley couldn't ask for more.

"When I went to the bathroom the other night, I saw a room with a weird coding on it and call it a hunch but it wasn't right."

Halley folded her arms. "I'm sure it's nothing."

Rex stood up and headed for the door but Halley saw the frustration from within.

"Wait, let's figure this out. What did the code say?"

She scribbled the coding through the condensation of the window and it read, HAR8378. Rex stared at it, as if the answers to jump out at him. Halley leant forward to wipe away the carvings by the hem of her jumper. As she reached over, she lost her balance and forcibly thrust her leg onto the ground for support. The Blackberry tumbled out of her lap and flipped open. Then Halley saw it. She switched her gaze from the phone to the coding on the window. Her heart pounded at the back of her throat and chills ran down her spine.

"Hal, what is it?"

She pointed at the keypad and her finger lingered from one number to the next. Rex tucked a tuft of stray hair behind his ear and followed her guide.

"I don't get it."

"Look, each number has a combination of three possible letters. So if we start with eight, it could either t, u or v. The next number in the code is three, which could be d, e or f."

"So you think it means something?"

"That's what we need to find out."

Halley created a list of the numbers and possible letters through the condensation of the window pane. Her finger traced along the frosted glass until she reached the bottom of the frame. The coding appeared nothing more than a large mess and perhaps Halley was further away from the truth. Maybe she was mad but it was worth a try. She rearranged the letters but it made no sense. Halley and Rex stared at the window together, they tried to decode the numerical system. HAR-*LESL* ... *HAR-VESU* ... *HAR-UDQU.*

"Hal, this isn't working," Rex complained. "Forget I even mentioned it."

"Wait." Halley bit her lower lip in concentration and rearranged the letters once more. "V ... E ... S ... T?"

Halley's jaw dropped open and she turned to Rex who glared at the letters carved onto the window. "Vest? That doesn't mean anything."

"Wait, what was the first part?"

"Eight, three ..."

"No, I mean the letters."

"Oh ... H, A, R."

"V, E, S, T."

"Harvest."

"Maybe we need to rearrange the letters," Halley exhaled.

"No." Rex thought in silence. "What - What's the name of this station?"

Halley glared at him blankly.

"Fuck! The registration number?"

Halley clasped her hands around her head. "Umm ... ORG ...

26."

"So the number two has a, b and c. Then six can be m, n and o."

Halley rearranged the letters as quick as she could and Rex did the same. She stood up and traced the letters into the corner of the window but nothing seemed to add up. She pressed her finger onto the window and was about to try a new combination but her finger quivered. There it was. "Oh my god … A-n. It spells organ."

She shuddered. Organ harvest. This place was not a research station but an organ harvest.

Halley emptied her stomach into the trash can. She clutched her stomach and prayed for the endless nausea to leave her abdomen. Rex held her waist to keep his balance and he whispered words of encouragement into her ear but Halley couldn't control herself. "We need to warn the others, come on."

Halley stumbled over her own feet and slammed against the hallway. She entered the lounge room to see the clones played a game of chess whilst Cyrus and Sebastian enjoyed a cigarette on the couch. The room was calm and made Halley feel crazy but she knew the truth. Sebastian did a damn good job to have concealed it.

"We need to leave," Halley puffed.

Apollo snorted and continued with his chess match. "What do you mean?"

"Everyone head for the door," Rex snarled and lowered his hands to his knees. No matter the cost, he would ensure nobody got hurt. His eyes locked on Sebastian. "This isn't a research station -"

Rex cut himself off, he wanted to conceal the evil truth from Kiara. He wanted her to forget this entire ordeal but her eyes beckoned him.

"It's an organ harvest."

Deadly silence drained the air from the room and the clones took a moment to digest the information. Kiara stepped forward. "Tell me it's not true."

Sebastian stood up and drew a long puff from the cigar. He blew the smoke into the air-tight room and walked towards Halley. "Halley, honey, have you gone insane? I know your husband died and I understand you are in a lot of pain but that is no reason to take out your anger on the clones. We are only here to help you."

"Don't listen to him!" Halley exclaimed. She only hoped the clones wouldn't be fooled by his act. "The apparent registration of this laboratory and that backroom are written in code. We all need to get the hell out of here!"

Sebastian plucked the cigar from his mouth and blew smoke in Halley's face. He leaned in close to her ear. "I offered you a way out princess, this is your last chance. Leave now and don't look back. Think of your baby."

Halley ground her teeth and peered over Sebastian's shoulder at the innocent clones. The faces of her experiment, those who never asked to be born nor did they ask to venture into Antarctica. They awaited a verdict, for somebody, to yet again, foretell their future. She looked over at Rex who stood by her side. His wet hair encased his fragile face and his eyes beckoned for help. She couldn't leave him, she owed her life to the clones and to Rex more than anyone. He carried Halley and the baby when she couldn't go on. He gave his life for her, now, she had to do the same.

"I won't leave without them."

Sebastian pressed the cigar between his teeth. The truth came out. "If that's what you truly want, then you can die with them." He reached inside his fur coat and extracted a gun and aimed it at Kiara's head. "Did you really think I would come unprepared?"

"At least let me know why before you kill me," Kiara stalled.

"I guess I did. It's the least I can do before I plunge a bullet between your eyes. All of you are clones, you are nobody. You have no identity, no birth certificate and are all perfect candidates for what's to come. Have you ever heard of the Chinese black market? The underground trade pays a fine price for human organs. Your eyes," Sebastian, tapped his temple with the barrel of the gun "are one of the cheapest organs at fifteen-hundred pound. Your heart, one-hundred-twenty-thousand pounds, liver, one-hundred-fifty-seven-thousand pounds and kidneys for a rich price of two-hundred-thousand pounds. Allow me to do the maths for you, two-and-a-half million dollars for all of your organs. Gabriel and I would've been retired before our fortieth birthday and all would've gone to plan if some rotten little bitch didn't get in the way!"

Sebastian clicked the gun and closed one eye. He repositioned his target on Kiara's forehead. "I wasn't going to kill you until the Chinese ship docked, the organs would be fresher that way. I guess I'll have to use more ice."

His thumb wavered over the trigger.

SLAM.

Rex knocked Sebastian to the ground and the gun fired into the air. Sebastian flung his body and Rex was thrown off. He swung around and was confronted with Apollo. The men took turns to throw punches and petty kicks. Apollo stumbled backwards and so did Sebastian, neither of their moves was enough to cause proper harm. Apollo jumped into the air and kicked Sebastian's face. His nose cracked into his skull. Chino leapt into action and gnawed at Sebastian's ankles. Once he lost balance, it was the perfect opportunity for Cyrus and Apollo. They positioned their hand-knives into his neck. Sebastian's own kitchen knives had turned against him. "Please … Stop," he pleaded.

Rex watched Sebastian lie limp on the ground.

"Last chance."

Sebastian spat in his face. Rex swallowed. Another dead body was all the more reason to cast the clones inhumane. A part of him would always be human, if he killed Sebastian, it would only push him further away from sanity. He looked into the fear stricken eyes of Sebastian, he was helpless yet there was no time for pity.

"Do it." Rex turned around.

Cyrus and Apollo drove the knives through his neck and Sebastian dropped to the ground. Blood squirted in all directions and the clones were speckled with their own victory. Sebastian gasped for air but his struggle didn't last long. He weakened beneath the clones' grasp and his head gravitated towards the ground. He reached a hand toward Halley but she stumbled away and slid down the wall, the sight revolted her. She covered her eyes and although the empty blackness was a pleasant escape, the sweet surrender didn't last long for she was soon shaken awake by Chino. He knelt beside her.

"Did you know about this?" he mumbled beneath the smear of a blood moustache.

"I knew that there was a ship docking to take me home but I had no idea … If I knew I wouldn't leave you all behind. I promise. I never intended on hurting you."

Chino dropped his head and collapsed into Halley's lap. He panted, an attempt to expel the unspeakable horror that had occurred.

Rex crouched beside them, his face was covered in blood. So was the rest of him. "We can rest for tonight but that ship docks in two days so we need to get a move on. I have a plan."

"So do I," Halley said.

Halley folded the last paper corner of the origami flower and handed it to Kiara. The clones walked in a straight line out of the living room and into the snow. Cyrus and Apollo led the way and carried Sebastian' dead body, where blood dripped from his hand onto the ice. Halley stared at the origami piece between her gloved hands and although she had no tears left to cry, she mourned Sebastian's death. Not for herself but for whoever knew him back home. The clones lined up along the edge of ORG-26 and Rex turned towards them, although his face was hidden by the fur-trimmed hood. "I know that we despised Sebastian but we gather here for Halley's sake. She saved us tonight and in exchange we shall farewell Sebastian."

Rex raised his fist high in the air, he yelled at the top of his lungs and the clones joined in. Their voices echoed as Sebastian's body dropped over the edge. He tumbled across the magmatic rocks and disappeared into the snow. Halley screamed until her voice grew hoarse. She gasped for air and in all despair, her clenched fists opened and the origami flowers blew over the edge. The clones copied and the paper flowers fell over the grave.

XLVI

The Truth Itself

Halley was hypnotised by the steam from the kettle. It warmed her face into a sweat but was a pleasant change from the cold outside. She poured a mug of peppermint tea. The heat burned through her hands when a faint jab protruded from her abdomen. Halley snuck her hands beneath the jumper and circled her fingertips across her skin. The baby kicked again, her movements like the flutter of moth's wings. Someone entered the kitchen and Halley was pulled her from the momentary daydream.

Chino flopped onto the couch and faced the floor. His porcelain skin was replaced with bruises and a swollen cheek. His fragile body was covered in unforgivable scars and the memory of Shackleton Ice Shelf could never be erased.

Halley cradled the tea and sat beside him. Chino raised his head and stared at her expectantly. As if Halley was the perpetrator of lies. His hazed eyes looked her over.

"Will it hurt?" Chino's question hung in the air. His hands trembled but he hid them within his pockets. "Will it hurt when I die?"

"I would never do that."

"Oren would."

The conversation caught Halley off-guard. Despite the jarred agony from within. She ignored the comeback. Oren was desperate, there was nothing more to the equation. Her chest tightened and eyes stung but she had no tears left to cry. She breathed out the pain and expelled it from her body. It was too sinister for the baby to feel. "You're safe now. That's all that matters," Halley whispered.

"I can only hope you are telling the truth." Chino switched his gaze to the hallway where the clones emerged into the living room.

The clones sat around the wooden table, with Halley at the head. She twiddled her thumbs and thought for some time. She glanced across the clones, who reciprocated her gaze with that of admiration. Halley was the only person who had not betrayed them and it was time to offer the clones a proposition for freedom. "We can all board the ship but if these Chinese people want organs then that is our only way out of here. So we need to replace all of your organs with someone else's."

Rex ran his hands through his hair, it was an insane task. He leant back into the chair and planted the heel of his boots against the table. Frost dribbled to the carpet and he placed a pick in the corner of his mouth and scratched at his teeth. Rex was entranced by his own thoughts. "You're saying we should have used Sebastian's organs?"

Cyrus leant forward. "I think someone can do the honours and donate their organs for the greater good." He nudged Chino.

Chino stood up and mumbled under his breath. "I was going to die anyway, so go ahead."

"Enough," Rex snapped.

Apollo leant his elbows against the table. He twirled a strand of hair between his fingers and felt the pointed edge against his fingertip. "Sounds like this is going to muck up my hair."

Apollo plucked a comb from his back pocket and slicked the sides back.

Halley extended an open palm. "I'll be with you the whole time. If nobody boards that ship, then neither do I. I have a plan. We can harvest seal organs, one for each of you."

They each linked arms around the table and silence filled the air. As if they were too weak to attest the plan. After all, it was their only way out. The meeting was dismissed as soon as it had begun and Halley darted into the kitchen. She opened the top drawer, it was empty. She cursed beneath her breath and pulled the second one open. She reached inside, drew out a small kitchen knife and tucked it inside her back pocket. The clones entered the room, their faces were covered with identical balaclavas, non-reflective glasses and furred hoods. Rex brushed his hand against Kiara's elbow, although he couldn't feel her embrace beneath the padded gloves, he knew she was near. "You should stay here and help Hal. We will be back soon. C'mon boys!" Rex raised his fist in the air to which the clones copied.

There was no doubt he was leader again, for Cyrus' reign proved to fall short. They cheered and headed out the front door.

Halley turned back to Kiara. "Let's get a move on."

She took to Sebastian's room. It was crammed like her own with an unkempt single bed in the centre. She peered underneath but was confronted with nothing more than dust. She had no idea what she looked for but that was besides the point. She switched her gaze to the tallboy and thrust open the drawers, rummaged her hands inside the messy array of clothes and protective snow gear. Halley grew impatient and dropped the clothes to the ground until the drawers were empty. Padded jumpers and socks with holes fell to the ground. She emitted a sigh of defeat.

She headed for the CD player besides the bed. Halley pressed a few buttons until the blue screen illuminated and the symphony of a Russian balalaika filled her hears. She beat her head to the instrumental tune and scoured the room. Where would Sebastian contain information of the ship? Unless there was not a ship and that was another lie. Halley trailed her fingers along her belly, there was the slightest bump there now. It reminded Halley not to loose hope, for she would not only let herself down but also the baby.

"Hal!" Kiara called out.

A crash emitted and Halley darted down the corridor when she saw it. The door of room HAR8378 was broken in and splinters lined the frame. There was a chair lodged inside the door that hung from the hinges and Kiara bore a wide-toothed smile. They pulled the chair away and left a hollow circle within the door. Halley entered first, although not so sure she wanted to. She clutched her belly and swallowed against the bile at the back of her throat. Halley flicked on the light switch of HAR8378 and the room illuminated. The walls were concrete and an old light hung by a wire from the roof. Halley walked forward and her boot snagged on a broken tile. She headed towards a retractable metal table. The steel edges were indented with scratches and dents. The cold exterior chilled her fragile fingers. Kiara entered the room and her boots crunched over shards of chipped tiles and crumbled concrete. She stood at the end of the table. Her gaze was fixated on the wall and then Halley saw it too. At the head of the table was a labelled diagram of the human anatomy. Along the side was a detailed description of the anatomy and hand-written prices besides the major organs. Kiara held her breath and glared at the image. "This was my fate. I should have died here and for some reason, I feel guilty for living." She turned towards Halley "Did you ever make other clones?"

"No."

Kiara wandered around HAR8378 and trailed her fingers along the walls of what would have been her grave. She reached for a messy pile of textbooks and loose papers pressed in a nearby corner. Halley crouched beside her and they flicked through the pages of the books. She dropped them to the floor, one at a time. They soon stood in a pile of papers that detailed surgery and dissection of the human body. A gut-wrenching sensation surged but there was no time to be sick. Halley reached for the next book and her vision began to blur, so she skimmed through it instead. Her clammy fingers stuck to the pages and her heart thumped at the back of her throat for what she may find.

"Here," Kiara pressed a bundle of stapled papers into Halley's chest. "This one mentions something about China and there's a bunch of numbers written on the front page."

Halley sunk her head into the file. It was a printed document which must have been over four-hundred pages long. She realised the file was of printed emails between Sebastian and somebody known as Li Wei. Halley traced her fingers along the page and slowed down. She looked up at Kiara, she found what they needed.

XLVII

We're Going Home

The Antarctic breeze swept through ORG-26 as the clones marched inside, they had returned from their hunt. Rex slammed a Weddell seal onto the floor. The corpse was slimy and its' eyes remained open. "We've paid our price to board the ship. One seal for each of us, now let's get to work."

Halley slumped in a metal chair along the back wall of HAR8378. She watched from a distance as Apollo flopped a Weddell seal onto the metal table. He glanced at Rex who held a scalpel in his hand was fixated on the human diagram. His eyes locked on the liver and he mesmerised its' shape. Bulky and purple, surely it couldn't be that hard to find.

"Please, take your time. However long you need," Cyrus said, bored.

"Well it's a bit hard when I'm using a fucking human diagram for a seal!" Rex snapped.

Rex returned his gaze back to the seal. He fiddled with the scalpel, not quite sure how to hold it. He decided two hands was easiest and he lowered the blade to the seal's body. He pressed the tip into its' abdomen and its' fitted skin popped open. The stench of blubber and blood lifted through the air and it broke Rex into a sweat. He dragged the blade along the seal's skin, severed the connective tissue and fat. He cut through a vein and blood poured over his hands. He clenched his jaw until his lips shook. Rex continued to cut and then once he was happy, he slipped his hands around a brown-purplish organ that was sloppy and almost split in half. "I think I found the liver."

"That looks more like a pancreas to me," Apollo gagged.

"The hell, I don't know what I'm looking at. Maybe I should dice it up a little more so it looks like a liver?"

Rex pushed the thought aside and plunged the organ into the cooler bag filled with crushed ice. "What time does the ship dock?"

"Eight in the morning but I still need to locate these coordinates. Have you got the compass?" Halley asked.

"Yeah," Rex said distantly with his entire fist submerged in the abdominal cavity of the seal. The clones assisted the organ harvest throughout the night. Once they tired, they switched roles. The night was long and Halley focused on the map she found in one of the textbooks. She circled Shackleton Ice Shelf and waited for the answers to seep out of the book. Conversation grew dry and everybody moved robotic-like as they worked their way to freedom.

The final seal was harvested by 6:49 am.

Halley splayed the crinkled map across the table and traced her finger along the coordinates, 81.5 degrees South and 175 degrees West. She hovered over Shackleton Ice Shelf.

"We are here and we need to reach Ross Ice Shelf, over here," she tapped the map. "It's about two-and-a-half-thousand kilometres." Halley exhaled from behind the balaclava and fogged up her goggles. "It should take about fourty minutes."

"There has to be another way," Rex thought.

"There is." Kiara tucked the side fringe behind her ear. "When I was out in the snow the other day I saw some kind of bus. It's around the back in a shed."

Rex stared at her gobsmacked. Her intelligence made his heart skip a beat. That's my girl, he thought.

Halley and the clones ventured around the back of ORG-26 and surely enough, there was a square shed covered in a blanket of snow. The doors were secured by a metal chain and padlock. Halley tugged on the lock but it was frozen shut. One of the clones shone a flashlight and Halley pressed her face against the slit between the doors. She squinted against the dimness and could make out the outline of a bus. She turned around. "Any suggestions?"

"One of us might be able to get inside, if everyone else holds the door open as far as possible," Rex said.

"Off you go," Halley said.

"I'm too big to get through there. Cyrus?" Rex cackled.

Cyrus slipped his hands beneath his armpits and bulged his scrawny biceps forward. He sneered at the remark but remained speechless. That was a first.

"Fine, I'll go," Halley sighed.

The clones pulled against the hinges of door from either side. It creaked open and Halley pressed her body against the opening. She squeezed inside and her organs compressed within her chest. She held her breath and finally stumbled into the blackened room. She glanced at the clones, who shone a torch at her.

The red-and-white Terra bus was encased by a layer of dust and bore a series of smashed windows. It was bigger than expected and Halley climbed along the drivers' side and the door was unlocked. She slipped inside and fumbled along the ignition. There was no key.

She tore through the splay of crumbled newspapers across the dash. She tossed notepads and gloves over her shoulder. Then she saw it. Wedged in the far corner was a set of keys. She turned the keys in the ignition and the engine roar to life. "Move away from the doors. I'm coming through!"

Halley clutched the wheel as the Terra Bus bounced over the ice terrain. The slosh of fluid leaked into her ears. She turned to Rex who held a cooler bag of hearts between his knees. He switched his gaze from Gabriel's compass then to the map. He traced the journey with his eyes.

The Terra Bus descended along the backroad of ORG-26. Outside the window was a corner of red carpet and half-hidden origami flowers that protruded over the snow. A tear trickled down Halley's cheek whilst the bus slowed down. A fragile piece of her heart dropped into her stomach. She extracted a toothpick from her shell. Halley snapped the wooden pick in half and spat the excess splinters out the window.

"It's time to go," Rex said.

He checked the compass and marked their coordinates on the map. "We're almost there."

Along the Southern West hemisphere of Antarctica they reached Ross Ice Shelf, although it looked like the rest of Antarctica. The clones stumbled through the snow, as the cooler bags weighed them down. They followed the guide of the compass and tracked along the edge of the ice. Through the mist the nose of a metallic black ship protruded. It was coated with Chinese symbols painted in gold and the banter of a foreign language escaped over the railing. It had to be Li Wei's ship.

Halley breathed in the mustiness and condensation from within the balaclava, for it would be the last time. She jogged forward and her knees burned with ache. The fog cleared and a retractable rope staircase hung over the side of the ship. Halley reached for it and placed her foot on the ledge. It rocked and her body brushed against the ship. "Let's go home."

Kiara's eyes fill with tears. "I'm right behind you."

Halley climbed to freedom and her bones rattled with uncertainty. She leaned sideways and bumped into the ship. The staircase twisted as the clones beneath grappled with the frayed rope. Halley pressed her head against her chest and reached upright, her bruised hands hauled her forward.

She dropped onto the deck and slipped the cooler bag off her shoulders. The sound of slush emitted again. Kidneys, seven of them.

Halley crawled onto all fours when Cyrus hauled her to her feet. She nodded for he couldn't see the smile beneath her balaclava.

"Let's go home," he said.

The passengers of Lei Wei were dressed in identical black uniforms with golden Chinese symbols embroidered across their chest. A figure parted through the crowd and headed towards them. He folded his arms and spoke of the Chinese language in a seriousness voice.

"Do you speak English?" Halley asked.

The man remained silent before he mumbled in Chinese again. He sighed at the single-sided conversation. "Russian man."

"I am with the Russian man, yes."

"Where?"

Halley gulped. "I brought what you asked."

She showed the cooler bag and the man peered at the organs within the cooler bag. Halley slowed her breath until she almost fainted.

"Come," he said.

The Chinese man disappeared amidst the sea of unfamiliar faces. Halley followed close behind. From the corner of her eye she saw a blue-and-white cooler bag.

"Chino, are you ready?" Halley asked.

Her knees shattered, Chino wasn't there. A uniformed figure carried the cooler bag. Halley gulped and spun around. A series of five men lugged the cooler bags in a systematic manner. One of them groaned and pushed past her.

"Where did you get this?" Halley waved her hands before the men's faces. "That bag."

The man slapped her face and Halley fell to the ground. Her cheek burned. She gasped for air, this couldn't happen. Not now. She encircled herself like a dazed deer. Then a thought crossed Halley's mind, someone must have known what they look like. Someone recognised the clones and took them. The blood-curdled thought pulsed her legs with adrenaline. She shoved past the crowd and pelted across the deck. She was oblivious to the foreign remarks and blatant stares. A crowd laughed and pointed fingers.

Suddenly, a horn sounded as the ship pulled away from the ice. In that moment, Halley saw a clearing among the crowd and the glimmer of disintegrated ice shimmered along the metal railing. She ran on instinct and gripped the cold circumference of the rail. She peered over the edge and there they were. All five clones on the edge of Antarctica. "No! What are you doing! Stop this ship, somebody!"

"It's okay," Cyrus called out. "You're going home but we can't come with you!"

"What do you mean?" Halley wailed.

Rex cupped his hands around his mouth and called out. "Halley, we're all letting you live your life again. We don't belong anywhere. This is our home now!"

Through the shaken bitterness, she couldn't manage a goodbye. She watched Rex remove his balaclava and the innocent eyes glared at the ship which departed all too fast.

"You saved me. Thank you," Chino's faint voice yelled.

Rex raised his hand high in the air and whispered something but beneath the weight of the Antarctic breeze, it was lost in translation. The clones now appeared half their size as they stood on the frozen ledge of the Ross Ice Shelf.

"I'm coming back for you! Do you hear me?" Halley screamed of the upmost promise.

She raised a fist in the air and then drew it across her chest. She knew the clones heard her plea for they each laid one arm across their chest in unison. Halley could hardly breathe as heavy tears and unbearable pain clouded her mind. She stared at the clones until they were no more.

When the time was right, Halley would return to Shackleton Ice Shelf.

She knew it.

She clutched her belly and a sudden movement pressed against her hand. A salty tear dribbled down the fabric of the balaclava and slipped between her chapped lips. She swallowed the bitterness and her fingers curled across her abdomen. There was hope. A tiny fragment of Oren lived on, within her belly. There were two passengers headed home.